BACON AND EGGS
AND
OTHER TALES

To Pamela
All the best
Linda Griffin
March 2024

by
Linda Pearce Griffin

Table of Contents

Chapter 1

For Starters

Chapter 2

School Daze

Chapter 3

Who Can Say Why?

Chapter 4

Extra-Curricular

Chapter 5

Play Back

Chapter 6

Legacy

Chapter 7

Never Judge a Book By Its Cover

Chapter 8

Country Girl

Chapter 9

Tales from the Valley

Chapter 10

Necessary Lessons

Chapter 11

Just Because

Chapter 12

A Matter of Perspective

Acknowledgments

"You should write a book," they said.

"You should publish your stories," they said.

Really? Okay……..

Well, folks, it's an easy thing to say but a tough thing to do.

Flashback (2017): When I retired, the first thing I vowed to do was to write about my family members – grandparents, aunts, uncles, and sometimes cousins – so that my children would know these people as I had known them. I was able to do that via Storyworth – a format that is perfect for non-tech-savvy folks and a small audience. Sometimes, I allowed friends to read those stories, and they all were very complimentary and said, "You need to publish this." And perhaps one day I will. But in the meantime (being worried I might be barred from future family reunions), I began writing a blog – thanks to the encouragement of my friend, Rebecca Moore, and the skills of my very kind and tech-savvy son, Alex. The Word Press venue allowed me to post stories I'd been holding onto and/or share some meandering thoughts that were itching at the edge of my mind. I have been grateful that family, friends, and complete strangers have read and subscribed to my blog, www.articulation.me

As I received compliments and encouragement from friends and readers, I began thinking of publishing a collection of random short stories that I had written about my life. However, I had no clue as to how to go about such a project, but I began investigating the possibility. Several author friends - Celia Hales, Linda Shuping Smith, and Rebecca Moore - suggested self-publishing, which sounded doable – maybe. But being a novice in the publishing world and lacking sufficient technical skills, I was clueless, reluctant, and despairing. Finally, with a big friendly push from dear Ray Morales, I dipped my toes in the water. I made a few tentative steps, but there is so much to learn, and it was overwhelming to me. Thank goodness I found KDP Partners. Maddy Green, Mark Oslo and their team took my hand and helped me to jump through all the necessary hoops. And here I am!

Certainly, additional acknowledgments must go to my multitude of supportive friends: Marty Kellogg, Maureen Morrell, Sue Jasinski, Judy Essick, Beverly Clark, Jackie Strickland, Phyllis Alford, Kathy Payne, Debby Floyd Raines, and Robin Hasslen. Their encouragement kept me pressing onward. I am also grateful for the kindness of readers (who are family and friends from everywhere) like my dear ASNC Sisters, Ann Palmer, Susan Pearce, Elaine Morales, JoAnn Lanzi, Hannah Stallings Headrick, Kim Strickland Setzer, Donna Thompson, Lynn Massey Orr, Susan Garber, Barbara Steele, Sheila Dreps, Meredith Mcgill, Susie Davis Concelmo, Jenel Maurer, Marie Holmes, Jackie Batten Utley, Pam Batten, Asia Sharif-Clark, Jeanette Hammond, Shelli Rowland, Mona Garrett, Kathy and Phil Tant, Lynn Marshbanks, Anita Dieters, Gloria Carroll, Shae Morales, Sharri Gaines, Lynn McLaughlin, Shannon Speller, Candace Heath, Susie Roberson, Sandra Johnson, Steve Stallings, Don Perry, Sheila Cooke Stancil,

Jennifer Mitchell Shipman, Allette Hale, Roni Adams, Karen Sparrow, Kim Walker, and if you're a reader and I forgot to list you, please accept my apologies and my sincere thanks for reading. I most especially owe enormous thanks to my long-suffering husband, Brad, and my patient daughter, Whitney. No project is ever done in isolation.

I am also grateful to Kindle Direct Publishing for making this venue available to those of us who know next to nothing about publishing a book. And without KDP Partners, this could not have happened. I am beyond grateful.

Dedication

I dedicate this book to the memory of my Grampa, John Wesley Pearce (Johnny to my Gramma and his friends) – who loved me well and taught me to appreciate a good story. He inspired my imagination from his front porch rocker to the back porch eating watermelon and everywhere in between – including sitting in the soft Carolina sand eating pretend ice cream. He has lived forever in my heart.

Author Bio

Linda Griffin is a Southerner – born in the Shenandoah Valley of Virginia and raised in rural North Carolina about 20 miles East of Raleigh in the small town of Zebulon. She has had varied careers including Registered Nurse, Bodywork Therapist, and an advocate for individuals with autism and their families. Linda has two adult children, a nephew she claims as her third child and six grandchildren. She is currently retired and lives with her husband and their two rescue dogs, Rosie and Honey.

Introduction

Once upon a time, there was a little girl who loved storytelling – the kind in books that her mama read to her, complete with voices. The kind her grampa told her while rocking in his chair on his wide front porch. The kind folks told which often started with "let me tell you this…" The kind she told herself – sometimes they were true, and sometimes she made them up….

My family was full of storytellers. My Uncle Howard could spin a yarn that wound around nearly a whole afternoon but was so rich with description and full of voices and sound effects that you never noticed the time. On evenings after supper, my daddy would tell us stories about his childhood: his dog named Joe, his favorite mule who was deaf, getting into trouble with his cousins or at school – all painted so clearly in my mind it was like looking at a picture book. And cherished times with my mama would begin with my imploring, "tell me about when you were a little girl…"

It's no wonder that I have always loved to write. Starting early in grade school, I made up all kinds of stories. One was about a village terrorized by a giant who ended up befriending the villagers and being their guardian – all based on my observations of an ant hill that I visited on the way to my gramma's garden or to the outhouse. My teacher was intrigued, and her response spurred me on to write a story about an ice cream family – the daddy was a chocolate cone, the mama was vanilla, and the daughter was strawberry. By middle school, I was writing a weekly serial about a girl named Charlie, which my classmates read eagerly and clamored for more as soon as the story made it around the room. In high school, I joined the Journalism Club and eventually became the editor of the school paper. I worked part-time at the local newspaper and dreamed of going to college and majoring in Journalism. Human interest stories were my choice, but maybe someday there would be a novel….

As it turns out, John Lennon was so right: "life is what happens while you're busy making other plans." And so it was with me. I became a lot of other things – a heartbroken young girl, a bumbling secretary, a wife, a divorcee, a miserable secretary, a wife again, a mother, a substitute teacher, a nurse, a massage therapist, an advocate for parents of children with autism…and through all of that, I wrote – bits of verse at times, snatches of thought and longing, but always stories – bits and pieces and sometimes whole stories with a beginning, middle and an end.

So here I am. Now. In this place. Still writing stories. And Lord help me! A blog and now a BOOK – a for-real, in-print book. I hope you will sit a spell. Take off your shoes. Curl up. Maybe have a cup of tea. Let's see where this goes….

Chapter 1

For Starters

Bacon and Eggs

I was standing on a wooden church pew beside my granddaddy, singing to the top of my voice, "Bacon and eggs; bacon and eggs; for there's no other way to be happy in Jesus but with bacon and eggs."

I loved bacon and eggs, and I loved my Grampa. I was 4 years old and in my Happy Place, visiting my grandparents. What a glorious morning! Why, we'd just had bacon and eggs that very morning sitting in my grandparents' kitchen, and now the whole congregation was singing joyfully about it.

The polished wood of the pews and podium gleamed golden in the morning sun. Jesus sat with his sweet lambs in the big oil painting that looked out at us. All was well in the world. I was with my Grampa and could climb onto his lap anytime I wanted while the preacher was preaching and the choir was singing. More than likely, I fell asleep that Sunday morning nestled in Grampa's arms.

Later that day, at the Sunday dinner table, I said, "I like that song about bacon and eggs." The adults looked at one another, perplexed. No one seemed to know what I was talking about.

"You know, the one we sang this morning…." and I began singing it for my audience. They all listened for a minute and then began to laugh.

"It's not 'bacon and eggs. It's 'trust and obey.'"

Really? What does that mean? I had no idea what either of those words meant. And, frankly, I was a little disappointed that there wasn't a song about bacon and eggs. From then on, I sang the right words with my mouth, but in my head, I could hear "bacon and eggs." I liked bacon and eggs better. I still do.

Hurricane

A hurricane is described as an intense tropical weather system of strong thunderstorms with well-defined surface circulation and maximum sustained winds of 74 mph or higher. They are categorized according to the strength of their winds on a scale of 1 – 5. A Category 1 storm has the lowest wind speeds; a Category 5 has the strongest.

In October 1954, one of the century's most intense storms, Hurricane Hazel, a Category 4, landed on the southern coast of North Carolina. Winds were clocked at 150 mph on Holden Beach. By the time she reached Goldsboro, the winds screamed on at 120 mph. Even as far inland as Raleigh, the storm roared on with hurricane-strength winds from 80 – 100 mph. Hurricanes seldom travel so far inland. Hazel flattened everything in her path, earning a nickname: "The Bulldozer."

Trees snapped like twigs, littering the highways by the thousands. World War II veterans likened the damage to a scene from the war. Hazel affected land and people from Jamaica to Canada. In NC alone, nineteen people died, more than 200 people were hurt, and more than 15,000 homes and buildings were destroyed. The Weather Bureau in Raleigh issued an official report stating: "all traces of civilization on the immediate waterfront between the state line and Cape Fear were practically annihilated." The NOAA report stated, "Every pier in a distance of 170 miles of coastline was demolished."

Three couples from High Point were trapped in a house on Ocean Isle Beach, then washed away by a tidal wave, along with members of a neighboring family. Only one of the couples survived. The other two couples left eight orphans to mourn them. A couple honeymooning on Oak Island was washed up in a tidal wave. They managed to survive by tying themselves together with a blanket and clinging to trees until the storm passed. Oak Island (then known as Long Beach) was completely devastated.

Hurricane prediction was not as accurate then as it is now. Still, people were aware that there was a hurricane in the Atlantic. It had destroyed three towns in Haiti and killed 1,000 people there. Hazel was predicted to head into the Gulf of Mexico and weaken. However, the freakish storm made a sudden right turn and headed north. Still, it was expected to pass the Carolina coast and go on out to sea. Needless to say, she did not follow the projected course.

My parents and I met Hurricane Hazel head-on that fateful day, October 15th, 1954. I was 4 years old at the time. I was not impressed. We were traveling in our Studebaker from our home in Harrisonburg, VA, to visit my grandparents in Zebulon, NC. Mama was pregnant with my baby brother, although that didn't mean much to me at the time. I was happily playing with my doll Bonnie when I first became aware of the storm. Daddy lifted me out of the back seat and put me in the front seat beside Mama. I looked out the windshield. The wipers were slapping back and forth in vain - making no impression on the rain gushing down against the glass. Daddy had pulled the car off the road and into the driveway of a farm house. There was a large oak tree in the yard. Daddy said that he was going to see if we could go inside the house to wait out the storm. I wanted to go with him. He said I should wait in the car with Mama. Mama told him to be careful. I wasn't sure why. When Daddy got out of the car, I asked Mama whose house it was. She didn't know.

"Then why are we going there?" I asked, very perplexed at this odd event. Mama said she and Daddy thought we might be safer inside a house than in a car. I remained puzzled. I felt perfectly safe. I decided to pay more attention. Mama and I watched Daddy as he made his way toward the house. The wind was blowing fiercely, and it made Daddy's clothes look funny. I noticed he put his hand up to his face to shield his eyes. He climbed the steps to the house slowly, it seemed. He did not knock politely at the door; rather, he banged on it with both his big fists. As he beat at the door, I looked at Mama. Her face was tense. I asked what was wrong. She said I shouldn't worry – that we would be alright. Her words did not convince me. Her face was saying something else, but what?

After a while, Daddy made his way back to the car. There were leaves and sticks flying in the air around him. When he got back into the car, he said that if anyone was in the house, they probably couldn't hear him knocking, what with all the wind and rain. His face was dripping wet, and he mopped it with a handkerchief from his pocket. By this time, I was quite aware that something was wrong. As if to confirm my fears, there was a sudden thud on the top of the car, a loud popping, and the windshield flashed with a very bright white light, and then something big, black and snake-like, slithered and danced across the windshield. Mama screamed. I pulled myself up into a little ball on the seat, a small knot of fear in my chest. Daddy put both his arms around me and Mama. He said that an electric wire had fallen on our car and we would be alright if we just stayed in the car.

The three of us sat in the car and watched the storm as it blew wind, rain, limbs, and leaves all around us. The sound it made was deafening. The small knot of fear in my chest began to grow, and I whimpered. Daddy hugged me to him and said not to worry, that we were going to be "just fine." He reached down and picked up my doll, Bonnie. He handed her to me and said, "You just play with Bonnie. There's nothing for you to worry about." And with that, the knot of fear dissolved – just like that! Even when the enormous oak tree in the yard was ripped up out of the ground by its roots and fell over into the yard, I didn't worry. In fact, that's the most I remember about the storm that day. How long we sat there or how we managed to get to my grandparents is unknown to me. I remember that we sang songs together and I played with my doll.

The next memory I have of that day is being with my grandparents. Gramma cooked me some scrambled eggs and cheese. Grampa held me on his knee and gave me one of his delicious Sundrops. All was right in my world.

I was too young to understand how wicked and powerful Hurricane Hazel had been. I was too naïve to know how very lucky my family had been to have survived our experience completely unscathed. There wasn't even a scratch on our car. All totaled, Hazel was responsible for 95 deaths and $281 million in damage in the United States, 100 deaths and $100 million in damage in Canada, and an estimated 400 to 1,000 deaths in Haiti; however, that number was never confirmed.

Hazel certainly made her mark in history, but I have to admit that I am always surprised when I read the statistics and records, even though I was directly in the path of her fury. It is as if I was at a still point there with my parents – secure in the knowledge that my daddy was taking care of everything.

Mr. Vance's Pansies

In our house on Wolfe Street in
Harrisonburg, Virginia (circa 1955), our next-
door neighbor was Mr. Vance. He was a
stocky, white-haired gentleman with a wide,
pink face and broad smile. He reminded me of
Santa Claus without the beard. He had lived
in the same house for many years. He shared a
side fence with us and a back fence with my
grandparents. He had known my
grandparents forever, and he knew my mother
as a little girl -- which seemed extraordinary to
me. Mr. Vance lived alone. My mother told
me that his wife had died some years before,
and they had one son who was grown up –
like my mother – which meant he lived in his
own house and not with Mr. Vance.   I
wondered who took care of my old friend. My
mother said that he took care of himself. That
seemed odd to me – a man cooking and eating
meals all alone. I am sure I wondered aloud
about it because I also learned that he had
been devoted to his wife, cared for her

tenderly during a long illness, and missed her very much.

The thought of that made me sorry for him, and I sometimes worried about him being sad and lonely. But his plump, happy face always dispelled my gloomy thoughts, and what I remember most was his joy in gardening. I often watched him from my bedroom window. He tended a fairly large vegetable garden in his back yard from which he shared his bounty – juicy tomatoes, yellow onions, red potatoes, fat cabbages. It seemed he was always taking produce to my grandparents or leaving a basket of goodies on our porch. Mr. Vance also tended a large rose bush and rows of flowers – zinnias and dahlias. As much as my mother appreciated his gifts of vegetables, she was equally delighted when he would bring her a bouquet of flowers. Mr. Vance's specialty was pansies, and it was he who introduced me to them. I could see the soft petals from my bedroom window congregated in their lush beds, looking like pallets of rich, thick paint. I was –

and still am – amazed that these delicate beauties could grow in such cold weather.

It was my good fortune that Mr. Vance loved sharing his pansies almost as much as he did tending them. I was delighted on cold winter mornings when my mother would call out, "Mr. Vance is here!" I would run to greet him and his shining face, knowing he would have something to share. I adored his presence. He felt like the sun and smelled like soap and wind. He would stretch out his flannel-covered stocky arms and bend down to tenderly offer me his precious gifts. Whenever I looked into his broad, leathery hands to find those splendid, velvet faces looking back at me, I would gasp a little in awe.

My mother would float the cuttings in glass bowls or dishes and place them on our sunny kitchen table or our dining table. I would climb onto a chair in order to gaze at their lovely faces -- purple, yellow, blue, or white -- each so unique - they seemed to have a personality of their own. Some looked cheerful and happy; others wistful or sad. Some were feminine, while others were decidedly masculine. I was intrigued by them all.

I am certain in my time alone with them, they spoke or sometimes sang to me. My parents thought it was my "vivid imagination." And so I mostly kept these sacred events to myself – until one winter morning when I was allowed to visit Mr. Vance as he knelt in his pansy beds. Timidly, I confessed that sometimes his precious pansies spoke and even sang to me. I wondered whether he had ever heard them. He continued at his work for a moment. Then he turned his sweet pink face to me, smiled, winked, and told me I was a lucky girl and that I should continue to listen - very carefully. Then he rose from his work and took me by the hand to join my mother at the clothesline before going in for a cup of tea. That was all he ever said about that subject, but I knew they spoke to him, too. After that, whenever I saw him kneeling at their beds, I understood his tender care and delight, and I wondered about their conversations. It made me feel better about him living in his house without his wife or son because I knew he wasn't really alone.

The Giant in the Crack

I remember living with my family in our house on Wolf Street in Harrisonburg, Virginia. I was between four and five years old. I can recall the lay out of the house and many of its furnishings. I even remember the windows and how the sun light shone through them and the patterns it created on the oak floors. There was a living room, dining room, kitchen with a walk-in pantry, and two bedrooms on the first floor. Beyond the kitchen, there were stairs in an enclosed space that led up to a big room which was unused while we lived there but was warm and sunny during the day with golden oak floors. My mother stored things there: suit cases, freezer containers, glass jars, and such that I was occasionally sent to retrieve.

Mostly, I loved that house – well, except for those stairs. The stairs were a problem for me. Actually, it was a crack in the wall on the way up those stairs that gave me trouble. About halfway up on the right wall, there was a long crack in the plaster. And in that hideous crack lived a horrible, ugly giant. I knew that because I had seen him! Originally, this giant lived in my "Jack and the Beanstalk" book. He was hairy and grizzly with a bulbous red nose and large buck teeth. He was enormous with hulking shoulders, muscular arms and legs, and gnarled, claw-like hands. I could see him lumbering to and fro in his giant castle, the floors and walls quaking with each step. His thunderous "Fee-Fi-Fo-Fum!" turned my heart to ice! Of course, in Jack's land, he fell out of the sky and out of sight -- gone forever, no longer a menace to Jack. Unfortunately, he had fallen into my world and now lurked in that miserable crack, just waiting for the opportunity to snatch me off those steps and into his evil lair! I was terrified of that possibility.

My parents thought I had a wonderful imagination and, therefore, were delighted with this story. I realized from their patronizing smiles, the pats on my head, and their chuckles when they related my plight to my aunts, uncles, and grandparents that I was doomed! If I were to survive, it would be up to me. I lay in my bed, snuggled under the covers, the silver moon spilling into my room, considering various strategies. I sat on the front porch steps, watching autumn leaves tumble and twirl while dreaming of being daring and brave. And I rode my tricycle like the wind, thinking how to outwit that wicked monster.

Finally, I settled on my womanly charms and tea, which has been served in a civilized manner for many centuries to many a beast. Every morning from my own hutch (a tin furnishing about 2 feet high with elegant red flowers on the sides and front doors), I selected a tea cup and saucer. I filled it with delicate, aromatic brews and carried it up those loathsome stairs and set it quietly at the mouth of the giant's lair. Then tiptoed down again, wanting only the tantalizing aroma of my offering to awaken the terrible, sleeping giant. Faithfully, at noon, I would peer up the stairs to see whether or not he had been pleased with my gift. Each time, it was evident that my potion had calmed the savage beast, and he was either napping contentedly or had wandered happily down a wooded path somewhere in his giant land. So, I would remove the cup and saucer, wash them, and replace them in the hutch. Then, I would select a burgundy goblet and luncheon plate, which I filled with some exotic wine and a dainty morsel of cheese and crackers or fine pastry for a delightful snack on his awakening or return.

At dusk, my heart would cringe as I thought of those stairs, the crack, and that evil giant, for I knew I must retrieve my dishes. I usually dragged some poor creature with me -- a doll or stuffed animal -- to the dimly lit landing, where I once again would peep and peer up the long steps, always thankful to find the goblet and plate empty. I would rush to retrieve them, usually unseen, but on occasion, I was heard or my retreating back side spied by the merciful creature who decided that the meal was just so delicious that he would spare me yet another day.

In fairy tales, magic happens suddenly -- with the wave of a wand, an incantation, or some other definitive means. However, in real life, magic happens slowly and indiscernibly.....and so it was with the giant who lived in the crack in the wall. As the days passed, the crack seemed to widen, and gradually, I was able to see inside by some dim glow filtering through the trees and leaves of that other world. My fear lessened, and I no longer dreaded my trips up the stairs. I sensed peace and harmony emanating from that place. And though I knew I could not enter the now intriguing other world, I could peer inside the crack and down a velvet green path strewn with leaves and mist. I imagined all sorts of fantastic places and creatures to be found there.

One sunny morning with teapot in hand, I was greeted by the giant's wife, who, you may recall, had been left in a castle in the clouds when the giant had crash landed into Jack's bean garden. She looked as homely as before, but her dismal, resigned expression had been replaced by a timid but kindly smile. Now, I cannot tell you how the giant and his wife had been reunited nor how their relationship had managed such a lovely reconciliation -- I can only testify to their contentment with one another. I, of course, felt certain that my soothing teas had somehow played a crucial part.

The giant's wife and I visited together on the stairs many times after that. Sometimes, the now content couple and I would have a tea party, and I would bring the tea service and one or two of my dolls. These were gay, pleasant occasions. I was relaxed and happy -- all my old fears were gone. I cannot now recall what we talked about. I do know that they revealed secrets to me about that house and all the places and noises that frightened me. I was able to meet their twin boys, who lived way back in the darkness of the pantry that slanted down under the stairs. And the dreadful bumping and scratching noises that paralyzed me with fear while I was in my bed at night, I now understood to be the giant family. I was assured that they protected me, and I was comforted by their presence in my house.

We moved when I was 6 years old. I cried to be leaving my giant friends as we all knew the opening to their world was in that house on Wolfe Street, and they could not travel with me. I would feel sad whenever I thought of them in that house without me. I wondered if the people who moved in after I left enjoyed tea parties with them. I even felt a little jealous. My mother said that maybe they had patched the crack. I was shocked. Why in the world would they want to do that? Who would want to close the door to such an enchanting place? The idea was inconceivable.

A Cat Named Clara

My family inherited a cat from a little old lady named Miss Barham when I was about seven years old. Miss Barham looked exactly like a gnarled old woman from one of my storybooks. I suspected she might be a witch, although not a bad witch. Miss Barham had been renting our house in North Carolina and had moved all of her belongings out a few days before we began the process of moving in. She had left word with my grandparents that she had taken everything except her cat, which could not be found when she was all packed up. However, she promised that she would be back to fetch the cat. My parents had spied the cat about the property and assumed it belonged to the old lady. I saw the cat, too, and secretly hoped that Miss Barham would not come to get her. I liked the look of her whiskered face, and I liked the idea of having a cat for my own pet – even though this particular cat did not come close enough for me to make friends. Miss Barham showed up as promised on the day we were moving in.

After cordial greetings were exchanged, my parents continued their work, and Miss Barham began looking around for her cat. She called "Here Kitty kitty" many times, but her kitty did not come. After quite a long time, someone spotted the cat sitting regally among some cabbages in a garden behind our house. Miss Barham chided the cat for not coming and beckoned her with more "here kitties," but the cat remained in the garden regarding Miss Barham with what seemed some disdain. Miss Barham tromped off to the garden, whereupon the cat hastily changed her position to a now plowed-up tobacco field beside our house quite a distance from the garden. When Miss Barham made for the plowed field, the cat made for the woods. Miss Barham shook her head, grumbled, and returned to our yard. Every now and then, Miss Barham would call out, "Here, Kitty-kitty."

After some time, the cat strolled out of the woods and sat herself down in the middle of the plowed field, her eyes looking directly at the exasperated Miss Barham. The old lady called her kitty over and over, but the cat was clearly not interested in coming anywhere in her proximity. At long last, Miss Barham admitted defeat – whether from exhaustion or embarrassment, I couldn't say. She had stayed her limit, and it was apparent she would not be able to take the cat with her. My parents had continued with their moving work. Still, they were aware of the current impasse between the old lady and her obstinate cat. They promised Miss Barham that they would feed the haughty creature. And Miss Barham promised that she would be back another day to collect the recalcitrant cat.

The cat appeared daily for meals and stayed for head scratches and belly rubs. As it turned out, we had all gotten a bad first impression of the cat. Although she had appeared regal, aloof, and indifferent, she was, in fact, quite the opposite - sweet, affectionate, and docile. Miss Barham had not introduced us formally, and as far as we knew, her name was Kitty. Be that as it may, any cat who allowed herself to be dressed up in my doll baby's clothes, set and stay in a doll's high chair, and pushed around in my dolly's baby buggy without complaint needed a better, more substantial name, in my opinion. I declared that she was the sweetest cat ever and that I was going to name her after my Sunday School teacher, "Miss" Clara, who was the absolute sweetest person I could think of. Neither my Sunday School teacher nor the cat seemed to mind, and since "Miss" Clara had laughed out loud and said it was a lovely compliment, I was quite sure that Clara the Cat was honored. For a while, I worried that Miss Barham would come back to claim her cat, but she never did.

Now, one thing you should know is that my daddy was not a cat lover – or at least, he did not want a cat for a house pet – but he was impressed by Clara's courteous nature. Unlike other cats he had known, she refrained from winding herself around his or my mama's legs, kept a polite distance, and only sought affection from me or my brother. The respectful Clara never once deigned to even step one little paw into our house - not that she would have been allowed to stay there, but that she knew her place further swayed my

daddy positively on her behalf. Clara also
occasionally left generous gifts on our
doorstep – dead things or pieces of them: mice,
rabbits, birds – which horrified my mama but
assured Daddy that she was a good hunter
and was earning her keep.

After some time had passed, during one
of her belly rub sessions, I noted that Clara's
soft tummy was overly fat. My parents told me
that she was likely to be a mother soon. My
brother and I were thrilled. My parents sighed
and rolled their eyes. I knew that cats usually
hid their kittens from prying eyes and
predators, and I wondered where that
somewhere might be. As it happened, Clara
had a big surprise in store for all of us!

In the middle of the night, my parents
were awakened by the meowing of a cat. The
meowing became louder and closer. Mama
wondered if it could be Clara. Daddy, firmly
assured of her usual genteel nature, was
certain it could not possibly be. He went to
their bedroom window, opened the curtain,
and there on the window ledge was the
pitifully wailing Clara. He was surprised but

thought that surely something was wrong for her to behave in such an unusual manner. He decided to investigate. Flashlight in hand, he went to the front door, opened it, and to his further surprise, there stood Clara.

Then, to his utter amazement, she walked right into the house as if she'd been there a hundred times before and headed straight for the basement door. Daddy figured there was nothing to do but to oblige the cat, and when he opened it, she went straight downstairs. By this point, he had deduced that the poor Clara was in labor and needed a safe haven to bear her offspring. Daddy followed her down but then escorted her to the garage and walked to the very back, where he had built wooden bins to house potatoes for the winter. He placed an empty box in one of the bins and lined it with a burlap bag. It seemed that he and Clara had reached a mutual agreement through sheer telepathy, for she quietly got into the box and nestled down to begin her business of child bearing.

Daddy came back upstairs, shaking his head and chuckling to himself. The next morning, I could hardly wait to go downstairs to see the new arrivals, but Daddy cautioned us that despite Clara's usual amiable disposition, being a mother might make her overly protective and unwelcoming to prying eyes. So, my brother and I went quietly to the kitten nursery and peeked into the box. Clara looked up at us with her sweet face, and although obviously tired, she was pleased with her litter. She rolled over just a little to allow us a peek at her six little kittens nursing cozily among her soft fur. We were delighted.

I was more than a little astonished at how Clara had managed access to our garage and even more so at Daddy's part in the little miracle. I didn't want to press too much – afraid Daddy's grace would only extend just so far – but I had to know more. I asked Daddy what he thought. He shrugged, "Well, it's spring time and sometimes tomcats come around and kill newborn kittens. I think she just wanted them somewhere she knew they'd be safe." (The reason for this being: so the female would go into heat again – which I learned later) "But how did Clara know which window was yours? And how did she know about the basement?" Daddy just shook his head. "She's a smart cat." What other answer could he give? It has remained one of life's mysteries, that's for sure. Later that day, Daddy opened one of the small garage windows, which were high up on the wall, and leaned a 2x4 board on its sill so Clara could enter and exit the garage at her leisure. I'm pretty sure Daddy earned some extra stars in his crown for that favor, but nobody in our family said a word - although my mama smiled at me and winked.

When the kittens were up and walking, Daddy allowed them to stay in the garage until they got big enough to move out on their own accord. Nothing is much cuter than kittens at play, and we all enjoyed watching them grow. As it often happened in the country back then, cats find their own way. As they grew, some of them lingered, but some left. Still, Clara stayed on our property for a number of years. And with every litter of kittens, she and my daddy played out their original agreement: she went into labor, and he let her use the garage for her nursery. Over time, it was no longer astonishing, although we continued to be reminded that Clara certainly was a remarkable cat.

One particular spring, when Clara was again with a new litter of kittens, we were all awakened by a great commotion in the garage – a clattering, thudding, loud squalls, shrieks, and hissing. Daddy leaped into action. He grabbed his shotgun and ran down to the garage. I heard him shouting, and a few minutes later, I heard him fire his gun. I was panicked. It was a little while before he returned. When he did, his face was downcast as he reported that a tomcat had come into the garage, and, of course, that was what all the commotion was about. Daddy said that Clara was a fierce mama and had fought valiantly to save her babies. Unfortunately, the old Tom had killed one of them before Clara could fend him off. When Daddy arrived on the scene, Clara had the intruder backing up the 2x4 board toward the window. At the sound of Daddy's voice, the mean old cat turned tail and ran out the window. Daddy ran out into the yard and fired buckshot at the cat's backside, which sent him into a forward flip and tumble across the field. The last Daddy saw was the attacker's frayed tail disappearing into the dark of the night. Daddy returned to check on Clara, who was examining her babies. Daddy removed the poor little thing who had not survived and buried him near our garden.

Being a country cat who mostly lived outside, Clara came and went as she pleased, and there came a time when Clara went but did not come back. I can't say what happened to her. Sometimes, in the wild, when animals know their time has come, they go off somewhere alone to die. My daddy said that's likely what she had done. There was no way for us to know how old she was, but we calculated that she was pretty old. She had lived with Miss Barham before she lived with us, and for how many years we didn't know. Then again, maybe she had never belonged to any of us. Perhaps we all lived on her property as far as she was concerned. All I know is that Clara was the best cat I ever knew. We were lucky that she chose to grace our lives with her presence. I like to think of her lounging in the sun – soft and sleepy and perfectly content.

Grampa and the Witch

Grampa, like most of his siblings, was an engaging story teller. Folks loved to listen to him. I was among them, and if he wasn't charming a crowd, I would sit on his lap and beg for him to tell me a story. My favorites were about his childhood - most of them I have forgotten except for this one, which enchanted me then and even now.

When Grampa was a small boy, a witch came to his house carrying a basket on her arm. She set her basket on the kitchen table. The contents of the basket were covered by a cloth and hidden from view. The old woman bent toward him, looked straight into his eyes, pointed a bony finger at him, and warned, "Don't you look in my basket, Johnny!" then she added, "If you look in my basket, I will know it. So keep your nose out of my things."

Grampa admitted that her stern warning frightened him, and he recoiled from her staring eyes and pointing finger. Then, the old hag whirled and left the room, leaving her basket on the table. Johnny was terrified. What could possibly be in that basket that was so valuable, so important that it required such strong caution? Was it something magical? Her wand, perhaps? Or did it contain a healing potion or evil brew? Maybe it was some poor creature that she had turned to stone or shrunk to near-nothingness. The possibilities of what might be began to grow. Under that cloth could be magical beans, herbs, or poisonous mushrooms. Witches had been known to steal babies. Perhaps she had a wee babe tucked under the linen cloth. My grandfather, it seems, was a hero even then because that particular thought was enough to nudge his curiosity into action. Johnny crept quietly over to the table. He looked around carefully to make certain that no one could see him. And he listened intently for any noise that would alert him that someone was coming. He slowly, quietly, cautiously lifted the cloth, taking care not to move the basket even a single inch. Then he peered into the old woman's basket. Every time he told me this story, I held my breath.

"What? What was there, Grampa?" I would ask, even though I had heard the answer many times before.

"Nothing," was the disappointing reply.

"What did you do then?" I would ask.

"I went on outside to play," he'd say. "But do you know what?"

"What?" I would breathe, my eyes wide and my heart racing.

"When that witch came back to the kitchen to get her basket, she knew I'd looked inside," he would say and nod his head for emphasis.

"How? How did she know?" Surely, she had a crystal ball or a magic wand that told her such things.

"Old witches just know things like that. She could probably smell where my fingers touched her cloth. Or else she saw me in her mind's eye," he would say.

Oh, my! I could see the old hag's nose twitching as she sniffed the air around the basket when she entered the kitchen. I would shudder. And then I would wonder what the Eye in her Mind looked like -- a Mind's Eye -- oh, Dear! Oh, my! I could see that one all-seeing, terrible eye looking out through her forehead and able to view all manner of things not within normal sight. It was more fearsome than her crooked, warty nose.

"What happened? What did she do?" I would press, and every time I asked this question, I feared the answer.

"She came out on the porch and called me over. She leaned toward me and pointed her long bony finger in my face, shook it, and said, 'I know you looked into my basket, Johnny, didn't you?' Her eyes were all wrinkled and squinty. I was scared to death she was gonna put a spell on me. But she didn't. She just cackled and went off down the road."

Oh, what a relief! She didn't turn him into a toad or a rat or a pillar of salt or worse yet into nothingness -- because she could have done that with a snap of her bony finger -- just made him vanish away into thin air. Where would that be??? I wondered why she had given him a reprieve. Maybe because putting his hand into her basket didn't amount to anything. There was nothing there for him to see. Oh, my grandfather was such a lucky fellow! Thank Goodness. What in the world would have happened to him if there had been something under that cloth -- one of her dark secrets? What would he have done then? Sometimes, as we sat rocking together, we expounded on one of the awful possibilities. Our imagination about all that wickedness and his bravery would wind on for hours.

My grandfather died when I was seven. I was heartbroken. I missed his booming voice, hearty laughter, bear hugs, candy surprises, and sharing secrets. Most of all, I missed sitting with him in his rocking chair, leaning against his chest as he told me fabulous stories that enlivened my imagination. They were his legacy to me. I filled the void his passing left in my life by revisiting his stories. Certainly, his encounter with the witch and her basket was the most impressive, and I was left alone to expound on the whys and what-ifs of that event. Sometimes, I would discuss this particular story with my grandmother or my parents, but they usually smiled and dismissed it rather carelessly, I thought. They did not seem to see the depth of the mystery.

Years passing did not dilute my fascination with that moment in my grandfather's young life when a witch had entered his world, and he had bravely disobeyed her warning. And moreover, he had escaped unscathed. There came a day when I was struck by a new thought about Grampa's story. Perhaps the event had unfolded exactly as the old crone had meant for it to. Perhaps she was only trying to lure him to put his hand into the basket. That would be just the sort of thing a wicked temptress would do to a curious boy. Perhaps his hand being inside her woven lair was the key to some other secret that only witches could know. That gave a whole new meaning to her evil laughter as she departed. She knew something that only she could know. My poor unsuspecting grampa,

the innocent young Johnny, had been part of a magical spell all those years ago. And because of that moment in time, the world had changed and was never the same again.
I wished mightily that I could visit Grampa again. We had much to discuss. I closed my eyes and imagined what that might be like: his strong hug, loud laughter, and the candy from his pocket -- all wonderful, but nothing as sweet as crawling into the rocker with him to have our discussion.

     My inner vision was strong. I could feel myself there in Grampa's presence: the sweet smell of his soap, the soft denim of his overalls, and the easy rise and fall of his chest. Then, just as I was about to present my latest theory, my memory rested on his fabulous thumb -- or maybe I should say *thumbs*, plural -- for my grandfather had what our family called a "double thumb" on his right hand. His large hand was normal in every way except for the two thumbs, which grew out of the place where everyone else had only one. Each thumb was fully formed right down to the joints and nails. They entwined with one another like ivy around a tree. Although they were inseparable, they could move independently of one another. I had often examined that thumb in a sort of absent-minded way as I sat in my grandfather's lap, listening to his stories and songs. Sometimes, I would attempt to separate the appendages, and Grampa would end the struggle by pinching one of my small fingers in between his two amazing thumbs. I would squeal with laughter. Perhaps I had been looking right at the result of young Johnny's disobedience all along without realizing it! Could it be?

My lonely introspection was too much for one young girl. I needed someone to talk to about this new perspective. Perhaps Daddy could help sort things out. And so I laid out the revelation and asked what he thought. He laughed and tousled my hair, "Honey, that old woman wasn't a witch. She was just an old woman with a wrinkled face that scared your Grampa. She was teasing him with her basket. She knew if she told him not to look in it, that would just make him curious, and he would be bound to do it. She didn't have any special powers. She just knew young boys and their natural curiosity. She went off laughing because she knew by the look on his face that he had done exactly what she'd said not to do." I was stunned and disappointed. I knew Grampa was a wise man, and he wouldn't have believed the old woman was a witch if it weren't true. And I said so. But Daddy remained firm.

"There are no such thing as witches," he said as he shook his head. I could see there was no convincing him. He went on with his chores, leaving me to consider his words. Here was a man who had told me on other occasions that he didn't believe in ghosts, evil spirits, or ugly giants. And now he was saying he didn't believe in witches. He probably didn't believe in fairies or elves, either. And yet he went to church regularly and prayed openly to God. You couldn't see Him either, so what was the difference? How did a person decide what was real and true or not? Now, there was another mystery to be solved. Whenever I posed this question to the adults in my world, their answer was invariably:

"You must have faith to believe in God." Apparently, faith didn't count in the matter of ghosts, giants, or witches. I began to think of all the incredible things adults believed in, like gravity, God, the Holy Ghost, the creation of the world in only seven days, the virgin birth, and germs. How could these things be absolutely true, but yet other mystical creatures and magic not? What did faith really mean? Mama and Daddy shook their heads and said things like:

"When you get older, you'll understand," or "Just have faith, and you will see," They didn't seem to understand that I DID have faith, and it allowed me to believe in ALL these things. It seemed my faith was different from theirs. My grandmother just laughed and hugged me. She didn't seem too worried about my beliefs or my faith. Other adults had reactions ranging from complete perplexity to just plain horror, and then they worried about my "salvation." In a rural

Southern Baptist church, even as a young girl, I knew enough to know that this was a grave concern, even though I really didn't comprehend the idea of salvation any better than their notion of faith. And so I decided to stop asking them questions. I knew that my grandfather had been a respected leader in our church as well as in the wider community. He had studied the Bible and had been ordained as a deacon of the church. He didn't seem to have any problem with believing in all manner of mystical things. I would have liked to have a discussion with him about his idea of faith. I had a strong feeling that our idea of faith was much the same.

So there I'd gone round and round in my thinking and was right back where I started. There was no question in my mind that Grampa had met a witch when he was a boy or that he'd had an extraordinary encounter with her. The real questions remained unanswered: Had the old crone let him go on his way unhurt, unmarked? Or had putting his hand in the witch's basket been part of a magical spell that created his double thumb and let something loose in the world that had not existed before? I supposed I would never know the answer to these questions. What I do know is that my grandfather was incredible. He was a deeply spiritual man who loved his children fiercely and his grandchildren with abandon. He wore a suit with a vest and pocket watch on Sundays, but during the week, he rambled about his farm in overalls and went barefoot as often as possible. He adored his wife, and even in the early 1900s, with all the work that needed doing on over 100 acres of farmland with only mules for plowing and no electricity, he took every Monday to help his beloved Bessie do her washing. It was well known among his nine children that he regarded washing as a chore to be shared because he acknowledged it as monstrously hard work. He was a gregarious man who loved people and entertained guests of various races and creeds, graciously sharing whatever he had, even during the dark days of the Depression. Many folks in our community remembered his kindnesses and spoke of them long years after his death. He had great gifts of inspiration, oratory, and imagination. I felt his immense love as a palpable and solid thing. And the joy of it was evident whenever he sat in the dirt with me and pretended to eat make-believe ice cream or rocked me in his front porch rocker singing hymns or weaving fantastic tales. Perhaps the old witch _had_ changed him that day -- maybe she conjured up his extra thumb. Perhaps his fabulous double thumb kept him open to other viewpoints and magical possibilities. Maybe what changed in the world that day was ....well, I can't say for certain.......but maybe it has to do with faith – the kind that allows you to believe in people and their stories, the kind that has kept my grandfather's story alive for me even after all these years. Whatever it was opened a doorway for my grandfather and for me. That's how this story came to be.

As an adult, I understand the responses of my parents about my Grampa's witch story. But as the granddaughter of Johnny Pearce, I choose to believe in magic. I believe there is more to life than we can see with the eye or explain by science.

Chapter 2

School Daze

Boyfriends

In Second Grade, I had two boys who liked me more than a little. I was flattered and very much enjoyed their extra attention. Otherwise, I had no idea what to do about this happy turn except to smile at them. That seemed to be quite enough – at least in the beginning – but I'll get to that in a minute.

I had known Steve for a while. He was the son of our family physician. Sometimes, we played together at his grandfather's house if my mama or brother had a doctor's appointment. I also knew many of his extended family members – aunts, uncles, and cousins. Additionally, Steve and I had been Senior Class mascots a couple of years prior to starting public school, and we had been thrown together on various occasions regarding that event. Steve was always well groomed, well dressed, and well mannered – a perfect gentleman, my mother said.

And then there was Earl. I had never seen or heard of Earl before entering Second Grade. Earl was a little rough around the edges but sincerely sweet. He was an athletic and scrappy boy. Despite his rowdiness on the playground and frequently scraped skin, he had a softer side. He liked to sing to me, which made me blush, but I had to appreciate his earnest effort.

In the beginning, Steve didn't know that Earl liked me, and Earl didn't know that Steve liked me. It was as if neither boy was aware of the other's existence. Not knowing a thing about love – family relationships aside – and certainly nothing about love triangles, it never occurred to me that this knowledge could be a problem. Everything was stars and hearts and flowers as far as I was concerned. Steve was the one that changed the playing field.

At recess, we all played outside under the shade of a huge old oak tree if the weather was nice. The ground was sandy and just right for drawing pictures or Hop Scotch patterns or making a circle for Dodge Ball. There was also jump rope and tag. Sometimes, we just raced from the side of the building down to a chain link fence to see who was the winner. One day, Steve suggested to a small group of us that the boys chase the girls to the fence. If a girl was caught, she would have to give that boy a kiss. I'm sure our teacher, Mrs. Rogers, was completely unaware of this game because I am very sure she would have nixed it had she known. I guess it just looked like a game of racing or tag to her. The girls that played giggled about it. I felt both delighted and terrified. And no matter how much I liked the fact that a boy was paying extra special attention to me, there was no way I was going to let that boy kiss me. No, sir!

Somehow, my mother had infused me with Southern Belle rules early on, and I knew innately that kissing a boy in public was a big "NO-NO." So, let the games begin! Yes, indeed. I ran like the wind – every single time. Not one of those Second-Grade boys ever caught me – including Steve or Earl. What did happen was that Steve realized that he and

Earl were both chasing the same girl. Earl also came to the same conclusion about the same time. And that's when the problem started.

The extra attention I received escalated from each boy. Previously, when Steve paid attention to me, Earl was usually occupied elsewhere. And when Earl paid attention to me, Steve was busy doing something else. But now their eyes had been opened, and a competition began. Steve began to bring me presents – sometimes a flower or maybe an apple. So Earl brought me presents, too - a pebble he'd picked up or a cookie from his lunch. (Mama said to say "no thank you" as politely as possible to the cookie because Earl needed to eat the lunch his mama had packed for him.) Steve also brought me a Nurse doll for Christmas, a box of candy for Valentine's Day, and hearts cut out of construction paper just because. Earl gave me a magnet that didn't work, a broken watch, and scraps of paper with squiggly hearts drawn in pencil on them. I treasured these gifts all the same. But that didn't slow or stop the competition. Mama cautioned me to "be nice" and not to hurt their feelings. I figured I could do that easily enough, but after a while, it got harder as the competition grew.

One day, Steve and Earl sat directly in front of and facing me and surprised me by asking whom I wanted to marry. Lordamercy! I was stunned. Certainly, I had never given this a moment's thought. Yet there they sat, each boy looking at me very sweetly and expectantly. Not having considered marriage at this point in my little life, I was at a loss for words. I knew that they were each considering themselves as possibilities and were waiting for me to end the competition then and there. Finally, I hit upon a response that I thought would avert further competition when I stated what was my typical response to grownups when they queried, "What do you want to be when you grow up?" My mantra in those days was, "I'm going to be a nurse when I grow up." And so that is exactly what I said to both of them.

Steve and Earl stopped gazing at me. They turned toward each other and glared. I felt pretty proud of myself – happy with my reply, which had postponed decision-making on my part and had averted a possible squabble between the two boys. But Steve wasn't giving up. He turned to me, smiled smugly, and with his chin high, he turned back to Earl and said with a slight air of arrogance, "Well, I'm going to be a doctor." Steve turned back to me, looking quite as if he might have won the prize. But Earl was clever and not about to be out done. He glared at Steve for only a moment before looking at me dreamily and replying, "Well, I'm going to be sick."

Sigh…….Boys! I sure had a lot to learn.

Coins and Reprieve

Having a school Annual was a big deal to me. Not only did the Annual capture pictures of our classmates and the school year's events, but friends passed them to friends to write in – thoughts on whatever – events that had happened, looking ahead, good wishes, and the like. They were a treasure – and still are. I desperately wanted one.

When I was in 5th grade, in Mrs. Gregory's room, Ann Davis (later Matheny) came into our room to announce that money would be collected the next day for school annuals. Ann was in high school on the Wak-high-an Annual staff. She was also my friend Susan's big sister. Ann was wearing a London Fog raincoat and penny loafers – the epitome of cool. Knowing she was on the Annual Staff made the Annual even more appealing. I watched her casual manner, wondering if I could ever attain such ease. I wanted to feel hopeful but figured if owning an Annual was out of the question, then maybe other things were as well.

Daddy's business was struggling to get off the ground, and there was no extra money for anything. I understood the phrase "pinching pennies" in a very personal way. Nevertheless, that night, I told Mama how much I wanted an Annual. Mama understood. She did not chide me for wanting something that would stretch our family's budget. She knew it was important to belong. She asked if I had any money in my piggy bank? Yes, I had some coins there, but not enough. Mama had some rolled coins, some change in her purse, and loose change stuffed here and there. She gathered everything she could find. Then we counted it, and happily, there was just enough. It was after banking hours, so there was nothing to do but put all the collected coins in a paper bag, which I took to school the next day. When the Wak-high-an staff showed up, I was proud to be among those who lined up to pay for my annual.

When it was my turn, I walked up to Ann Davis and self-consciously handed her my paper bag. Without a word, she looked inside and then plunked down at Mrs. Gregory's desk, poured out the money, and began counting. Mrs. Gregory rolled her eyes and sighed audibly, indicating her displeasure. I was beyond embarrassed. I expected that Ann might communicate agreement with my teacher, either verbally or by another impatient gesture, and so I apologized. Ann looked up at me, shrugged, and said, "Money is money." Period. Then, she nonchalantly continued counting the coins.   It was clear that she couldn't have cared less if I had handed her all pennies. I felt reprieved. I suspect Ann never thought another thing about that day, but I have never forgotten it. I was so grateful for her gracious attitude that relieved me of my embarrassment. Her actions endeared her to me for life. It was the first year that I was able to have a school annual, and I was so proud when they arrived that I was able to stand in line to collect mine. I still have it.

Cuban Missile Crisis Plan

The Cuban Missile Crisis occurred during October and November 1962. It was probably the closest our country came to engaging in a Nuclear War with Russia during the years now referred to as the Cold War. Without going into the whole political turmoil, the bottom line is that Russia had delivered nuclear weapons to Cuba, which were then aimed directly at the United States. When the United States learned of this threat, President Kennedy drew a line in the sand, and there were tense conversations and negotiations between the United States and the Soviet Union. The American people were kept abreast of the stressful situation by the nightly news that strained everyone's nerves. And whenever there was official word from the President, it was not comforting. Fear was at a peak. The military, politicians, and ordinary people prepared themselves as best they could. Part of this preparation included discussion and practice for what should happen in the event that a missile strike should actually happen. School children practiced "duck and cover" – which meant hiding underneath their desks. It was a terrifying time, and even though most adults tried not to discuss their fears and plans in front of their children, it was impossible to avoid the overwhelming dread. As a twelve-year-old child during that turbulent time, I was not ignorant of the raging unrest.

Riding home from school on the bus one day, my friend Billy and I were discussing the whole mess. We had practiced "duck and cover" that day, and both of us were pretty sure that hiding under our desks would not be much protection if our school building collapsed. We figured we had a better chance outside if worse came to worse. Where we really wanted to be was home with our mamas. And so we began making plans for our personal safety – to hell with "duck and cover"! After some consideration, Billy and I decided that if some terrible thing really did happen, what with school alarm bells ringing, sirens wailing, lots of commotion, and the teachers' own fears, we could easily just rebel.

No "duck and cover" for us. We would run like rabbits – straight for home.

We both had younger siblings – he had a little sister about 3 years younger, and I had a little brother who was in 2nd grade. Their existence added to our problem. We couldn't abandon them, and that was that. We calculated that each of us would run to our sibling's classroom, grab them, and drag them along. Their teachers would be no better prepared than ours and would not expect a rebellious older kid to show up and snatch one of their charges. After fetching our precious cargo, we planned to meet at the big tree near the Teachers' Dormitory and head out for home. We plotted our course and how far we could travel together before we'd have to split up. After that, each of us would be on our own. The only problem we could foresee is that our little siblings might not come with us quickly enough. They might be frightened by the chaos and be confused about what to do. So, we would have to give them prior instructions. There was some concern that they might reveal our plan to the adults in charge, but it was a risk we had to take.

We each left the bus that afternoon with a plan in mind. Once I got home, I waited for an opportunity to talk to my little brother alone. I reminded him about the "duck and cover" routines we'd been practicing at school. His little head nodded in agreement. I explained that if "the bomb" really came, I didn't want to hide at school; instead, I was planning to run home, and I wanted to take him with me. My little brother continued nodding, and so I gave further instructions. "When the teacher says for you to 'duck and cover,' you do it but be watching the door, and when you see me open that door, you get up and come with me right away, do you hear?" He nodded in all earnestness, his eyes wide with fear. I hated to see his poor little face look so scared, but there was no avoiding it.

The next morning, on the bus, I consulted with Billy. Yep. He had talked to his little sister, and she was on board, too. Both of our little siblings had been sworn to secrecy, and we just had to trust that they would hold true. In any event, we had a plan, and we were sticking to it. Billy and I discussed it every afternoon on the bus ride home. Sometimes, I'd remind my little brother about the plan. He had not forgotten. I never discussed my rebellion with a single adult. I ran it over in my head before going to sleep at night, and every time, we had to practice "duck and cover" at school. Whenever the drill started, I felt the same knot of sick fear at the pit of my stomach but then steeled myself for the resolve that I would need to begin my great escape.

The Cuban Missile Crisis resolved, but Billy and I maintained our pact – just in case. I stopped scaring my little brother with ominous reminders. But every now and then, I rehearsed my escape route in my mind – just in case. I'm not sure when I actually let go of that vague dread, but eventually, it dissipated. Perhaps it happened as I was moving along with life like the rest of America.

Learning to Drive

I grew up in the country, and like many country kids, I learned to drive a tractor long before I learned to drive a car. In fact, I learned to drive my daddy's tractor when I could just barely reach the brakes. There wasn't much to it, really. Changing gears on a tractor is relatively easy, and the fact is you can drive pretty much in one gear and get to most places a tractor ever needs to go. My mama wasn't too keen on me learning, but Daddy ignored her and taught me anyway. The day he jumped on an old board with a huge rusty nail sticking out that thrust itself clear through his work boot and into his foot, Mama said she was mighty glad I was able to drive the two of us back home. It was the first and only time I ever heard my daddy come close to cursing: "SON OF A GUN!!!" is what he yelled with such a groaning rage that it frightened me.

I knew something was wrong. I had seen my Daddy jump from the top of the tractor onto a pile of old lumber, and when he landed, there was a solid thud and an immediate roar of pain. I watched him pull his foot and boot loose from the board and its nail. I was horrified. He said, "you'll need to drive us home, Little Girl." He climbed back onto the tractor, and I put it into gear and set off for home. In retrospect, I'm sure that he could have driven us home. Still, I suspect he knew that putting me in charge of the situation gave me something to put my mind to besides the awful accident that had just happened. What I remember most about it was how proud I was that I'd taken care of my daddy when he was hurt!

I didn't drive any other vehicles until the summer when my schoolmates and I were slated to take driver education Classes. I was pretty nervous about the upcoming classes mostly because of the instructor, who was the high school football and basketball coach. The man was revered because he could drive his boys to win ballgames, but he was gruff, loud, rough around the edges, and had a reputation for his impatience and short temper. I mentioned my anxiety to the guy who lived next door who was also a classmate – not to mention that he played ball and knew my fears were not unfounded. He suggested that I could practice driving "the Blue Goose" – his dad's old Chevy pickup that had been through some rough weather and tough terrain and could probably take a jolt or two. The old truck was a straight stick (meaning you changed the gears manually on the column), which was how the Drivers Ed car would be as well - so it would be good practice. As with most farm boys back then, my friend had been driving that truck around the farm for years, so his driving instruction would only be a formality for his license. He didn't need to learn much of anything save the rules of the road. My brave friend drove me up to a stretch of his farm that was clear of any major obstacles – well, other than a barn, some trees, a pond, and a fence. I managed to get the Blue Goose going, but changing gears on a column was new for me and much more delicate than changing tractor gears. And you'd think being off the highway would be a plus, but the ruts and bumps encountered on a dirt road are graceless and unforgiving. I lurched and chugged and bounced along until I ran into a fence and gave up. The poor old Blue Goose was no worse for the wear, and I was certainly not cheered by my efforts. I awaited Drivers Ed like a man doomed to the gallows.

And like a doomed man, there was no escape, and so Drivers Ed began. The classwork was interesting and easy, but I knew the hard part was yet to come. The fateful day came, and I crawled into the driver's seat with the instructor/coach sitting alongside me. For those of you who live in my hometown of Zebulon, we were on Wakefield Street. I started the car, put the car into first gear (good start, right?), and Coach Chapman said, "Now let off the clutch slow and give it some gas." We bucked and lurched along the street until Coach slammed on the brakes on his side of the car (back in those days, the instructor had a brake on their side). Ugh. Sigh. Coach said very slowly and deliberately, "Okay, let's start again. This time, let off the clutch real slow…." And so I begin again. Once again, we buck and pitch along the street until Coach slams on the brake and shouts, "Slow, G—Dammit! I said SLOW. S-L-O-W. Do you know the meaning of the word???!!!" Gulp. And off we go for the third time.

This time, I get the complete meaning of SLOW, and I'm off – totally humiliated but going. Somehow, I manage the rest of my session without any misstep and no further shouting or cursing. At the end of my session, I am totally spent. Worn out. I climb into the back seat and observe the next student's misery. When I arrive home, I tell my mom I'm not going to drive the next day. My mom says we'll discuss it at dinner. My dad listens to my recounting and looks sympathetic but says that I must drive the next day. "That's just his way," he says and insists that I should not let Coach know that he has upset me. "Don't let him know that you're scared of him. It will only make things worse." (Nowadays, the dude would never have been allowed to act like this guy did on a regular basis. However, this was a totally different climate…. But I digress.)

The next driving adventure was mostly okay for me – no bucking, no lurching, no yelling, no cursing. Still, I was a bundle of nerves and glad to finish my turn and crawl into the back seat. From there, I witnessed another student's torture and felt nothing but pity for her distress.

On the third day, things began well enough. Still, somewhere in the middle of my stint, I pulled up to a stop sign that was on a slight incline, and, added to that, there was a huge tree that obstructed the view of traffic coming from the left. I came to a full stop but then eased forward, taking care with the clutch and brake so the car wouldn't stall, allowing me to increase my field of vision before moving forward from the stop sign. Just about that time, a huge lumbering dump truck came from the left. Of course, I full-on braked to allow it to pass, but Coach let loose a hailstorm of criticism. "Damn! Are you trying to kill us???!!!" I made no reply and continued driving. But from that moment on, every time Coach saw a big truck, he would point at it and yell, "There's a truck, Linda. Why don't you see if you can hit it???" I began to come undone.

Finally, we pulled into the driveway of another student, and Coach said, "Yeah, we'll let Linda back out onto the highway and see if she can do it without killing us all." That was it. I'd reached my limit. I stopped the car, got out, opened the back door, and got in. I was done for the day. For a few seconds, there was dead silence. I sat there waiting for Coach to explode and realized I didn't care what he said or did - I was DONE. Period. At length, he began to chuckle. Then he shrugged his shoulders and said, "Well, I think I've pissed her off, boys." And he motioned for my classmate to get into the driver's seat. He didn't say another word to me.

I didn't tell my parents about the incident. I guess I was waiting for the next day's fallout. The next day arrived too soon for me, and I walked out to the car to find Coach calling the previous driver an "egghead." I took a deep breath and got into the driver's seat. Coach settled down on his side of the car and said, "Now watch this,

Egghead. This girl is a perfect driver." I was momentarily stunned but, without a word, started the car and set out to drive – yes, perfectly from then on – no more yelling or cursing from the Coach. In fact, he hung out the window, drank his "cough syrup," waved at friends along whatever route he commanded, and generally enjoyed the ride. And just like that, I had learned to drive - perfectly.

Shoes

My husband thinks I have too many shoes, and I would agree that I have a considerable number. But I'm certainly not the infamous Imelda Marcos! In fact, I suspect that I am in the low range compared to the average woman. So, let's talk about Imelda for a minute. It has been estimated that the Philippine Dictator's wife had over 3,000 pairs. I currently have 73. I know this because I counted them. And 73 is nowhere NEAR 3,000 – never mind that I hate Math and can't do ratios. However, when I consider the number of shoes I have now compared to the number I had growing up – well, maybe then I'd sorta look like Imelda Marcos.

When I was growing up, what you had, at the most, were 4 pairs of shoes. In the Fall, we went shopping for everyday school shoes, a pair of Sunday shoes, and maybe a pair of tennis shoes. In the spring, you got to buy a new pair of shoes to go with the Easter outfit and a pair of sandals for warmer weather. Sometimes, I also had a pair of flip-flops. And this was pretty typical for the girls I knew. I felt lucky. I knew some folks couldn't afford but one pair of shoes that had to do for everything.

I did NOT feel lucky the day my parents took me to the foot doctor because I was "pigeon-toed." I'd never noticed this deformity, but apparently, they had. I suppose they discussed it privately because it was a big surprise to me. Mama showed me how I wore out my shoes unevenly and said it would be important to correct the way I walked if I wanted to wear high heels later. That certainly motivated me to get off on the right foot. Is that a pun? If so, how convenient.

Initially, I have to admit I was kind of excited to be going to a foot doctor, and Dr. Dameron was a nice man. So, I was okay with the whole thing UNTIL I saw the shoes. Ugh. They were saddle oxfords, which were "sorta" in style - only no one else's looked like mine. Mine were clunky, square-toed, and heavy. They had metal weights inside, which forced my feet to swing forward. And they were built up on the inside to train my feet not to roll inward. My mother thought they looked fine – "just like the other girls," she said. But they weren't. Other saddle oxfords were made from softer leather. The toes were more curved, and they came down lower on the foot. Mine laced up to my chin – well, almost.

During my first years in Corrective Shoes, I was in 4th and 5th grades, and I managed. The doctor allowed me to have a pair of Sunday Shoes that I could wear to church. Period. And there was no going barefoot – ever – even in the Summer. And there was no wearing sandals either. Or tennis shoes. But, like I said, I managed. I guess fashion wasn't that important to me in those years.

By 6th grade, I was tired of my heavy and far-from-glamorous Corrective Shoes. By 7th grade was just plain sick of them. I watched every girl's feet in school. Although saddle oxfords were still being worn, they were, like I said, NOT like my clunkers. If I had taken those clodhoppers off and thrown them at anyone, they could have died from blunt force trauma. Or, at the very least, suffered a concussion. No kidding! Girls were wearing penny loafers, sweet little Mary Janes, and adorable Capezios. Whenever I complained, I had to hear about arch support and ankle support. I sighed and secretly yearned for a pair of soft leather flats in some fashionable color.

Finally, in 8th grade, Dr. Dameron consented to something other than those awful black-and-white tie-up clunkers. Even so, I had to hear yet another lecture about arch and ankle support. Afterward, I skipped off shoe shopping with my mother, glad in my newly found freedom. I knew that Capezios wouldn't make the grade, but I was going to find something fashionable and NOT black and white tie-ups. I was thrilled when my mother picked out a pair of Ghillies. They were soft gray leather and beautiful. They also met the doctor's criteria. I was so giddy with excitement that I fairly floated to school in them. I wondered if anyone would notice that I'd lost my clodhoppers. No one did.

During high school, I owned a pair of burgundy penny loafers, trendy golden palominos, a couple of slingbacks, green and brown suede stack heels, pale yellow Pappagallos with dainty leather flowers on the toes (my all-time favorites), and real, honest-to-God high heels. Back then, no one ever really knew how much I appreciated and admired every single pair of shoes I owned – always feeling something akin to being pardoned from a prison sentence. Nowadays, when my husband mentions I have too many shoes, I just chuckle to myself. Yep. 73 pairs, and not one of them are black and white saddle oxfords!

Chapter 3

Who Can Say Why?

Devil's Advocate

We were staying at my Gramma and Grampa's house in the front bedroom -- Mama, Daddy, my baby brother, and me. I was about five years old. My Aunt Mary and my ten-year-old cousin, M.C., were staying there, too -- in the back bedroom.

I liked it there because there was always something going on -- my gramma cooking or bustling around in the kitchen or digging in her garden -- my grampa telling stories or finding candy in his pockets --my cousin doing something daring or getting into trouble. Another aunt lived across the yard with her husband. So there were plenty of adults around churning up life.

I hated going to bed at night. There was so much going on, and I had to miss it. I slept on a pallet of quilts that my Gramma made on the floor at the foot of my parent's bed. There was a door that opened onto the front porch. I would lie on my pallet and look out the screen door. I could see the pale gold light of the living room spill out into a little pool on the front porch by my Grampa's rocking chair. I could hear snatches of conversation -- adult and mostly incomprehensible -- but sometimes bursts of laughter. On a couple of brave occasions, I crept onto the porch and inched near the front screen door to peer in and feel their voices. But the great darkness that loomed out past the edge of the porch forced me back to my safe pallet.

One sunny afternoon, another adult rolled into our lives -- my Uncle Jack. He was tall and dark-haired with ruddy cheeks, twinkling eyes, and a broad smile. He was loud, jovial and friendly. I thought he would be fun. But Gramma seemed stiff and distant. Mama and Aunt Mary exchanged knowing glances. I sensed something was wrong. Later, out in the yard under the apple tree, I could see Gramma, Aunt Mary, and Mama through the kitchen window getting dinner on the table. Grampa, Daddy, and

Uncle Jack had walked out to the barns. I pondered the change I felt in our house. I must have voiced my uneasiness because M.C. began to try to enlighten me.

"Uncle Jack has seen the devil, you know," he offered casually.

I was incredulous, "Really?" Then, thinking he was up to one of his tricks, I asked, "How do YOU know?"

" 'cause he told Gramma he saw Satan standin' right there by the apple tree, and I was with her. Uncle Jack had a big rock in his hand. He was gonna throw it at him!" M.C.'s eyes were wide as he recalled the horrible day. And I moved away from the tree and looked around it.

"Here?" I queried and pointed at the gnarled trunk.

"Yep." M.C. nodded.

"What did you do?" I asked.

"I stood behind Gramma," he said, and I realized that he had been afraid. The story took on truth and a more frightful meaning because I didn't know *anything* could scare M.C. -- certainly not his Mama's spankings.

"What did Gramma do?" I asked.

"She was mad and told Uncle Jack to put the rock down," he said, and I knew he was still a little amazed by her bravery.

"What happened?" I questioned.

"He threw the rock," he remembered with an even wider gaze into that distant day. "But Uncle Jack said he missed him and that the devil was laughin' at him. Then he yelled and cussed, and Gramma took me inside and got Grampa." he nodded for emphasis. My heart pounded thinking of that evil and chaos right here at my Gramma's house -- suddenly, nowhere in the world seemed safe. I was gripped by the claws of this ugly knowledge.

"What did the devil look like?" I bravely asked, daring to know the truth.

"I didn't see nuthin'." M.C. shrugged and regained his usual aloof composure.

"But Uncle Jack saw him?" I asked. I was confused.

"Yeah. Gramma says when you're bad, you can see the devil, but good people can't." "Is Uncle Jack bad?" I was shocked.

"Yeah, he'd been drinkin'." M.C. shrugged, andI figured it must have been some evil brew -- certainly not my Gramma's delicious sweet tea or my Grampa's beloved Sun Drops.

I shuddered and watched M. C. straddle his bicycle. I thought I would go into the kitchen with my mama since M. C. was leaving me alone. But he leaned toward me to share one last horror:

"The devil's not red, you know." "He isn't?" I squeaked.

"No. He's green with horns and a tail," he stated matter-of-factly and then pushed himself off into the wind, pedaling fast and making clouds of dust and gravel fly up around his spinning tires. I watched him for a few minutes, thinking about his horrifying tale. Strangely, I almost envied his experience

-- being in the presence of such bravery as my Gramma's and yet such vile blackness -- good and evil in its purest forms. I shuddered. Then, aware of the western sun reflecting on the kitchen window and feeling very alone, I ran into the house.

During dinner, seated at the long table, I watched and listened very carefully to Uncle Jack. He didn't seem like the sort of person that would consort with the devil. I guess you never can tell. Whenever he smiled at me or teased me, I felt a little flutter of terror in my belly. I hoped he would talk about his encounter with the green monster. I wanted to ask him, but I knew M. C. would never trust me again, and so I kept silent. But it stayed on my mind the whole evening while the women cleared the dishes, my Grampa took a chew of tobacco, and my daddy and Uncle Jack smoked. I sat with Grampa for a while, listening to a story and his hearty laughter. He gave me an orange slice -- a gummy soft candy coated with sparkling sugar. Darkness fell outside, and the living room took on an amber hue in the soft lamplight. I regarded each adult's face for any sign of trouble but saw none.

Mama washed me off at the kitchen sink, and I fussed about going to bed. She promised she would read me a story before I went to sleep. I kissed everyone goodnight and ran to the front bedroom, picked out a book, and hopped into my parent's bed. I don't think I heard a word my mother read, and when she was done, I could no longer contain myself. I told her M.C.'s story. I thought I would feel better, but it just hung there like a stained curtain. She fluffed the pillow, kissed my head, and dismissed the event with one lone comment, "Oh, Uncle Jack was drunk."
I am sure her remark was meant to negate my fear, but not understanding it, I was not consoled. Then she was gone, and I was alone in the darkened room. A pale silver light filtered through the screen door. I strained to hear the adult voices, but they were oddly muffled, and I worried about what that could mean. I lay very still and squeezed my eyes shut. But my Gramma's clock ticked out the long minutes, and finally, I had to open my

eyes or die of curiosity or fear. I looked around the room to find everything in its place but darker. I could see an unfamiliar shape between the door to the next room and the wardrobe. Slowly, it took the shape of a man of slight but muscular build. I strained to see more clearly. Lord! Have mercy! It wasn't a man but Satan himself with slick green skin, stout horns, and a long tail that swayed slowly back and forth like a snake. And he was smiling a very wicked smile. I screamed for help, and mercifully, Mama came. Of course, she could not see the apparition and tried to convince me that what I had seen were clothes hanging by the wardrobe. But I knew what I'd seen and I was terrified.

After that I decided I could not be afraid of Uncle Jack. Perhaps he was like me -- not bad, just misunderstood. After all, we'd both seen the devil -- and he was green.

The Girl with the Shaved Head

I had seen her before that day in the cafeteria – just around school - on the playground, in the hallway. She wasn't in my room. Maybe she wasn't even in my grade. She was thin, olive-skinned, and had large chocolate-brown eyes. She could have been pretty, only she reminded me of a rabbit – cautious, timid, careful, and ready to run if necessary. But that day in the cafeteria was the first time I really noticed her, really paid attention to her. Someone at my lunch table pointed her out and told our group that the girl's daddy had shaved her head. That's why she was wearing a scarf. I looked up at the kids standing in the lunch line. Sure enough, the girl was wearing a scarf folded into a triangle and tied beneath her chin. No one would wear a scarf on their head inside for no good reason. The girl was in line with her classmates, but her shoulders were hunched, and her body leaned against the wall – whether it was an attempt to hold herself up or to try to melt into it was hard to tell. Her doe-eyes mostly looked down but every now and again would flash furtively about. She looked scared, sickly, and pale – her olive skin notwithstanding. I peered intently, and, yes, I could see stubbles of hair that had been shorn very close to her head – almost like a crew cut except shorter, and there were bits of smooth skin, too. I was horrified at the truth of my classmate's report.

"Why did he shave her head?" I wondered aloud.

My classmate shrugged and said, "He was prob'ly drunk."

Our lunch table fell silent. I suppose we were all letting the information and its ramifications sink in. No one laughed or snickered, and we all moved our eyes away from the girl to the food before us. Even so, I couldn't stop thinking about the girl and her shaved head. Why did this happen? Was her daddy mad at her? What had she done to make him mad – so mad that he would take the trouble to find whatever tool he had wielded and proceed to commit such a violent act? Certainly, he had wanted to shame her.

What could a young girl do to bring down such a horrible punishment? And this girl was so meek it was hard to imagine that she could have done anything intentional? My parents didn't drink, but there were plenty of folks in my family and community who did, and I had heard whispers. I knew "bad things" could happen when a person overindulged. Still, basically, I was naive and had never really considered what those things might be. Here was one of those things. And it was bad.

How did this happen? Didn't she have anyone who could have protected her? Grandparents? Her mother? Where was her mother? Suddenly, I realized that she had suffered alone – even if there had been a room full of people present for the event. She alone was subjected to this cruelty and had nowhere to hide. Even now. I thought briefly: if my daddy had shaved my head, I would have been so embarrassed I wouldn't have gone to school the next day. And in the next instant, I realized that maybe going to school was safer than being at home. That very thought made me feel sad and sick.

I looked up to see her carrying her lunch tray. She looked too frail to carry that big brown tray. It appeared much too heavy for her. Her shoulders hunched forward so much it seemed possible that she might topple over. I watched her set herself and her tray at a table a little way from me. The sadness on her face was too much to take in. I never saw her take a single bite.

After that day, I continued to see her cowering about here and there, wearing the kerchief to hide her bald head. Eventually, her hair grew in, although not prettily. It was short and brown and always looked uncombed and ratty – as though she had just got out of bed and forgot to brush it. As time passed, I saw less and less of her until she was completely gone. I don't know if she moved away or maybe she just quit coming. It's been over fifty years since I've seen her, but I've never forgotten her. I am ashamed to say I don't remember her name. But still, I think of her. I don't know where she is or what happened to her. I wish she could know how deeply she affected me – how utterly she changed the naïve girl I was. I mean that in a good way – in the way that opens your eyes and shows you something else about the world you didn't know before. But I hope she never reads this. I hope she has forgotten her sadness. I hope she is somewhere lovely and peaceful. And I hope she is not afraid.

Freedom of Choice Or A Girl Named Gail

In 1954, the U.S. Supreme Court ruled that school segregation was unconstitutional and must end. Mostly, it didn't. In 1955, the U. S. Supreme Court ruled that integration should happen with "all deliberate speed." And yet, when I entered high school in 1964, our school remained all white. North Carolina, along with a number of other schools throughout the United States, had a Freedom of Choice Plan, which gave students the right to choose between white and black schools, independently of their race. Therefore, many schools remained segregated. So much for integration, right? However, in 1965, my Sophomore year, 3 black children chose to attend my school. Two students were in Elementary School. One was in high school – a Freshman. A thin girl with skin the color of cocoa named Gail. It caused quite a stir!

I am sad to say that many students treated her cruelly. She was not in any of my classes, but I heard boys in the hallway and stairwell jeering and calling her hurtful names. Otherwise, she was ignored – which was every bit as painful, I'm sure. She walked alone and stood alone at break times. I heard she ate alone in the cafeteria, although I never saw her because we must have had lunch at a different time. I felt sorry for her. I could only imagine how lonely she must have felt. She looked completely miserable and terrified. Only one student in all of my school had the nerve to seek her out and attempt to befriend her. That girl had a cross burned in her yard. Although it was reportedly a group of young boys and not the KKK, the message was as clear as it was awful.

I wish that I could say that I was that one brave person who attempted to befriend the forlorn girl. I am ashamed to say I wasn't that person. The next year, Gail did not return. That she had survived the previous school year was a miracle, in my opinion. That she didn't come back was completely understandable. I thought about her – wondered what had become of her. I felt guilty about my own lack of action. I had certainly felt compassion, but I had failed to show it. So, what good was that? There was no way to absolve my sin or resolve my guilt. Over the years, I tried not to think about it too much.

Many years later, I was grown and working as a nurse in a chemotherapy clinic when I met another girl named Gail. She was a delightful person who laughed easily and always had a twinkle in her eye. I enjoyed her company. We had lunch together often and talked endlessly – about all sorts of things. We became good friends. Gail was my first friend of color with whom I was comfortable talking about race relations. I was grateful for her openness and honesty.

One day, she shared this story: Black churches were instrumental in moving the Civil Rights movement forward. During the era of Freedom of Choice in the 1960s, her church decided that they should select some children from among their members to attend a white school. Gail was one of those children. She attended an all-white school during her Freshman year. It was awful. She was taunted, ridiculed, humiliated, and terribly lonely. After that miserably wretched year, she was so depressed that her mother did not insist she return. It took her a long time to recover.

I was stunned. Oh, my God!!! Here was the poor little girl I had so sorely wronged all those years ago. What could I say to take that pain away? Words of apology were necessary but inadequate. I wanted to throw myself to the ground and grovel at her feet. I wanted to cry but felt I didn't deserve such release. Nevertheless, with tears in my eyes and an enormous lump in my throat, I told her how sorry I was that this had happened to her and how I regretted my sorry inaction.

At first, she was confused. Through a jumble of confusion and words, we were able to discern that she had not attended my school but a different school in a different county in North Carolina. She was not the Gail of my memory. It was a simple coincidence of names. Or perhaps not – I guess it depends on whether or not you believe in "coincidence." In the end, I asked her how she had managed to survive and how she could even tolerate white people. She touched my arm gently, smiled kindly, and bestowed more grace with these words than I could ever have given myself: "There comes a time when hate must end, and you choose to forgive."

In that moment, if the heavens had opened and a golden crown had been set upon her humble head, it would not have surprised me. Yet nothing visibly miraculous happened. Even so, I believe that Gail's choices of grace and forgiveness are indeed her crowning achievement. Would that the rest of us could learn these lessons as well as she.

Chapter 4

Extra-Curricular

Appendage

I was ten years old and supposed to be in some sort of program at church that Mama was in charge of because she was the leader of the Baptist Women's Circle. But I was sick – sick as a dog. I was so nauseated I could hardly hold my head up, my mouth full of that sickly, salty taste that floods in right before you throw up - only I wasn't throwing up. I just wished I would. I told Mama I didn't feel good. She looked doubtful and reminded me that I "had a part in the program." Great. Now I felt nauseated AND guilty. Thanks, Mama. She went into the bathroom and started putting on her lipstick. I followed her and sat on the edge of the tub.

"Mama, I really don't feel good," I said again and wished mightily that I would throw up that very minute so she would know that I was completely serious. She said I should go lie down, which I interpreted as being dismissive and irritated. It didn't occur to me that she was just in a hurry and distracted which I can see clearly now as an adult. The trouble was that I really did feel guilty about not "doing my part" – it was just in my DNA, that guilt thing. I don't remember now whatever it was I was supposed to say or do, but you can bet your bottom dollar that I had rehearsed it to the hilt and was prepared to do my best. I just couldn't do it the way I was feeling, and I knew it right down to my toenails. I continued to feel guilty, but I felt much worse physically than I did mentally, so I made my way back to my bedroom, where I crawled into bed, hoping I would die so that my mama would feel guilty.

My grandmother from Virginia, whom I called Bobo, was visiting, so she stayed with me that evening. I suppose that Daddy and my little brother went to church, too, but I really don't remember. I was too sick. By the time they returned from church, I barely remember Mama calling my name. Daddy carried me to the car and took me to the doctor. The only memory I have of that visit was Dr. Stallings pressing my abdomen and the pain I felt. It was excruciating and made me throw up. Mama said I screamed, but I don't remember. Dr. Stallings sent us directly to Rex Hospital in Raleigh, where I met his surgeon friend, who explained to me that my appendix was inflamed and needed to be removed. I had no idea what an appendix was, but if that's what was making me feel so bad, I was all for whatever it was he was planning to do. My mama must have asked more specifically about the surgery because I recall him proudly announcing that the surgery had been perfected and I would only have a tiny "bikini" scar on my right lower abdomen. I was too sick at the moment to care. The next thing I knew, I was being wheeled into the Operating Room, where my big feat was to count backward from one hundred. I think I said, "One hundred, ninety-nine..."

The next time I opened my eyes, I heard someone yelling, "Nurse! Nurse! Give me something for the pain!" – just like an actor on television. Maybe it was a program on television? And then I realized that someone was me. What? Why? Oh, yeah. I was really in pain – like nothing I'd ever felt before. I couldn't figure out where I was hurting or why I was hurting. And I had no idea where I was. I wasn't at home. An unfamiliar face appeared before me – a woman with a nurse's cap on. She said something to me, but I couldn't say what, and soon everything was swirling, and I was falling down into a black hole of sleep.

The next time I opened my eyes, the sun was shining through a big window, and I was swaddled in white and lying in a hospital bed with rails on either side of me. A nurse was saying "good morning" as cheerfully as if I'd just arrived at Sunday School. There were other beds in the room with lumps in them, but I couldn't tell much else about my roommates. What I wanted was my mama, and I could feel myself wanting to cry. The nurse told me she was going to adjust my bed so that I could sit up. And when I tried sitting up as I usually did, I realized why she was helping me. Ugh. Once I was upright, she pulled a tray over to me with breakfast food – I couldn't say now but it was likely eggs and toast but it didn't matter. I knew I couldn't get any food past the lump in my throat. I didn't want this cheerful nurse nor any of the food she claimed would be delicious. I wanted my mama.

I was struggling not to burst into tears when I saw Mama's face at the door. The sight of her was so wonderful that something tipped over and the tears spilled out. No angel could have been more welcome. When she put her arms around me, I began to sob and apologize for not "doing my part". I was surprised by her laughter as she caressed my face and said that nothing mattered except that I was alright. And so I learned that the program had gone on without me. My absence hadn't ruined a thing. I must say that I was both relieved and surprised. And then I wondered if anyone had missed me at all. Mama laughed and said, "Of course".

In retrospect I learned quite a lot from that experience. Mostly I learned how good it makes you feel to have people take good care of you and to have people let you know that they are thinking of you. I got flowers and cards and visitors. I was fussed over by my parents and other relatives. My little brother was especially sweet. The surgeon told my parents that I had arrived at the hospital in the nick of time as my appendix was on the verge of rupture and that would have been a life-threatening condition that would have made recovery more difficult. I also learned what an appendix really is and a bit of its medical history.

The appendix is small pouch like structure that hangs from the side of the colon. It actually looks a bit like a worm and is attached to the first part of the large intestine. It was discovered by anatomists in the 1500s but they had no idea of its function although they knew that it could be inflamed and cause serious illness. The first appendectomy was performed around the mid 1700's but there was no general anesthesia until the mid 1800's. Can you imagine? And, yes, they really performed the surgery without it – which required a lot of folks holding the patient down. Lord have mercy! I cannot even imagine. You'd be scarred for life – physically <u>and</u> emotionally. Once general anesthesia came into being surgery became almost the gold standard treatment for appendicitis.

Nowadays laparoscopic surgery has mostly replaced open surgery and a laparoscopic appendectomy is considered one of the safest, lowest-complication surgical procedures. That said, the appendix remains a mystery. The cause of appendicitis has yet to be identified and no one understands why the appendix will rupture in some patients but recover in others. As recent as 2007 research showed that this tiny body part appears to play a role in both the digestive and the immune system as it stores beneficial bacteria that can be used when the GI tract loses its gut flora. More recently, professionals are wondering whether antibiotics would be just as effective as surgery – noting that men on submarines that could not surface for six months during the Cold War received antibiotics instead of an appendectomy and recovered relatively well. I understand there is an ongoing study in California attempting to verify whether or not antibiotics would be just as good as surgery – certainly it would be less invasive.

Appendicitis is most common in children and young adults between the ages of 10 and 30. In the United States, appendicitis is one of the most common causes of sudden abdominal pain requiring surgery. Each year more than 300,000 people have their appendix surgically removed. Left untreated the appendix can rupture and the death rate for a perforated appendix may be as high as 50% according to The Science Direct.

What I have <u>never</u> learned, however, is how to <u>NOT</u> feel guilty – and I feel guilty a lot – sometimes about stupid stuff. A doctor I used to work with told me once that he could probably make me feel guilty for WWII if he put his mind to it. See what I mean? Too bad that surgeon couldn't remove the "guilt gene" while he was removing my appendix. Sigh…….

Swinging

I was at the park watching a young girl swinging – leaning forward to face the wind and then leaning back her face to the sky – her hair flying in the wind and her face awash with pure bliss. For a moment I was her – caught up in the sound of her laughter and remembering the pure joy of such a simple, nearly forgotten pleasure.

I recall learning to swing – a thing that you cannot explain how to do to another person. Rather it is a rhythm that you learn all alone. I was lucky to have had my parents, grandparents, and older cousins to push me in the beginning. But after a while, my parents – the ones around most often and most likely to be the ones to push me on a swing – insisted that I should learn to swing by myself – especially since they had bought me a swing set so that I could entertain myself. Mama tried to explain how to do it but the words made no sense. I remember the frustration of leaning forward and leaning back and very little happening. But then I figured out that if I gave myself a little push with my own foot that I was on my way. And oh, wow! Did I soar??? I could swing myself so high and hard that the swing set would bounce up on one side. My mama warned me that I would tip my swing set over but I never did. Nor did her warning ever keep me from swinging as far as I could go. There was nothing like the wind in my face, my hair flying loose and wild, my feet stretching toward the sky, and the feeling that I could soar into the stratosphere.

And as much as I loved my swing set the very best swings were at the park where the ropes were many times longer than mine at home. Those swings could catapult you into a space very near the clouds – or so it seemed to me. I could never get enough. I felt I could always go a little faster or a little higher. It was intoxicating. And after having swung my body backwards and forwards, upward and downward, time after time after time – when I finally stopped the swing and got off it seemed as if I had been weightless so long that it was a heavy burden to carry my own body through space in such an ordinary way. It always surprised me a little how heavy and humdrum it felt to walk away. It was those moments that I envied birds the most, I think.

Once when I went to visit an older cousin, she took me to a Lawn Party (which is like a small fair for those folks who may never have heard of a Lawn Party). They had games and some rides. One of the rides was called The Swing and it had individual seats that were suspended from very long chains that were attached to a carousel. When the apparatus was turned on you and your seat were swung outward and around. At first my cousin thought I was too little to ride it but the operator said I would be fine and lifted me onto the seat and put a bar into place that I could hold onto. Looking at it I wasn't confident in its ability to hold anything much besides your attention and I elected to hold onto the chains on either side of me instead. My cousin took the next seat suspended beside me and after she was in, she gave me a little worried look and asked if I was alright. Her expression gave me pause but I wasn't about to act like a baby. I figured I should be safe enough. Nobody died on these things, right? I nodded and tried to smile. And then I heard the motor rev up and my stomach gave a little lurch. I clutched the chains and determined that I was going to be just fine. And as it turned out I was. In fact, I think I was more than fine. I had chosen the outermost seat which flies the highest of all. And even though I was just the tiniest bit scared I was also thrilled. I flew through the night air faster than I ever had and it was exhilarating beyond words. I looked out across the lights and sounds happening below and up into the soft indigo of the summer night sky. The stars seemed to be spinning – but, no, that was me spinning among them. The only bad part to that evening was when the ride was over and I had to get off. I could have flown through the air like that the whole evening. My mama fussed about it when she heard about my adventure. It seems that there had been tragic accidents now and then involving such swing rides. Mama declared that they were too dangerous. Maybe so. But it sure was fun and I was glad she hadn't been there to stop me.

Porch swings are nice, too, although not nearly as exciting. Although I guess it all depends on whom you're sitting with on that swing. In my personal experience the idea of a porch swing is more romantic than they actually are. If you're trying to enjoy a glass of iced tea, it's tricky to drink and swing at the same time, and I've learned that you need to come to a complete stop in the swing so that you can set your drink down without incident. The most fun I ever had on one was lying down on the seat while one of my cousins pushed me. But you don't go far or fast and then you always have to get off and give them their turn which is just how it goes – 'cause no way are you able to push yourself while lying down – at least I never figured out how.

As an adult the most fun I've had on a swing was on an enormous swing that hangs on the screened porch of a house our family stayed in on Lake Lure. The swing is as big as a sofa. The bottom is cushioned and there are plenty of pillows. You can't swing far or fast but I could swing gently on it surrounded by all six of my grandchildren, listening to them chatter and giggle, smelling the autumn air, and wishing the day would last forever. I never even had to push.

Birthdays

I recently celebrated another birthday and the day brought with it memories of other birthdays over the years. Growing up my brother and I were allowed to pick whatever cake we wanted for our special day. Mama would ask us what kind of cake we wanted several days before the actual birthday so that she would have time for grocery shopping in case of some special request. That prelude made the coming birthday seem all the more exciting. Sometimes it would take me a day or two or even three to decide. Knowing I would be mulling it over for a while Mama would offer suggestions or show me pictures from one of her women's magazines. Every year I chose something different. Among the many delicious cakes she made for me these were the ones I remember the most:

- A layered yellow cake with sliced bananas and cream between each layer. It was something I had just imagined would be delicious and Mama had never made such a cake before. She warned that the bananas might darken. However, that scrumptious cake didn't last long enough for that to happen.

- A coconut cake with some of the coconut dyed blue and some dyed red so that my cake was red, white and blue. I remember that she poured coconut milk over the cake allowing it to seep through and make the cake super "coconut-y". Yum.

- A layered white cake with crushed pineapple icing on the top and between the layers – boy! Was it juicy.

- A layered yellow cake with strawberry icing and big fat strawberries on top. It was almost too pretty to eat.

- A carrot cake with cream cheese icing – my all-time favorite.

- A chocolate cake with chocolate icing – which sounds boring but it was exciting for me because it was not a typical dessert for Mama to make.

My brother was less adventurous. He chose a German Chocolate cake – every single year. I am rolling my eyes as I type this but I must admit her German Chocolate cake was indeed spectacular.

My birthday is in July and that meant that the weather was usually hot and humid. I grew up in the North Carolina Piedmont, after all. And in my childhood most folks did not have air conditioning. In fact, it was a rarity. So what a treat it was when my parents hosted a party in the basement of our home for my tenth birthday where it was nice and cool. We strung crepe paper all over everywhere and blew up lots and lots of balloons. Our usually drab basement where Mama did the laundry became bright and festive. Kids brought their roller skates – the kind that fit on your shoes and you tightened with a key. No one was very practiced at the sport. We fell as much as we rolled but we laughed all the while. It was grand fun.

In middle school Mama let me have a slumber party with girlfriends from my class at school. What a brave woman she was to suffer the squeals and giggles of middle school girls who ran around in shorty pajamas and bare feet for an entire evening and way past midnight. The bunch of us slept on quilt pallets in our living room – well, we didn't actually SLEEP that much. Apparently, the whole idea of a slumber party is to see who can stay up the latest. Mama rose early and made pancakes, eggs and sausage for a more subdued crowd of yawning young girls. Parents arrived midmorning to claim their well-fed but very sleepy daughters. I'm pretty sure everyone went home to take a nap. I know I did – and I think Mama did, too. She'd certainly earned one.

My sixteenth birthday dawned sunny and bright with a knock on the door that turned out to be a delivery from a local florist. Mama called me to the kitchen where I found a large rectangular box with my name on it. Mama was as excited as I was, I think. Flowers from a florist were an uncommon event at our house. I opened the box gingerly and even now I can recall the heady perfume that wafted out into the air. Mama and I both gasped as we saw luscious green ferns cradling the rich red petals of sixteen long stemmed roses. I was both delighted and stunned. The card read, "Happy Sweet Sixteen! Danny".

The boy next door that I'd known my whole life was the "Danny" on the card. We had been playmates for years. We were also classmates but since high school our relationship had been confusing for me. He would ask me out on dates – movies, restaurants, dances, etc. – and we always had such fun together. We were never at a loss for words and we laughed a lot. But back at school with our friends he would hardly look at me - much less speak to me. Yet he would tease and laugh with all my girlfriends. I found it confusing and infuriating. My daddy said it was because he liked me but that made absolutely no sense to me. And still here before me was a present that said perhaps my daddy was right. Danny was away at Football Camp and so I knew he'd made arrangements for those flowers before he left. I was impressed but completely bewildered. Mama smiled at me and said, "Let's get these in some water." She helped me snip the stems and arrange them in a vase.

At supper that evening after my daddy and little brother had properly appreciated the fragrant roses, I moved them into the living room. During our mealtime conversation I expressed what a surprise the flowers had been and then went on to complain about the way Danny treated me when we were in a crowd. The two acts seemed conflicting to me. I admitted that I was befuddled. Daddy chuckled and said, "That boy likes you." A refrain I had heard before and still I could not comprehend it. I shook my head and shrugged. Daddy grew somber and said, "Now that boy likes you enough to have spent his hard earned money on those flowers for your birthday. If you don't like him, don't string him along. That wouldn't be right." I was astonished at his suggestion - that I would consider such deception – never mind that I wouldn't have known how to go about such behavior in the first place. I decided to respond with a simple, "Yessir" and let it be. He nodded and left the rest of it for me to figure out. And that was considerable. Being sixteen is hard. So is young love. It has taken a few birthdays to figure things out. And even with all the birthdays I've had much of life remains a mystery…….Perhaps that is just as it should be.

Chapter 5

Play Back

Paper Dolls

Cleaning out the attic I ran across a couple of tattered boxes containing my old paper dolls. Inside I found my old friends - not as tattered as the boxes but definitely worn. When I was a little girl, I spent endless hours playing with these paper friends. In case you are unfamiliar with the term "paper dolls" they are figures cut out of paper or thin cardboard with separate clothes that are also made of paper, which are held onto the dolls by paper tabs that fold over and around the dolls.

I was probably five or six when I received my first paper doll, Sally, who had "magic" stay on clothes rather than the usual tabs. Of course, way back then they really did "magically" (or magnetically, I should say) stay on. After years in the attic Sally is still smiling but her "magic" has gone so none of her cute outfits stay put any longer. Now she is clad only in the appropriate underwear for a young girl of the 1950's – plain cotton panties and an undershirt with a tiny flower at the breast bone. Some of Sally's clothes were plain white, asking for crayons, which I obliged with various clumsy colorings. Sally always reminded me of Dick and Jane's little sister in the 1st grade reader. Of note: the original price sticker is still on Sally's box. It seems she was purchased from J.C. Penney's department store for 66 cents.

I liked Sally quite a lot until Rosemary Clooney came along. Rosemary was a real-life singer and actress popular in the 1950's. Most notably she appeared with Bing Crosby in the movie, "White Christmas". Rosemary, the paper doll, like the real-life Rosemary was sophisticated, stylish, and shapely. I thought Magic Sally could be Rosemary's daughter in my pretend world but it was a difficult "pretend" since they were not the same scale. Poor sweet Sally became a bizarre, giant child beside the chic Ms. Clooney. Rosemary did not have a box because she came in a "book" like many paper dolls of that day. All her clothes were on sheets and had to be cut out. A few of the fashions remained in Rosemary's book - not cut out with my trusty little scissors like the rest. For some reason, I did not prefer them. I look at them now and admire their style. My taste has changed a bit, I guess.

One of my favorite paper dolls was my namesake, Linda. She came in a book, too. Linda was a member of the Mickey Mouse Club Show which was a television show hosted by the Walt Disney character, Mickey Mouse. The members wore shirts with their names on them – Linda, Doreen, Annette, Cubby, Lonnie, Bobby, Tommy are the ones I remember. They also had hats with mouse ears on them, which I coveted. Once I had an opportunity to own one but I had to choose between the mouse ears and a baton. I chose the baton – Linda could twirl one quite deftly and I thought I would learn this skill. But I never gained proficiency and always regretted my choice. I would have loved wearing those trendy mouse ears and looking like an official Mouseketeer. Like most of the Mouseketeers,

Linda was bright and talented. She was a dancer and I envied her pink toe shoes and imagined myself twirling and leaping as gracefully as she did.

And then there was my paper doll, Peggy – the one with "real" hair. Oh, what fun she was! She had bows to go with most of her outfits and they could be attached with a bobby pin. Back in the day I thought her hair was long and luscious. Now it just looks like a sad clump of matted fur. I suppose years in the attic didn't bode well for Peggy's lovely locks.

There were also miscellaneous paper dolls that I had cut from magazines at my Gramma's house. She always lovingly saved the issues for me – knowing I would be delighted to have another paper friend. To be sure these paper dolls were smaller and more fragile than the others but they lent themselves nicely to my world of make believe. There were different models in each issue and they were all on the same scale so I could have sisters and cousins and friends sharing clothes and all sorts of adventures.

Paper dolls are still being made today but I suspect their popularity has waned significantly to those of my childhood days. I've heard there are Paper Doll Conventions held here and there these days but I doubt if my old friends would be invited. And, even if they were, I wouldn't let them go. No one could ever see them through my eyes – not as they are now but as they once were. And wouldn't that be a shame?

Tree House

My daddy built a tree house for my brother at the edge of the woods across the field from our house. It was a sturdy platform wedged securely among a few young but tall hardwoods. It had two walls but the rest was open to the surrounding woods. A small, shallow creek gurgled softly nearby. The entrance was by a hand-made ladder. My brother was delighted. My daddy was pleased with his gift and proud of his work – as he should have been. But my feelings were hurt. I felt left out. Daddy so obviously made it for my brother – not for the both of us. Of course, I knew my brother, always sweet and generous, would allow me to play there whenever I wanted. So, I nursed my hurt feelings in silence.

That tree house was a magical place. It was a fort, a castle, a magic carpet, a hideaway. It was any place it needed to be whenever it needed to happen. I sat nestled there among the trees a many a time reading, writing, or simply daydreaming. But I spent many times in that tree house being a myriad of other things: Rapunzel, captive and waiting for her prince; a queen commanding armies; a jungle girl whose best friends were wild animals; Diana the goddess of hunting and the moon; a cloistered nun; an evil sorceress living in a stone tower; a forest nymph caring for the trees and wildlife; a solitary woman who lived deep in the forest collecting herbs and such for magical brews; Wonder Woman living among the Amazon Women on Themyscira; a tree fairy; a magical girl whose best friend was a flying tiger; a tortured poet writing meager verse; a starving artist living in a lonely loft; a runaway girl hiding from some evil something.

My brother played there often, sometimes alone, sometimes with me, sometimes with friends. And I know he thoroughly enjoyed it. But I am absolutely certain he never enjoyed that tree house more than I did.

For a long time it bothered me that my daddy saw that tree house as belonging to my brother. I'm sure he never meant to hurt my feelings but Daddy was "old school" and he saw things in strict categories – like male and female. I suspect it never occurred to him that a girl would want to play in a tree house. Girls liked doll babies, dollhouses and dress up. He knew I had a big imagination but I'm pretty sure he didn't realize how alive and vibrant it actually was. I don't fault him for that. Most of my imaginings I kept to myself. I figured some of my imagined characters might have been up for questioning or conversation about sin or being of sound mind. And I wasn't up for any of that. I preferred to have my magical world all to myself – free of judgment and possible condemnation. Besides, I had secretly decided that the tree house was really mine. And some things are just better kept to yourself.

The Bicycle

I wanted a bicycle so bad and was too young to do anything about it except hope that I'd get one for Christmas. I had learned there was no such thing as Santa Claus and so I understood the relationship between how much money your parents had or didn't and what you might or might not get for Christmas. When I told my mama that I wanted a bicycle for Christmas she said they'd see. Later on, while helping her with the dishes one night after dinner she said "Bicycles are pretty expensive" which I figured was a way of saying that I might better pick something less expensive to put on my Christmas list. Still, I was hopeful. Another night Mama asked if I would be disappointed if my bicycle wasn't a new one but one that had been recycled. Heck, no! I didn't mind. I just wanted a bike. I couldn't care less whether it was old or new or dented or had an ugly paint job. I just wanted a bike. So, you can imagine my delight when on Christmas morning I found a beautiful maroon colored bicycle with a big red ribbon on the handlebars all ready for me to learn to ride. I could hardly wait to ride it. I had been picturing myself cruising along on a bicycle for so long that it came as quite a surprise to learn that riding it wasn't as easy as I had imagined it would be. At first my parents helped me on and then with the balancing of myself. Then they'd give me a push. Off I'd go, a bit unsteadily, sometimes for a short burst, sometimes for several yards. But the ride always ended with me out of control and flailing and invariably in the dirt. Finally, my parents told me to just keep trying by myself – that I would "get it" eventually – that I just needed to practice. And then they left me to it. I whined. I cried. I hated myself. And most of all I hated that doggone bicycle. I decided I couldn't do it. The bike was ugly. If it had been new, I would have mastered riding it more easily. I lived in the country where there was lots of sand and the sand threw me off balance. If I lived in town where there were sidewalks it would be easier to learn to ride. I hated everything about my life – even my parents who had abandoned me in my greatest endeavor. I could barely contain my irritation at the supper table but I knew better than to be disrespectful. I went to bed sour and out of sorts with the world.

I didn't awaken the next morning in a better humor and refused my own silent mental goading to get my bike and try again. Instead, I sat in my room feeling sorry for myself. In the afternoon, my mama came into my room and asked if wanted to try my bike again. I shrugged. I didn't have the nerve to tell her I'd given up and that I hated that bike. She said she'd help me balance a few times but that sometimes people fell off their bikes before they learned the balance necessary to maintain the ride. She tried to assure me that once I learned the art of balancing it would be a breeze to ride. I didn't believe her but I didn't say so. I just put on a jacket and went with her to the garage to get the now dreadful bike. I pushed up the kickstand and wheeled the bike slowly onto the back driveway. I could see the dirt and rocks waiting to greet me when I met them on the ground. Perhaps Mama felt my hesitancy and she suggested that she would ride it first and I could watch. I agreed and watched her push off and ride it around in a short circle. I am ashamed to admit that when the driveway turned to sand, I hoped to see her flounder. But she didn't. Instead, she rode on smoothly giving me tidbits of advice as she circled the yard. Then it was my turn. Inside my head I was sulking and feeling obstinate but I climbed on the Maroon Monster and began again. Mama held onto the back of the bike and the seat, keeping me upright as I maneuvered down the path to the barn. I could hear her running alongside me. The bike felt unsteady for just a minute and then it didn't. The wind was in my face and I was gliding down that path all alone. I was doing it! When I got to the end of the path, I wasn't sure about the turning thing and I toppled over. But when I got up that time I was smiling and Mama was running toward me laughing and saying, "Yes!" I think she helped me get going a couple more times but I'd felt that balance thing and it had infused me with the energy to keep trying. And I did. I fell down a lot, I'm sure, but I stayed upright and balanced more than I fell. I learned about turning corners, going up and down hills, riding through mud puddles and on graveled roads, sandy roads, and eventually on paved streets in town with my friends. I rode that bike everywhere. I rode fast and slow and laughed and daydreamed and felt entirely free. And I loved that beautiful maroon colored bike. It may have been used by someone before me but I know whoever it was never loved it as much as I did. My brother inherited it when I discovered makeup and corsages. Apart from that I don't know what happened to that marvelous machine. It should be in a museum somewhere with a sign that says, "This is what trying something new looks like."

Little River

If my mama had known that my little brother and I were playing so close to the river that ran by our house she would have had a hissy fit. Not to mention the times we actually played IN the river. And the time I walked across the dam would have given her heart failure and earned me a sound spanking, I'm pretty sure. But luckily for me she was blissfully unaware of our exact whereabouts on those beautiful days of our childhood in the Carolina countryside. Mama was a city girl who had moved to the country – an unfamiliar landscape for her but she had known the freedom of walking city streets with her siblings and friends and playing outside for hours on end without her parents knowing her exact whereabouts. And although she was more guarded in my earliest years, as time passed, she became comfortable with her new environment – sprawling fields, woods, a nearby stream and the river – and allowed us to play and roam as we pleased.

Little River is a tributary. It originates in Franklin County and crosses through Wake, Johnston, and Wayne Counties where it eventually joins the Neuse River somewhere around Kinston, North Carolina. The Neuse goes on to enter the Pamlico Sound, which eventually flows into the Atlantic Ocean. A portion of Little River flowed about 150 yards away from our house in the Wake County countryside between Zebulon and Wendell, North Carolina. I'm pretty sure my mother never considered this bigger picture – with a bird's eye view of the rivers and how way leads onto way. Or maybe she did the time my next-door neighbor, Danny, and his friend, David, decided to canoe down part of Little River in the dead of winter. Unfortunately, on their return home, they ended up tipping over into the freezing water. The young boys righted the canoe, climbed back in, and continued heading upstream. Night was beginning to fall, and by that time, a search party (which included my daddy) had been rounded up. The men were relieved to find the boys wet and chilled to the bone but otherwise unharmed. Danny said he thought his was in big trouble until he saw the look of relief on his dad's face. Mama had rung her hands anxiously until Daddy got back and reported the good news that the boys had been found more or less intact. Right then, Mama gave me and my brother a little "talkin' to" about being careful, which, of course, we didn't really think applied to us because we were always careful. To soothe her we nodded solemnly and decided via telepathy that we weren't going to share any of our daring adventures that involved the river.

Directly across the river was Tarpley's Mill – an old grist mill that had been in full operation through at least 1955. I actually found an old advertisement from a 1955 local paper that read:

"Tarpley's Mill has a complete new corn-shelling, feed grinding, mixing and molasses blending plant. We also have platform scales, electric truck dump to make your trip to our mill a pleasure. This new plant will be in operation by November 7 to 10. Everyone interested in seeing grain or feeds of any kind is invited to look our new

plant over as soon as we can get it going. Yours for More and Better Service. J.W.Tarpley, Route 2, Wendell. Phone 5386."

Clearly, Mr. Tarpley was expecting a bright future for his newly outfitted mill. Unfortunately, the electric portion of the mill proved to be its demise as it created a huge fire and the mill was never reopened. The building was abandoned and the dam that had been built now served no useful purpose. With no prying eyes to observe our escapades on or in the river my brother and I were free to explore, stomp, splash, and climb as we pleased. When there had been lots of rain the river would overflow its banks. Depending on the amount of rain the flooding could be a little or a lot. It was pure delight to take our shoes off in the summer and splash through the gushing water. Climbing around the twisted and tangled tree roots now submerged in water was exciting, if not a little scary. During a drought the water level naturally fell and yielded new ground to explore. It was particularly tempting to put our bare toes on the soft moss or make footprints in the soggy black silt. Sometimes the level was so low there was no water flowing over the dam. It was on one of those hot days that I dared to crawl up onto the dam, balance myself, and walk across to the other side. I had the good sense to forbid my little brother (who was five years younger) from joining me. I often considered walking across the dam when the water was flowing over it because it looks so cool and inviting. Probably lucky for me that I never did.

There are thirty-eight different species of snakes in North Carolina – six are venomous and reside in the Piedmont area of the state (where I live, in case you're wondering). Even though I was well aware of this fact, it never occurred to me to worry about meeting up with any of them. Now, that's not saying that I like snakes. In fact, they freak me out – poisonous or not. It just never crossed my mind to think about anything other than being a carefree kid. I was more worried about the monster under my bed than I was a snake. And I should have been way more concerned and careful because Lord knows! There were plenty of water moccasins (also called Cottonmouths) in and around every river in the country. How we missed encountering one is nothing short of a miracle. My daddy used to say: "The Lord protects children and fools." I'm pretty sure he was right. When I think of it now, I am reminded of the Bernhard Plockhorst painting, "The Guardian Angel," showing an angel and two little children close to an abyss. Our assigned angel probably worked overtime on occasion.

The only time Mama ever really worried was when we didn't respond to her calling us. She would stand on the back steps and "yoo hoo" adding our names until we called out, "Coming!" Somehow, we always managed to hear her no matter what we were doing – except on one particular occasion. My brother and I had gone next door to play with neighboring children, Vicky and Danny (yep, the same fellow who tipped over in a canoe with his friend). Danny was my age and sometimes boyishly surly or off on his own adventures. Vicky was an age between me and my brother, Douglas. On this summer day,

146

Danny was not available, but Vicky was up for adventure. I was on my bike, and Douglas was following behind, furiously pedaling his trusty little tractor. Vicky grabbed her bike, and we headed down a path that led behind an orchard, through a bit of woods, and over a small creek.

We were caught up in some imaginary world when Vicky's dog, Brownie, an old hound mix, lumbered down the path toward us. Brownie was a sweet, lazy old soul, but on this day, infused with high imagining, Vicky declared that the fur on her neck and running along her spine was standing up, and this was a most unusual occurrence. Since she wasn't my dog, I had to take Vicky's word. I wondered aloud what this might mean, and Vicky diagnosed it immediately and emphatically as "Rabies!!!" Rabies? Really? Oh, no. We need to get away from the rabid dog as quickly as possible.

I commanded my brother to get off his tractor and "Come on! Hurry! Run!" And the three of us proceeded to run as fast as our little legs could carry us. Whenever we looked back there was Brownie loping along behind us, which simply heightened our fear and we began to actually "run for our lives" scrambling up the slight incline toward Vicky's house. Gasping for breath, we reached the back door steps and yanked open the screen door. Sure enough, there was Brownie right at our heels, and we imagined her foaming at the mouth and in hot pursuit when, in truth, she was merely loping along, thinking what a great game this was. Once inside, we locked the screen securely, thinking to ward off the "mad dog" in case she tried to break down the door. Poor Brownie.

In the meantime, Mama had been back at our house, calling us to come home. Now count our huge garden, my daddy's bird dog pen, the chickens, another branch that led down to Little River, a field, an apple orchard, and all the way to the little bottom between the trees where that little bridge crossed the small stream. And now remember that we were caught up in the terror of a rabid dog chasing us while we ran for our lives. It was no wonder we didn't hear Mama's sweet soprano "yoo-hoo" floating across the summer air. It was most unusual for us not to respond, and when we didn't, Mama began to worry. Soon, she set out on foot to find us.

Eventually, Mama saw the tracks our vehicles had taken down to the little stream between the woods. There, she found our abandoned bikes, along with my little brother's tractor, turned on its side and lying in the dirt. She also found my little brother's red baseball cap without its owner. Douglas never took that cap off his head unless Mama made him. Fear struck her, and she began running and calling our names loudly. When at last I heard her, I called out from behind the locked screen door, "Mama, we're here." By this time, Vicky, Douglas, and I had armed ourselves with weapons – croquet mallets – ready to do battle with the Monster Brownie. When I next heard Mama's voice, it had an edge to it, and I peeked out tentatively from the screen door. I could see she was anxious, and maybe she was mad. I could also see the dreaded Brownie. I yelled out, "Mama, watch out. Brownie has rabies!" Mama looked at the old hound with her sweet eyes and happily wagging tail. Within two seconds, Mama ended that fantasy as easily as a pin might pop a balloon,

"Linda, what are you talking about? Come here! Why didn't you answer me? You have scared me half to death."

I remained cautious of the possible rabid dog. Still, I was also eager to assure my mama that I had not been ignoring her. I wanted her to understand we'd been dealing with our own set of problems – big ones, too! And then there were three of us all explaining to her at the same time – our words tumbling out and over each other. Mama hugged us and began to laugh. When she had made sure Vicky was alright and convinced us that Brownie was just fine, we headed home to wash up for supper. On the way, I decided to change the subject. We didn't need a lecture about being careful, and she didn't need to know every single detail of our adventures. It might put a picture in her mind that would do me no good in the end. That night at supper, she recounted to Daddy how we had scared her, and we got a stern warning from him: "You answer your mama when she calls." We both said, "Yessir," and we mentioned that we'd been busy running away from Brownie because we thought she had rabies, which made Daddy laugh. And that was the end of that adventure. After that, we kept keener ears and sharper eyes 'cause way down deep in our souls, we knew we were doing plenty that would have scared Mama way more than she was on the day of the rabid dog incident, and we cherished our freedom.

I remember my adventures on Little River fondly and am so glad for the role she played in my childhood. I'm glad my mama never knew what we were up to because we had a wonderful time and learned things they don't teach in school. I'm also glad my own children didn't grow up there. If they had done the things I did, I would have had a hissy fit!

Tag

Lots of families have activities they enjoy doing together. For some, it is card or board games; for others, it might be hiking, sailing, or some other outdoor sport. Like those other families, my childhood family enjoyed being together, too. Sometimes, we played cards, board games, roller skated (Daddy just watched and cheered – no roller skating for him), went for walks, went to ballgames, and spent time at a lake or beach. But what my brother and I liked best of all was a family game of tag.

It wasn't often that we could coax Daddy into playing with us. This industrious man owned a landscape company, which meant physical labor from sun up to sun down, Monday through Friday, whatever the weather. I could not truly comprehend the meaning of "tired" in those days. For one thing, my daddy was the strongest, hardest working man I knew – or have ever known, for that matter. He seemed superhuman to me - so that was one thing. The other thing was my own youthful ignorance. I mean, how tired do kids really get? And for how long? In my childhood, I might be tired from some physical exertion, but give me a little break, and I was up and ready for the next adventure. So, when my brother and I would try to start up a game, and Daddy would wave us away with his hand and say, "Go on now. I'm tired," we'd give it a couple more tries – because we didn't really comprehend anyone being too tired to play. You never could tell if Daddy was just bluffing. Sometimes he did that. And if he ever joined in the game – then it was ON!!!

The game usually began after dinner when Daddy had pushed his chair a little ways from the table and lit a cigarette – a clear signal that he was done with the meal. Then one of us - me or my brother would get up and move around the table, tap his arm or knee, and move quickly away while saying, "Tag! You're it." Like I said, it might not happen, and he would shake his head, wave his hand, and say, "Nahhh. Not now," or something like that. We might press it a time or two. Still, we'd either eventually read that it was definitely

NOT going to happen, or Mama might say, "Leave your daddy alone. He's tired." Sometimes, Daddy would bluff and say, "No," and then leap forward, and the chase was on. Sometimes, he would leap toward you right after the first tap. You couldn't predict, and it was always good to be on your toes. Once we had done the tap and proclaimed him "IT," then it was best to back quickly out of reach and be ready to run. You never knew just what might happen. He might start the chase after a bluff or two or three or right away. And he might chase after the first one to tap him, or he might turn around and tag somebody else – Mama or whichever kid wasn't the initiator. Whatever happened, the fun had just begun.

Our version of tag was actually two games in one. There was no "home base" where you couldn't be tagged (as usually happened when you played with other kids), and it included Hide and Seek. Additionally, the entire house – upstairs as well as downstairs in the basement and garage was open territory – including the surrounding yard and fields. So it was WILD and more fun than words can describe! There was always lots of yelling, screaming, laughing, scrambling, running, and general chaos. Even our family dog barked and ran and joined in the pandemonium. My wise mother had learned early on to quickly set the storm doors to the "stay open" position to avoid injury to people or property. The kitchen table got pushed to the wall to give a wider berth through that room, the living room furniture ended up against the walls, and every rug in every room of the house would be askew with the ensuing mayhem. We hid behind doors and in closets usually because we wanted a hiding place where you could set off running if you were caught and tagged. Burrowing underneath a bed or into a small confined space was a problem if you got tagged since you'd have to wiggle out from whatever place you'd squeezed yourself into before you could start full-on running, and by then, the person who had tagged you was long gone. And, of course, you ran the risk of being tickled first, which further set you back in your ability to make a clean break. And, for sure, Daddy was as likely to tickle you as not. The whole game could last an hour or more and was super exhilarating and the most fun a kid could ever have. And even though Mama fussed a little about having her house turned upside down, she was an enthusiastic participant on every occasion. She laughed and squealed like a young girl. Daddy never screamed or squealed, but he sure could holler and bellow with the best of 'em. His belly laughs were the best!

During one of our wild games of tag, a lady from our church happened to stop by our house for some reason that no one remembers – and probably she wouldn't remember either. But I'll bet money she never forgot the scene she encountered. No one had heard her pull into the driveway – what with all the screaming and yelling and whatnot going on. We found her standing timidly on our front porch, looking a little like a rabbit about to head off to safety. Sweaty, hair tousled, and breathless, Mama came upon her and began to laugh. Then, realizing the poor woman's

confusion and uneasiness – had she just
entered the scene of a family brawl or what???
– Mama quickly composed herself and invited
the visitor inside. Reluctant at first, Church
Lady finally stepped through the wide-opened
doorway inside to the Living Room – only to
find my mother's usually tidy house in
complete disarray. Her eyes darted wildly
around the room as she surveyed the scene.
Mama moved on into the kitchen and
motioned for the visitor to follow. The kitchen
was no different. The table slammed up next to
the wall, chairs helter-skelter about the room,
and Mama calmly opened the refrigerator to
make glasses of iced tea for everyone. Our
visitor moved into the kitchen with
trepidation. By this time, Daddy had come
inside – also sweating and breathless. My
parents chuckled and explained to the uneasy
guest that she had happened to have come
upon a family game of Tag. The lady laughed
a bit half-heartedly, and, in truth, she sounded
slightly nervous. She also declined the iced tea
offer, stated her business, and made a hasty
retreat to her car. The four of us – Mama,

Daddy, my brother, and I watched her go. Then we all looked at each other and fell into hysterical laughter. There was no telling what the poor woman really thought, and for sure, there would be a report to the church crowd about the wild shenanigans in the Pearce household. We could only imagine. The thought of it was almost as much fun as our game of tag – and it allowed my brother and me to forgive the unexpected visitor for interrupting our lively game. In fact, the whole scenario has lived on as gleefully and vividly as any one of those crazy games of Hide and Seek Tag.

Chapter 6

Legacy

Bird Dogs

My daddy loved dogs, and he especially appreciated a good bird dog. There is true beauty in watching dogs running over a field, sniffing out quail, standing point when they find their mark, and seeing other dogs in the pack honor the first point. Although I never went hunting with Daddy (because I didn't like the shooting/killing part), I've watched him train young dogs and have walked fields with him and his dogs. It's an amazing thing to witness.

Daddy had bird dogs for many years. There are many kinds of dogs used for hunting quail, but Daddy preferred English Pointers. These noble working dogs are lean, muscular, and focused. They love to run and are tireless. Their short, slick coats are a definite plus in the South, where the climate is hot and the terrain often filled with sheep burrs which could be of particular bother to dogs with longer coats. Pointer coats can be patterned or solid and come in several colors. All the ones Daddy owned were patterned and either black and white or liver and white. Their height is around two feet high, with males weighing as much as 75 pounds, while females are generally smaller and can be as light as 45 pounds. These loyal dogs carry themselves quite regally, and Daddy was always proud of his pack.

Folks used to say that Wallace Pearce's dogs lived the high life. It was certainly true that he took good care of them. Although he was affectionate toward them, and they clearly loved him, they were not house pets. Daddy built them a large wooden house – one tall enough for him to walk into and stand upright (and my daddy was 6′2″). It measured about 12 ft. x 20 ft., had a shingled roof and a cement floor with a loft area bed a few inches above the floor, which he kept covered with clean wheat straw. If it was hot, the dogs could lie on the cool cement below. There was a large trough for their food and a water spigot to give

easy access to fresh water. One side of the
building opened onto a large fenced area that
was shaded by Catawba trees. Even so, the
dogs dug large tunnels for themselves within
their confine to offer an additional layer of
shade. These tunnels were so large that my
little brother would often crawl inside them to
play. If he lay down inside one, he would be
completely hidden from sight, which gave my
mama a couple of bad frights when she
thought her little boy had gone missing. The
friendly dogs didn't seem to mind his
company one bit and never gave away his
hiding place. It was a relief to Mama when
he'd finally poke his little head up after her
searching high and low over the property. It
got so if he went missing, that's where she'd
look first.

My brother got to go hunting with
Daddy when he got his first BB gun. He
marched proudly out through the field on that
first hunt. At length, one of the dogs went on
point, and when Daddy commanded the flush,
a large covey of quail flew up into the sky.
Now, if you've never heard a covey of birds

rise into flight at close range, let me just tell you it is LOUD and can be particularly unnerving if you're not expecting it. My little brother was expecting the quail but not the terrific sound that comes from the cacophony of so many wings beating at the same time, moving underbrush and air. Daddy, of course, calmly raised his gun and downed two birds. He turned to his young son and asked, "Did you get one?" My poor little brother hadn't even raised his trusty BB gun, much less fired it. He was still stunned from the resounding noise of that covey lifting off. Nowadays, my brother chuckles at the recollection and, knowing my daddy's generous nature, says, "If I would've gotten off even one shot, Dad would have declared one of those birds was mine."

One time, Daddy's cousin, Walter, who lived way off in California, decided to ship my Daddy what he claimed was the best hunting dog in the world. It was a Weimaraner. Daddy was deeply honored by such a generous gift. I was excited and couldn't wait to see what this famous German dog might look like. I wasn't disappointed. He was indeed a very different dog – bluish-gray, sleek, and quite handsome. His name was Butch, and although he was large, he was young and untrained. Sometimes, Daddy allowed him into the house, much to Mama's dismay, and he romped around, creating havoc until Mama chased us all outside. Butch was very affectionate, and I would have loved to have him as a pet, but I knew that he was a working dog and bred to hunt.

After giving Butch some time to acclimate to his surroundings and "getting some of the puppies out of him," Daddy set out to train him. I had witnessed this before, and it was grand fun. Daddy secured a couple of quail, which were moved from their cage on training day to a small wire basket. With the dog out of sight, the basket would be hidden in a thicket of grass, weeds, or bush. Then, the dog was brought into the field, unleashed, and given the command "hunt." Daddy was pleased with how quickly Butch caught on to what was required of him and declared that he was "a smart dog." And so Daddy took him out for a hunt with his three other very seasoned dogs. Butch ran like the wind. Butch could cover some ground, and Butch could find quail. And Butch could point. Yessir! BUT there was one problem: Butch could not seem to honor a point. That means that whenever another dog sniffs out the quail first, the rest of the pack must immediately become perfectly still – thus "honoring" the point of the first dog. They might not be in close proximity and might not even be able to smell the prey; nevertheless, they must stand perfectly still – no matter what.

Poor Butch. No matter what Daddy did to punish him, which ranged from leaving him behind in the pen to shaming him unmercifully, Butch simply could not honor another dog's point. Daddy said that, in fact, another dog would go on point, and Butch would boldly and defiantly flush the birds – a BIG no-no! among hunting dogs. After his rebellion, Butch would immediately get on his belly and crawl towards Daddy to await his punishment. So it seemed it wasn't a matter of not being able to do it or not understanding his

duty. Butch simply _refused_ to do it. Period.
Daddy realized the truth was that Butch was
flat-out jealous of the other dogs receiving any
kind of praise. He wanted to be the one to
point, be allowed to flush on command, and
then receive his reward. And if he couldn't be
THE dog, then damn the consequences! He
simply wasn't going to let that praise be given
to any other dog. That sad realization caused
Daddy to let Butch go to a friend, another
quail hunter who often hunted alone. He said,
"Butch is a smart dog, and he's a good hunter,
but he can't hunt in a pack." I was sorry to see
Butch go, and I think Daddy was, too, but I
had come to understand that working dogs
need to work to be happy. And Butch loved to
hunt, so it would have been a shame to deny
him that life.

If you ever get the chance to watch bird
dogs hunt quail and go on point, you don't
want to miss it. It is truly fascinating. As for
quail – if you've never eaten it, I can guarantee
you will never taste anything quite so
delectable.

Christmas Trees

The first Christmas trees I knew were cedar and chopped down in the woods near our house. When I was five, Mama and I made paper chains to circle our tree, and she cut stars out of cardboard that we covered with aluminum foil. I didn't know it was because she couldn't afford to buy ornaments. Those foil-colored stars remained among our treasured decorations even in the years when we had shiny glass balls and silver tinsel galore. Their quiet glow always warmed my heart and reminded me of those winter mornings with my mama.

A much taller cedar was the anointed tree in the sanctuary of the rural Baptist Church I attended with my family. I suspect a local farmer and member found it in the woods that wrapped the fields and roads in those days. The scent of cedar will forever remind me of Christmas.

My cousins across the road most often had a fir tree, which was a very strange-looking tree to me as it was not native to the

Piedmont region of North Carolina. Frazier firs are commonly found in the mountain region of the state, so I suppose they purchased their tree. Money was slim in our house, and purchasing a tree was not in my family's budget. So, imagine my surprise when Daddy actually purchased a Christmas tree for us. Of course, being his usual frugal self, he felt it was a wise purchase, as this particular tree would last for many years to come. Yes. It was an artificial tree – a spectacular silver aluminum tree that came in a box. After the base was set up and the main upright poles secured, the limbs were fitted into the appropriately drilled holes. Once all the limbs were attached, the aluminum tree fairly gleamed.

Daddy had also purchased a special light that had a slowly revolving plastic disc with colored lenses so the tree could reflect a variety of colors – red, blue, and yellow. It was the 1960s and quite fashionable. The 1963 Sears Christmas Book declared: *"Whether you decorate with blue or red balls...or use the tree without ornaments – this exquisite tree is sure to be*

the talk of your neighborhood. High-luster
aluminum gives a dazzling brilliance. Shimmering
silvery branches are swirled and tapered to a
handsome, realistic fullness. It's really durable….
The needles are glued and mechanically locked on.
Fireproof… you can use it year after year."

I was impressed that my parents were so cool and very pleased with this stylish expression of Christmas spirit. My little brother and I loved putting the tree together and decorating it. My mother was happy to be freed of the daily watering to keep our usual cedar tree from drying out, as well as the daily sweeping up of the constantly shedding needles. Daddy no longer lectured on the possible fire hazards – but he still made us turn the tree light off at bedtime and whenever we left home. I used to beg to leave the revolving light on so that I could see its beauty radiating from our living room window when we returned home. That never happened – apparently, the danger of fire lurked somewhere in his mind.

My parents continued to use that tree year after year – just as Sears had promised –

long after it went out of fashion. They didn't care, and neither did I. That fake tree held as many happy memories on its branches as any green cedar ever did. By the end of the 1980s, many aluminum trees were sold in yard sales or relegated to the trash. By that time, my parents were grandparents who lived in a small apartment. Eventually, they elected to have a small tabletop tree that was less difficult to erect and store. What happened to our grand silver tree, I cannot say.

In recent years, the old has become new again, and there has been a resurgence in the popularity of the aluminum Christmas tree. Collectors began buying and selling them – especially on Internet markets. As a matter of fact, a 7-foot tall pink aluminum tree sold on eBay for $3,600. If you recall "The Charlie Brown Christmas Special" from 1965, this might have been the very one that Lucy Van Pelt told Charlie Brown to get for their nativity play.

"Get the biggest aluminum tree you can find, Charlie Brown – maybe painted pink," she said. But, of course, Charlie Brown set out to find a

tree as well as the meaning of Christmas and ended up with a sad little tree that was not aluminum – rather a real green one in need of a home – or so Charlie Brown thought. Some folks think this may have contributed to the decline of the aluminum tree. And you must admit that Lucy's line, *"Let's face it. We all know that Christmas is a big commercial racket. It's run by a big eastern syndicate, you know,"* may have a ring of truth. Even so, commercialism has always been with us, and fake trees have been around long before the aluminum ones showed up. There have been artificial trees made from dyed goose feathers attached to wire branches and trees constructed of tinted pig hair. And, of course, there are many thousands of glass and ceramic trees, although most of these are not used to put the presents under.

One of my mama's best friends, Crettie, made a green ceramic tree in her Ceramics Class for Mama one year – complete with multicolored "lights" lit from inside the hollow tree with a single bulb. Mama was delighted with her gift. She kept and treasured it for all of her life. I inherited it and put it out each year, mostly in memory of their sweet friendship. A year or so ago, I gifted it to my daughter. For her, it is a memory of Christmas at her grandmother's home.

The first Christmas my husband and I were together, we were not married. He was a Vietnam veteran and musician finding his way. I was as lost as he, and it was something of a miracle that we found one another. We tromped into the woods, cut down a small cedar, and dragged it home - along with a great deal of Carolina sand. Decorations were meager and mostly handmade, but the scent of cedar made it smell like home. By the following Christmas, we were married. We had a tiny baby girl sleeping in a crib and another cedar with a few more decorations on it than the previous year. We graduated to a house and bought green trees from a tree farm. The kind that looks just right on the lot but is always too big when you get them home. I came to understand my mother's feelings about watering a dying tree and constantly sweeping up evergreen needles. Eventually, we bought a fake tree, but it was green and looked about as real as a fake tree can look. By the time we strung lights and hung our decorations, it was as magnificent as any tree we had ever seen – real or fake.

The Christmas our daughter was in college and living in Scotland, I generously suggested that she not come home for Christmas but instead enjoy being abroad. We flew her first cousin to be with her and bought both of them Eurail tickets as Christmas presents. Knowing how life can be, I figured it could be an opportunity that might not come for her again. I was feeling proud of myself and relatively happy until it was time to put up our tree. I took to bed sobbing, feeling very depressed, and totally lacking in Christmas spirit. After allowing me to wallow in self-pity for a time, my husband came into our bedroom. He announced that we still had one child at home and we couldn't abandon Christmas. And right in the middle of putting up our tree, I found my Christmas spirit. It didn't make me miss our daughter less, but it helped me find the joy in her experience as well as our own.

The first Christmas after I lost both my parents, I was grief-stricken. My daughter was all grown up and on her own, but our son was still at home. I tried to summon the energy to open the attic and make the first move towards putting up our tree. But the energy didn't come, and my husband did not insist. Instead, he suggested that we find a small tabletop tree with lights and let that be our tree. I agreed but felt guilty that I was allowing my grief to cloud my son's Christmas joy. So, I took a deep breath and decided to discuss all things Christmas with him. As it turns out, I learned quite a lot from our discussion. Alex has autism, and he sees the world differently. I was strongly reminded of this during our conversation. I began by telling him that I was feeling sad because I missed my parents. I said that sometimes the holidays could make people miss their family even more, and since that was true for me, I did not feel like putting up our big tree.

"Daddy and I were thinking we would just get a small tree with lights and put it on the table in the living room this year. Would you be okay with that?" I asked. Alex stared into space for a few minutes and then volleyed, "Does that mean you aren't going to move the furniture?"

"Well, I suppose so," I pondered.

"Good. I hate it when you move the furniture," he declared. I was stunned. Then I offered that I would at least get down the fireplace jumping jacks. I had a collection of several wooden jumping jacks that I hung on our mantel. Most of them looked like some rendition of the famous Nutcracker, but there was also a soldier and an angel among them. All their joints were connected by a string, and by pulling a string at the bottom, they moved into various positions. Alex's eyes widened, and he said,

"No. I hate those jumping jacks. They look strange and scary." Another surprise revelation. And all that time, I had thought they were so cute and that my children enjoyed them! Oh, well. (Here, I shrug my shoulders). That Christmas, we had one small tree sitting on a table in our living room. No furniture was rearranged to accommodate it, and no Christmas Jumping Jacks hung from our fireplace mantel – only stockings. And Christmas came just the same as it always did – except I learned a little more about my puzzling son, and I found joy waiting quietly beneath my heartache. I believe that such joy dwells in the green of cedar or in the sparkle of aluminum but mostly in the spirits of those we love – wherever they are.

Good Boy

"My dog had puppies, and they're so cute. Do you want one?" I was in the sixth grade riding home on the bus, seated with my friend, Carolyn. And, Boy! Did I want one?!? You bet I did. I would ask my mama the minute I got off that bus.

Mama frowned and shook her head. She talked about responsibility and began listing all the problems that come with a puppy – peeing and pooping all over everywhere, chewing everything everywhere, and dog hair. Of course, I solemnly promised that I would be in charge of every single thing that had to do with a puppy – from training to feeding to minding its whereabouts. She was unconvinced. And so, I waited until suppertime when I could present my case to Daddy. He listened and asked what Mama said. I ignored his question and proceeded to explain that I would be in charge, that it would be MY dog and my responsibility. He chuckled, Mama rolled her eyes, and he ended the discussion with the famous line, "We'll

176

see," which could mean anything and possibly nothing. So, for the time being, I had to live vicariously through my friend, Carolyn, who kept me posted on the progress of the puppies. She said they were too young to be taken away from the mother, so there was more waiting to be done no matter what was ultimately decided. When I had given up hope one particular Saturday morning, Daddy said I should get dressed and go for a ride with him. As it turned out, he took me to my friend's house to pick out a puppy. I can't tell you what any of them looked like because the minute I saw MY puppy, I was in love. He was a white ball of fluff with a black nose and black eyes. I named him after my favorite candy – Sugar Baby. My daddy harrumphed at the name, but I persisted. I usually just called him Baby, although my daddy mostly called him Bebo.

Baby turned out to be the best dog ever. Potty training him was a breeze – I only ever cleaned up a single puddle. Throughout his puppy years, Baby never chewed up anything but bones. He seemed to understand that whatever belonged to the humans was not his to trifle with. Mama said it was a miracle. I think he was trying to stay in her good graces. And that little white dog also stayed miraculously white – no matter where he'd been or what he'd been doing. It was nothing short of amazing and probably made Mama think he was cleaner than other dogs – which probably gave him a leg up (if you'll pardon the expression). Certainly, it added to his reputation.   We lived in the country, and the only dogs kept in pens were my daddy's bird dogs. Otherwise, dogs roamed free. They never got lost, but crossing the road could be dangerous, and we had lost a couple of dogs to this danger. Baby learned not to cross the road, and it earned him years on the planet.

When it was time for me to live elsewhere, the dog I'd had to beg my mama for suddenly became HER dog. Huh? How did that happen? But apartment life was no place for Baby, so it was just as well. Mama, Daddy, and Baby had learned to dance together. When it was mealtime, Baby went outside the dining room but laid down where he could keep his eye on my daddy (who did not want a dog around the table begging at mealtime). The moment Daddy pushed his chair away from the table, Baby rose to his haunches and waited for Daddy's signal that he could enter the room. At a snap of Daddy's fingers he trotted over to Daddy's chair and hoped that there was a morsel left for him. Whether the treat came or not, he was patient. If the treat was allowed, there was another finger snap, and he would sit up on his hind legs and wave his front paws for the reward. Good boy! Whenever Mama got out her broom to sweep the kitchen and den, he went directly to the backdoor so he could go sit on the porch until she had finished sweeping. Good boy! If there was leftover toast after breakfast, Mama always took it out to the backyard for the birds. Baby never partook of it because Mama forbade him. It was just for the birds. So, Baby just watched from the steps as the birds came to feast on it. Good boy! However, at one point in time, a very aggressive mockingbird moved into the backyard territory. The bird frequently dive-bombed poor Baby. Eventually, Baby had enough of the torture. When Mama put toast out for the birds, Baby waited for Mama to go back into the house. Then he trotted out to the toast, picked it up, and promptly hid it under a large bush in another part of the yard. Baby knew he was not supposed to eat that toast, but By Golly! he wasn't going to allow that hateful mockingbird to have it! Mama was thoroughly amused by Baby's behavior and found him all the more endearing. What a good boy!

When Baby came to live with us, we lived out in the countryside of central North Carolina. However, during his lifetime, my parents moved two different times. Their first move put them in a little village in the Shenandoah Valley of Virginia. The property was situated on a small lot, and there was not as much room to roam as Baby had been used to. Still, luckily, this little dog was easily adaptable. He took to his new home as if he'd lived there all his life. He quickly and easily became friends with all the neighbors. The next move was a few miles away but still in the beautiful Shenandoah. This house was in the country with lots of room to stretch, sniff, and roam. That little dog was such a happy soul. He would have managed anywhere.

Baby was much beloved by every member of our family, but he always let me know that he was really my dog. Whenever I came home to visit, he came to sleep by my bed every night that I was there – no matter what house my parents lived in. In his heart, he knew where he belonged.

Years passed. Baby began moving slower and lying longer in sunny spots. Mama let Baby out one morning, and he disappeared. My family looked for him and called and whistled and clapped for him to come, but he did not return. The neighbors saddled their horses and rode the fields looking for our beloved dog, but there was never a sign of him. I was particularly grieved to think of that sweet old soul dying somewhere all alone. He was nearly sixteen years old. In vain, I tried to console myself by thinking that maybe it was just his time, and he knew it innately. Like many other animals do, he left his pack and went off alone to die. Mama said that Baby had never been in any trouble in life, and maybe he just didn't want to be any trouble in death either. Daddy said, "That dog didn't die. Elijah came down from heaven in his chariot to get that dog because he was such a good boy." I have decided to believe that very thing.

Kitchen Table

Our kitchen table was the center of the Universe when I was growing up. As tables go, it was plain – even drab – an unassuming rectangle with chrome legs and a Formica top, Circa 1960, with matching chairs, of course. It seated our family of four at breakfast, lunch, and supper most days – although Daddy was seldom home at lunchtime except for the weekends. When the company came, there was an extra leaf (or two) that made it able to accommodate more folks. Mama could whip out a tablecloth and put flowers in the middle to dress it up – which was important if her mother was visiting or my rich cousins from Charlotte. They would have my Great Aunt Rena with them, and you could bet she would tell us that she couldn't eat 'so and so,' but she'd just have a bite of it – and then she'd end up eating a whole big serving – which you couldn't say a word about until after she'd gone.

Other times having the table dressed up didn't matter at all – like on Saturday mornings or having a snack after school or when Daddy made homemade ice cream. Or when my friends came to visit after school. We were supposed to be studying, but we were mostly having fun.

Lots of other things happened at that table besides eating. Mama cut out patterns and set up her sewing machine to make everything from pajamas to dresses. My brother and I did homework, made posters for school, and dyed Easter eggs. I cried many a night doing Math at that table - sometimes so hard I had the snubs - and I grew to hate Math and anything to do with numbers. The colors of my Easter eggs never looked quite as vibrant as they did on the package of dye. But some things were sweeter and richer at that table than anywhere else. Like eating oatmeal with butter melting on top, sweet cream surrounding it like a moat, the sun streaming in the kitchen window, and my mama just being there in the kitchen with me. Or learning where babies really come from. Or playing Monopoly with my brother on a Sunday afternoon. Or having major family discussions about religion or politics or the mean old rooster who stalked my little brother and what we were going to do about that.

Gloves

I have always admired gloves – their style as well as their ability to keep hands warm, dry, clean, and safe - whether for dress, weather, gardening, or cleaning the kitchen. Gloves were a fashion accessory long before my time, of course, but in the 1950's and 60's they were definitely part of any woman's dress ensemble – in cold or warm weather. Even as a very young girl I always had white cotton gloves to wear to church on Sunday. By high school I owned various colored gloves to match certain outfits. Gloves ranged from wrist length to above the elbow, depending on the attire and the event. When I first donned an elegant pair of long white gloves that extended above the elbow to wear with a sleeveless evening gown, I felt positively regal! (Even now you can hear me sigh recalling this moment in time…...)

I especially loved leather gloves. There is nothing quite as exquisitely soft as a pair of kidskin gloves – however, owing to their expense; I could only admire my grandmother's. Once when I was elected to the Homecoming Court, Mama bought me a pair of brown pigskin leather gloves that buttoned at the wrist with a brown pearl button. I felt very chic!

The only down side of gloves for me was my short, stubby fingers, which rarely filled out the pinky finger of my leather gloves – and sometimes, even the glove's ring finger was a bit lacking. I was always left admiring folks whose long, tapered fingers made their gloves look so classically graceful.

The gloves I know the least about are boxing gloves. My cousin Tommy had a pair, but he wouldn't let me wear them, and I had to pretend I didn't give a fig! But the truth was I really wanted to try them on and punch something - just to see what it felt like. And, strangely, for a little girl, I knew quite a lot about punching because I watched the Gillette Friday Night Fights! Every Friday night, I used to snuggle up on my daddy's lap to watch the boxing bouts. Daddy would talk about the various fighters, explain what was happening, and critique their moves, as well as the referee. Sometimes, he would become animated as he watched. His large, muscled arms would move and flex, and occasionally, he would utter a groan or an exalted "yeah!" It was dramatic and lively, and I loved it! What I didn't know as a little girl watching those fights was that he had been a boxer himself.

Eventually, I came to know this fact, although I'm not sure how. Perhaps he or Mama told me at some point, but it certainly wasn't because he ever talked about his career. In fact, he said next to nothing on the subject. What I know is that sometime after his high school years Daddy began boxing. He was sponsored by a well-to-do gentleman from Zebulon, Mr. R.H. Bridgers (who was mayor of Zebulon at some point). He went on to New York to fight professionally as a heavy weight. I have pictures of Daddy in the boxing ring looking muscled and handsome but very serious, his gloved fists raised and legs ready to move. I asked him once why he quit boxing, but he frowned, shook his head, and said, "Everybody in that business is not on the up and up." The end. I didn't ask again.

A few years ago, Tim Richardson, a fine fellow from Zebulon whom I have known most of my life, asked me if I had a picture of my dad in his boxing trunks. I said, "Yes," I did. Tim said he'd like to have one to hang out in the building behind his home, where he houses a ton of memorabilia. I was happy to accommodate. I like knowing that someone else admires my daddy as much as I do.

Tim is a couple of years older than me, attended the same school, and married one of my classmates (Sandra Chamblee). He's a nice guy - well-liked in the community. Tim is also quite a character – full of fun and with a good sense of humor. Here's what Tim had to say to me when I delivered the framed boxing picture to him:

"You know, I worked for your Daddy one summer. Wallace Pearce was a fine man. And he was strong, too! And worked hard! One time, I drove one of his dump trucks over to Wendell like he told me to, but when I was backin' under the shelter there, I didn't account for the height of the

truck, and I tore the roof of that shelter clean off. Lawd! It liked to have scared me to death! Your daddy was a big man, and I was kinda scared of him. I thought I was gonna have a nervous breakdown while waitin' for him to get there to pick me up. As soon as he got there, I started sayin', "Mr. Pearce, I'm so sorry. You can take the cost of that shelter out of my pay." But your Daddy put his big arm around my shoulders and said, "Boy, that's why I got insurance!" And that was the end of it. He never said another word about me tearin' that shelter all to pieces."

"I know somethin' about your daddy boxin'. When folks come 'round here and see this picture of your daddy, I'm gonna tell them what a great boxer he was – and that he could've been a really great boxer. My daddy had seen your daddy box and followed his career. He told me one time that Mr. R.H.Bridgers said, 'I could take Wallace Pearce and whip the world.' You know, he never got knocked out, and most times, he could knock the other guy out by the third round. That summer that I worked for him, I asked him about his boxing days, and he said, 'Listen here. I'm gonna tell you this, and then I don't ever wanna talk about it again. They asked me to throw a fight – they wanted me to lose on

purpose. But I got in that ring, punched the guy out, took off my gloves threw 'em at 'em, and said, 'I'm goin' home!.' And that's just what I did.' After that, he never said another word about boxin' to me, and I didn't ask. Your daddy was a fine man, and he didn't want nothing to do with somethin' that was dishonest."

I know this statement to be the absolute truth - without a shadow of a doubt!

As a boy, my daddy was daring and mischievous. He grew up in the country and ran wild over the fields, woods, and rivers. The games he played with his brothers, cousins, and friends were often rough and dangerous. He got into his fair share of scraps with his brothers and schoolmates. And he got into more than his share of trouble at school. Even so, he managed to learn the lesson of fair play and truth-telling very early on, and he developed a moral compass that never veered from True North. It guided him through his whole life.

When I think of boxing gloves, I think of my daddy as a strong, capable young boxer who wore those padded leather gloves

proudly – until he couldn't. Instead, he put on
a badge of honor and left those gloves behind.

Family Differences

Even though both of my parents were Southerners, they came from two very different places south of the Mason-Dixon. There was my father, who was from the sandy soil of the North Carolina Piedmont. He grew up on a farm where he had plowed with a mule, chopped tobacco and cotton, and toted water from a well. He had worn overalls and eaten grits and red-eye gravy. Then there was my mother, who was from Virginia's Shenandoah Valley. She could roller skate and ice skate with ease. She learned to sew in Home Economics Class and to cook only after getting married. Her biggest chores growing up were polishing the floor in the front foyer and checking out and returning books to the library for her mother. She had been a fashionable city girl.

My father's parents were simple folks who ate biscuits for every meal at a plain table with minimal fuss. My mother's family enjoyed casseroles and dined at a table covered with lace or linen cloths and freshly cut flowers.

My father's family was Southern Baptist. They attended an old country church, and my father was baptized in a nearby river. Sunday morning in those oak pews rang with slow nasal twangs whining out "the Old Rugged Cross" to a banging upright piano. My mother's family was Methodist, and at her baptism, she was sprinkled with water held in a marble basin. My daddy's Baptist relatives raised their eyebrows at this, and Daddy teased her. "Barely saved," he often joked. Her church's stone archways echoed with the strains of J.S. Bach reverberating through a pipe organ.

At times, my parents' Southern heritages meshed completely in attitude and understanding. They both abided by the strict social rules regarding politeness and decency. My brother and I were taught to say "'ma'am" and "sir" and to address every cousin older than 21 by "Aunt" or "Uncle." Men and boys removed their hats from the house. Girls kept their knees together when seated. And only heathens would dare to curse aloud in public!

My parent's cultural differences were sometimes subtle, sometimes striking, and some lost themselves along the way in their fifty years together. However, there was one abiding issue that has not been resolved to this very day. It involved mealtimes.

Now, both my mother and father agreed that the first meal of the day is breakfast. But after that, communication broke down! My mother referred to the midday meal as lunch. My father sneered at such nonsense. He thought lunch was a dainty serving of sandwiches for sissies. Real people, hard-working folks, had dinner. And, by the way, this is pronounced "dunnah." This noon meal consisted of steaming fresh garden vegetables, meat of some sort, and, of course, biscuits. This point of reference was the evening meal for my mother. My dad insisted that it was "supper." Mother staunchly contended that "supper" was a late meal served after 8 o'clock, and since our family ate at 6, this was too early for "supper."

From this eternal war of words, I learned to be specific about the time when making plans. Arrival or departure is never associated with the words "lunch" or "dinner" time, as this could create havoc with scheduling. Nothing could ever be said to occur before, during, or after lunch or dinner without causing extreme frustration among my family participants. An <u>exact</u> time needed to be stated whenever plans were made. This includes Christmas dinner, which my father believed was to be eaten at 12 noon and my mother believed was at 6 o'clock sharp!

Chapter 7

Never Judge a Book By Its Cover

Perfume

Hunter's Dime Store in Wendell, North Carolina, was my favorite shopping place when I was a child. The store was small with two aisles that were really just a long rectangle, which ran down one side, along the back, and then back to the front. Items were random, and there were so many they defied the eye to take them all in with one glance. There were plates, bowls, cups, miscellaneous serving and baking dishes, cookware, linen cloths, handkerchiefs, jewelry, toys, hats, clothes, handbags, creams, lotions, perfume, and countless other items – all of them stuffed here and there and everywhere – high and low. In the middle of this merchandise, madness sat tiny Mrs. Hunter, surveying her kingdom and ringing up purchases on her ancient cash register.

When I was very little, I was accompanied by my mother and forbidden to touch anything, which was pretty hard to do as we squeezed down and around the crowded aisle. One Christmas, Daddy gave me some money and allowed me to take my little brother into Hunter's and shop without adult accompaniment. Mrs. Hunter watched us like a hawk but finally decided we weren't planning to wreck the place. The two of us searched for Christmas presents for our parents. We left proud of ourselves and our newly found independence. After that, Mama would frequently let me shop there unaccompanied while she did errands. Of all those shopping trips, I can only remember three distinct purchases. One was a pink-sectioned dish that I gave Mama for Christmas. The other was a purchase for Mama's birthday and Mother's Day.

On her birthday, I had a hard time deciding but finally settled on an embroidered linen handkerchief and a bottle of perfume. All of the perfume came in small bottles of various shapes and colors. I chose a striated glass bottle with an indigo-colored top. "Ben-Her," it said. To this day, I have no idea why I decided that was THE perfect gift for my precious mother. Perhaps I thought it had something to do with the handsome actor Charlton Heston. The Lord only knows!

Mama opened my gift and exclaimed how beautiful, how wonderful, how much she loved it. I was pleased with myself, and my little chest puffed with pride. And so, of course, I bought another bottle of perfume for her on the very next occasion – Mother's Day. Blue Danube, it was called. It was in a heart-shaped glass bottle with a pale blue top. I had a pink music box that tinkled out "The Blue Danube" waltz, and I was sure the heady perfume was every bit as feminine and lovely.

Mama kept the perfumes on her dresser forever. I would ask her occasionally if she was wearing the perfume, and she would say, "Oh, I'm saving it for a special occasion." I never wondered why the level in the bottles did not dwindle. Many years later, I ran across the perfumes. I opened them and took a sniff. No wonder the levels had remained unchanged. I chuckled to myself and was touched by how my mother had cherished these gifts. Blue Danube still looked lovely. But Ben-Her had now become a mystery to me. Why had I chosen such a masculine-sounding perfume? What had I been thinking? All I could think of was a brave and daring Charlton Heston racing those white horses around the Roman Coliseum. That vision had nothing to do with my sweet, delicate Mama. I shook my head and laughed. It is only now, having seen my mother battle with Ovarian Cancer, that I know what lay underneath her seemingly soft exterior. Perhaps as a little girl, I sensed the strength that lay beneath the surface of her love.

Of Mice and Mama

My mama was a small woman – just a little over 5 feet tall. And prissy! Lord, that woman was prissy! She wouldn't leave the house without lipstick. She believed in good manners and "acting like a lady" – hands in your lap (gloved if possible), knees together, and absolutely NO cursing. She could give you the stink eye but hold it together in public even when she was mad as fire. The woman could also faint – always conveniently so that my daddy could catch her. (Excuse me while I roll my eyes here….) She could also sew and bake – her pies were legendary! She could whip up a meringue like nobody's business. She loved hosting – anything from birthday parties to sit-down dinners – which she could do on the spur of the moment without going to the grocery store, no kidding! Mama taught Sunday School and Bible School – charming kids with her smile and storytelling, which she perfected with the use of a felt board. She was warm, friendly, and generous with her time and energy. My friends liked her, and so did I.

She was a genuinely classy lady – a true Southern belle.

All that said, there was one thing my mama could not abide, and that was a mouse in her house. If she suspected such a loathsome creature was anywhere in the vicinity, the woman went immediately to DEFCON IV. That mouse was going DOWN! Traps were set, and bait was laid without delay. And if she happened to SEE one scurrying about – well, God help that poor mouse because my mama went into Full Attack Mode. And let me tell you, hell hath no fury like my mama on a mouse! Forget jumping up onto a chair and squealing like a girl - which you'd think someone who could faint would do…..but nope. All her priss, sass, and class went out the window.

One fine summer evening, my daddy had gone to the coast fishing, and I had gone to the movies with my boyfriend. It was late – around 11 o'clock – when I arrived home to find all the lights in the house on, which was unusual for the hour. My boyfriend wondered what could be going on and remarked that it wasn't past my curfew. I said maybe it was a few minutes past, but not much. We proceeded to open the front door to find my mama armed with the vacuum cleaner under one arm and a broom in the other, followed by my little brother (around ten years old) wielding a bat. Mama's face had that look of a Woman On A Mission. I was shocked into place. The boyfriend took a couple of steps back. Then, questions and answers collided. I asked, "What?"

My date squeaked out, "Are we late?"

My brother shouted, "Mouse!" And I knew immediately what was happening. My mama never gave us a passing glance as she careened around a corner with her weapons at the ready. The boyfriend was shaken and bewildered. He could not grasp what in the world could be going on that had transformed the usually genteel lady he knew as my mother into this fierce Warrior Woman. I'm pretty sure he was expecting a warm welcome and the offer of a slice of pie and a glass of milk. But nope! It seems he had fallen down the rabbit hole and ended up with the Queen of Hearts, who might at any minute proclaim, "Off with his head!" I tried to explain, but he was unconvinced that he was truly welcome and beat a hasty retreat from the potentially violent scene. By the time I had bid him farewell and made it back into the house, Mama had corraled the poor little mouse in my brother's room. With the strength of an army, my little mama had moved a chest of drawers into the middle of the room. Now, the terrified creature was left shivering on a baseboard in the corner of my brother's bedroom. Warrior Mama deftly aimed the vacuum cleaner wand at the mouse and sucked him neatly and swiftly up into the bowels of her Electrolux. Then, for added measure, she grabbed one of my brother's tee shirts and stuffed it into the tubing. She hauled the vacuum cleaner into the middle of the Living Room where she could keep a close eye on it in case the unfortunate mouse might somehow escape Electrolux Prison. Mama then perched herself on the sofa where she continued her vigil - determined to guard her home against the evils of Micedom.

When my daddy arrived home much later, he laughed out loud and chided her, "You don't think that mouse is still alive and able to crawl out of there, do you?" Mama was not amused, nor was she moved to feel any sort of sympathy regarding the fate of the trespasser. She said she was just "making sure," and her chin had that set about it to say she meant business. Daddy chuckled and took the vacuum cleaner outside to empty out the now-deceased prisoner. Once the criminal was removed, Mama resumed her role as Lady of the House – putting everything back into its rightful place and waving us all off to bed.

The next evening, my boyfriend showed up for our date. Still, he lacked his usual confidence and was tentative on entering the house. He was greeted by my mama's usual good humor and welcoming smile as she graciously offered him a slice of pie and a glass of milk. Later on, he said to me, "I'll tell you what. I sure wouldn't want your mama mad at me!" I laughed and said he didn't need to worry – he wasn't a mouse.

Chapter 8

Country Girl

Picking Beans

I had a lot of chores when I was a kid, but there was none that I truly hated more than picking beans. First of all, if you know anything about North Carolina, you know that the summers can be sweltering. And if you don't know anything about summer in the Carolinas, know this: Carolina summers are hot and humid and full of bugs. So there's that. Secondly, when my daddy planted a garden, he clearly planned on feeding the world because the rows were L O N G. Thirdly, Bean plants make me ITCH!!! And despite what my mama said, that itching was NOT in my imagination.

So, when my mama said it was time to pick beans, I knew I was in for a day from hell. Of course, I could never say such a thing to Mama because the word "hell" was not allowed into my vocabulary unless you were at church or otherwise talkin' about hell as opposed to heaven. Any other use of that word was considered cussin' (or cursing, if you didn't grow up in the South). And my mama was strongly opposed to cussin'.

On Bean Pickin' Day, you had to get up early in an effort to avoid the heat of the day – although some days, the heat lived all through the night and was still there in the morning – offering no relief at all. The problem with gettin' out to the garden early is that the dew is still on everything – from the grass you walked through to get to the garden to every single leaf and bean in the garden. Ugh. And you'd think that a girl that grew up working in the summers barnin' tobacco would know something about getting up early, wet leaves, and sweatin' – which is very true. However, barnin' tobacco is done with a crowd of folks that, in my experience, are mostly fun to work with. Bean pickin' is not exactly solitary, but let's just say it lacks the allure of a crowd, which may be hard to understand and even harder to explain. The bottom line is there was not one glamorous thing about pickin' beans.

I'd start pickin', and the sound of those first beans droppin' into the bucket sounded like a death knell. I knew that bucket had to be filled and filled and filled again.

The day began wet with dew, which eventually gave way to plain ole sweat, trickling slow and salty from every pore in your body, lying in dark creases around your neck, rolling over your face and into your eyes, burning like little pots of fire. The purgatory proceeded to include all manner of insects, which could be harmless grasshoppers that might startle you with their sudden jumps or graceful dragonflies that could be enchanting enough to lure you away from the task at hand before a sharp reminder from the busy taskmaster. Or you might meet up with some irritable ole hornet who'd just as soon sting you as look at you. But the worst was the blankety-blank (fill in any cuss word here that I was not allowed to say) mosquitos and flies – especially horse flies, which were the meanest, hatefulest critters ever invented with the absolutely nastiest bite you can imagine. And they bit you just because they wanted to.

Ugggghhhh!!!! They were surely Satan's minions!

About halfway through the first row (what? You thought my daddy only planted ONE row of beans? Oh, if only....) I'd start itching – mostly my arms, but sometimes my legs, too. And I tried with all my might not to scratch because once I started, the worse it got. I swear I could have scrubbed my arms raw and to no avail. It was awful. I could complain and certainly did my share of it, but I had learned that didn't accomplish anything except to make my mama mad, and what good was that? I'd just end up hot, sweaty, itchy AND gettin' the stink eye from Mama OR worse – and no matter what, I wasn't gettin' out of pickin' those beans. So there!

Even so, I have to say that it wasn't all bad. Walking outside on a summer morning with a fine mist hovering over the fields, birds singing joyfully, and morning glories showing off their prettiest blooms is a completely fine way to start the day, no matter what else is in store. And there is nothing quite like the sounds of summer in the country – those insects and birds, be they loathsome or lovely, could compete with any orchestra with their whirring and buzzing and trilling and cawing and chirping perfectly laid against the backdrop of hazy blue skies and a blazing ball of sun beginning low on the horizon and creeping slowly, steadily toward noonday. Then, when you're done, you feel mighty good about the bountiful harvest and very proud of your own hard work – not to mention the approving smile from Mama. And sittin' in the kitchen with her smile, my little brother, an electric fan blowing the air happily about while we cooled our insides with a glass of sweet iced tea, is just about the best reward there is.

Nowadays, I relish buying beans that somebody else has picked, for all these years later; I can still recall how much I hated pickin' beans. And yet, what I wouldn't give to have one more summer day with my mama in that bean field.

Outhouse

For those of you too young or refined to know what an outhouse is, let me explain. Also referred to as a "johnny-house," it is a small structure situated some distance from the house used to cover an earthen latrine and protect the user from the elements. Typically, it has one opening for one user, but sometimes it has two. Such structures were quite common back in the days when there was no indoor plumbing. These toilets were not heated, and during inclement weather or in the dark of night, folks often used a chamber pot indoors, which was emptied outside when conditions were more favorable. I have read that some people had fancy two-story outhouses, although I've never seen one. Most were square and made of wood, but I read that Thomas Jefferson built two octagonal brick structures. However, brick structures were permanent and immovable, which made them relatively impractical for modest folks, and I have to wonder if it is somehow connected to the expression "built like a brick $#& house"?

Nowadays, outhouses are mostly found at national parks or on mountain peaks.

All that said, what I know about outhouses comes from personal experience. Although all the houses that I remember living in had indoor toilets, my grandparent's home in North Carolina did not. As a child, I didn't wonder about this, nor did I consider it strange. It's just the way things were. And kudos to my mama for never pointing this out, as she was a city girl who grew up in a big house with indoor plumbing. I suppose in her day, these differences were not as stark as they would be considered today. It is only as an adult, looking back, that I realized how differently my two sets of grandparents lived. I enjoyed being with either one equally. The only differences to me were that one lived in Virginia, the other in North Carolina, and one in the city; the other in the country. Otherwise? Who cared? There was always something fun, delightful, or delicious happening at either place. Besides, back then, there were lots of folks around who had outdoor toilets, so it was just no big deal, really. Of course, most of those people had "one-seaters," which I considered rather lonely and sad. My grandparents had a very comfortable "two-seater" in which I enjoyed many fine conversations with Mama, Gramma, or one of my many girl cousins as we swung our legs and did our business.

Some years after my North Carolina grandfather died, it was decided that my grandmother needed an indoor bathroom. I am fairly sure her children made this decision because I happened to know that Gramma thought it was a foolish waste of time and money. Despite her initial protests, the point was pressed. Eventually, Daddy and my uncles installed a small bathroom in a corner of my grandmother's bedroom. The new addition contained a toilet and a sink. Period. It seemed that Gramma drew a line when it came to something as frivolous as a tub or shower. When I asked her why there was no tub, she snorted, clenched her jaw, and declared she didn't need one.

The rest of the family shook their heads at her stubbornness and whispered fearfully among themselves that she might never use the lovely convenience. That first cold winter, I'm sure she was silently grateful for being moved into the modern world. Still, I know for sure that it was her absolute practical nature that drove her indoors rather than her lust for luxury. By then, I was a teenager, and having an indoor toilet was nearly a necessity. I had become privileged. Having gained some perspective today, I can see that having a bathroom is indeed a luxury. Sixty percent of the world's population does not have safe or indoor toilets. And as unbelievable as it sounds, there are a half million Americans who do not have indoor plumbing, which includes (more understandably) rural and indigenous communities as well as (surprisingly) some urban communities, according to the Plumbing Poverty Project. (Who even knew such an organization existed?!?) Personally, I am very grateful for the comfort and convenience of an indoor toilet and realize that there are people in the world who would consider my bathroom an extravagance. And yet, when I think of myself swinging my little legs in my grandparent's comfy two-seater outhouse and chatting with one of my cousins, I am pretty sure that I was as happy as any queen on her throne. The end.

Roosters

I've personally known a couple of roosters in my time. My first was a little banty rooster gifted to me by Mr. Raeford Driver – probably to win my affection or offer an apology after making me mad as fire at church by calling me a "pretty little boy." I was four or five at the time, and he teased me mercilessly. At first, I would argue with him, trying to tell him that he was wrong and that I was a girl, for Goodness sake! But he was unmoved and would shake his head and say that couldn't be right. Every Sunday that I saw him, it was the same, "There's that purty little boy!" (big smile) and me (big frown) arguing, "No! I'm a girl." He clearly enjoyed the interaction, but me? Not so much. One Sunday, as we were leaving the church, I said to my parents, "Mr. Raeford makes me SO mad, calling me a boy!!" They laughed (again, not funny!) and told me that he was only teasing, but I was unconvinced. I suppose Daddy may have told Mr. Raeford what I said because one day, Mr. Raeford showed up at our house with a big smile, a twinkle in his eye, and the small, beautiful rooster as a present. I was thoroughly delighted. It didn't stop him from teasing me at church, but I stopped arguing. Instead, I just smiled 'cause you gotta forgive someone who gives you a rooster, right?

Daddy allowed the rooster to live uncaged, and so he hung around our yard, mostly in our garage, with our dog, Buck, who had the freedom of our backyard and garage but was tethered by a very long chain so that Mama could reign him in easily if company showed up. He was a sweet, loving dog to my immediate family. He was also loyal to a fault, and, in his mind, if you didn't live there, you didn't belong there. My Uncle Leamon and Uncle J.E. (actually, J.E. was a cousin, but in the South, an adult cousin moves to the rank of "uncle") hated him because, despite their attempts to befriend him with tasty treats, Buck remained firm in his opinion. He would chase them the length of his chain and then stare at them, growling and making it clear they were unwelcome. Mama would have to pull on Buck's chain and tell him it was okay for them to come in. Uncle J.E. always shook his head and laughed it off. Uncle Leamon cussed under his breath about "that damn dog." Once, Mama heard someone hollering and ran to the door to find Uncle J.E. standing on the roof of his car and Buck barking and growling at him from below. It seems that Uncle J.E. thought he could pull up close enough to the door to gain entry before Buck could get him. But finding the screen door locked, his only avenue of escape was the top of the car. When Mama arrived to save him, he asked her why in the world she kept the door locked when she had Buck???

You may think that Buck was ill-tempered and dangerous, but not so. He was sweet and patient with me and my little brother, who was in the crawling, toddling stage around that time. I played on and around him every day while he ate, sniffed around, or slept in the yard, garage, or sometimes in our house. He never bothered our cat or any of her kittens, either. And when the banty rooster came to live with us, he did not seem to mind one bit. In fact, that brazen little fowl had the nerve to roost right on top of ole Buck when he was lying down. It was common to find the two of them napping together - Buck snoozing with the little rooster hunkered down on his back. I don't remember what happened to that little fellow, but he was a character – strutting about, crowing and flapping, and allowing me to rub his sleek feathers and eat food out of my hand.

As a side note about Buck: he was a large black and white Pointer that Daddy used for bird hunting. Interestingly, whenever Daddy took him off his leash and Uncle J.E. showed up to go hunting, Buck showed no signs of animosity toward J.E. Clearly, Buck was able to separate his jobs into distinct categories that did not overlap – guarding our family and hunting quail. It's probably why J.E. could so easily let go of Buck's firm position when he was guarding and Leamon could not. Leamon didn't bird hunt. J.E. did – and he could appreciate a good bird dog. And Buck was a good bird dog.

The next rooster I knew personally was some years later. I was around ten, and my brother was maybe five (at least he hadn't started school yet). We had a brood of chickens, and it was my job to help gather eggs, which I mostly loved doing – except for one ornery brown hen who invariably pecked me whenever I reached under her for eggs, no matter what clever trick I employed to outwit or distract her.

Mostly, the flock stayed in their pen, but sometimes, they would fly over the fence in their clumsy, graceless way and peck around in the surrounding field and garden. No matter, Daddy could easily corral them back into the safety of their enclosure before nightfall. Besides, the girls were protected both day and night by a very large and handsome bird who was surely the King of Roosters and, in his mind, absolutely the King of All He Surveyed. He was a typical rooster – strutting around proudly, flapping his wings in grand display, and crowing to alert the world that he was alive and well. He led his girls to safety and scratched up treats for them,

hiding under rocks, leaves, or sticks.
However, his benevolence extended only to
his flock of hens. All others he eyed keenly
and with suspicion. His haughty flapping was
warning enough for dogs and cats and me. I
gave him a wide berth whenever I had to
gather eggs, and he kept his sharp eye on me.
Unfortunately, at some point in his reign, he
decided that my brother was a threat to his
domain, and the battle was on!

One fateful day, wee Douglas ventured
too near the King's perceived borderland, and
the ostentatious rooster flew onto his little
back and latched on with his great talons,
spurs out, squawking loudly, flapping his
enormous wings, and pecking mightily. It was
a terrible sight to behold!!! And it was
especially terrible if you were the big sister
watching your baby brother being assaulted.
No amount of yelling, screaming, swatting,
beating, or flailing was to any avail. The
rooster was wild and strong, and I was
helpless against it. Fortunately, Mama came,
armed with a broom, and beat the attacker off.
That evening at dinner, we all related the

horror to Daddy. I don't remember what he had to say about it, but I imagine he thought we were being overly dramatic about the incident. After all, the old rooster had never displayed such aggression to or around him. Not to mention, Daddy was 6'2", so the rooster probably didn't seem big or scary to him in the least. I suspect that if he had witnessed the awful scene himself, that would have been the end of that ole bird right then and there.

At any rate, the rooster became my poor little brother's constant nemesis. If the chickens were all safely enclosed, there was no problem. But if the King happened to be out and strutting about, then anything from a minor skirmish to a full-on battle was likely to ensue. Sometimes, he would just chase Douglas – who learned to run pretty fast. Sometimes, he would attack full-on. It always ended the same way: Douglas crying, helpless, and running; me screaming, flailing my arms, and trying unsuccessfully to beat the wild bird away; Mama coming to the rescue and knocking the attacking bird off her baby boy with a broom. One evening at supper, after we had recounted yet another such brutal incident, Daddy looked at my brother and asked, "You know what we're gonna to do about that ole rooster?"

My wide-eyed little brother slowly shook his head. "No." And Daddy said, "Well, come Saturday, I'm gonna get my hatchet, and we're gonna chop that old rooster's head off and cook him for Sunday dinner. What do you think about that?"

My brother nodded and smiled with both relief and glee, "Yes!" he nodded affirmatively. I figured that he thought Saturday couldn't come soon enough to suit him.

Now, if you know me, I assume that you think I would have been opposed to such a callous course of action against one of God's creatures. And, as you know me today, you might be right. But let's look at this in the light of the 1950's. First, and most importantly, there was my little brother to consider. I had adored him from the moment of his birth, and I had only grown to love him more. In fact, seeing him tormented by this pitiless beast time after time only fueled a fierce charge over his small being. I had come to view the dutiful rooster as a spawn of Satan. And secondly, I was a country girl who knew about Fall hog killing time and slaughterhouses. I'd seen my sweet gramma walk calmly through the yard with her chickens clucking and pecking all about, snatch one of them by the head, deftly swing it around in circles a few times, and begin plucking feathers from its lifeless body while she strode back to the house to cook it for dinner – all so swiftly and gracefully executed that the chicken never made a sound. And neither did I. I knew it wouldn't be long before I was eating her heavenly fried chicken and good ole biscuits. It was just farm life.

Saturday came, and there was an air of excitement at our house akin to the State Fair. Big stuff was going to happen, and our whole family was going to be there to see it happen. So, when Daddy decreed it to be THE TIME, Mama, Douglas, and I marched out to the site of execution like folks going to a gallows picnic. Daddy had a block of wood used for such occasions and his trusty hatchet laid out.

There was some distant squawking in the chicken pen, and Daddy emerged holding that big old rooster by his feet and strode up the path to where we were awaiting the main event. He asked Douglas if he wanted to do the deed, but much as he may have wanted to, one look at that large, fierce bird, and young Douglas shook his head "no."

I was unprepared for the swiftness of the execution, for it took less than a minute for Daddy to have the rooster's head lopped neatly off. And because there was no need to have hold of a headless bird, Daddy had let go and stepped away. That's when the true horror began for my poor brother. In case you've never witnessed a chicken get its head chopped off, let me enlighten you to the fact that its body does not need its head to continue to move around for a while after the deed is done. This now headless fowl was no different. His brain had already sent the signals to his rooster legs to run and for his rooster wings to flap – so run and flap he did, with blood spurting out of his neck all the while. The bizarre zombie bird began running

in crazy spiraling circles that grew wider and
wider. In the first turn, he appeared to run
directly toward my brother. Of course,
naturally horrified, Douglas took off running,
too. Regrettably, my brother chose the same
wildly spiraling course as the crazy beheaded
rooster. As Douglas ran, he glanced back at the
unholy creature, and each time, the blood-
spurting, headless, flapping rooster seemed to
be running directly for him. Douglas' eyes
were wide and round with fear, as was his
mouth, but I'm not sure that he even made a
sound. The only sound I could hear was the
sound of my parent's laughter. In the end,
Douglas headed up the hill toward our side
door, and thankfully, the engine running the
dead bird wound down. The zombie bird
landed with a thud onto his side – stilled at
last and relieved of his duties as King of the
Chickens. My parents' pity for their small
son's ordeal overcame the hilarity of the event,
and they retrieved him from the porch where
he was trying in vain to open the storm door
so he could retreat inside the house. Mama
hugged and comforted him, but I could see the

corners of her mouth were still smiling. Daddy put his arm around Douglas' shoulders and walked with him to see that the devil bird was at last defeated – and rightly so, by the King of the Castle!

I honestly don't know if I laughed while the whole experience was unfolding because, to tell the truth, it was mind-boggling to witness. I think I was just staring in unbelief. But I have to admit that I have laughed quite a lot since then, remembering that unanticipated, incredulous, and hilarious spectacle! From my brother's point of view, however, it was the stuff nightmares are made of. He probably needed therapy afterward, but hey! It was the 1950s, and we lived on a farm. So there – and here's where I shrug my shoulders.

P.S. As an adult - and a big sister who cannot help herself - I occasionally relish giving my little brother a replica of a rooster as a Christmas gift. (He's an adult now and hopefully has had some therapy, so why not?)

And one more P.S.: I'll bet you'll never hear the term "running around like a chicken with its head cut off" without this scene coming to mind. (wink)

Homecoming

I was raised in a rural Southern Baptist Church when the only air conditioning in the summer was hand-held fans with pictures of Jesus on one side and funeral parlor advertisements on the other. There was plenty of hellfire and brimstone on Sunday mornings, Prayer Meetin' on Thursday nights, and lots of hymns sung with gusto both on and off key. A huge oil painting of Jesus sitting in a meadow with his flock of sheep hung behind the pulpit. I have stared into that painting more times than I could count. The folks in that church were sincere and sweet. I felt loved there, and that is a powerful thing. It was the best ingredient for Homecoming Sunday when everybody brought their finest home-cooked dish, which was spread out on a huge table crudely constructed amongst some old oaks but graciously shaded by these same trees.

To be sure, there would be a rousing sermon prior to the meal and then a blessing for the food that included the cooks, along with a heaping helping of general praise and

likely a little something for the sinners as well.
The blessing always turned into a prayer that
usually wound on a bit too long for us kids
who sneaked peeks at the bowls and dishes
covered with towels or aluminum foil – our
mouths watering in anticipation. My favorites
were fried chicken and deviled eggs.
Everybody had their own rendition, and it was
delicious fun to taste the varieties. Besides
fried chicken, there would also be pork, beef,
and chicken done every which-away from
fried to baked to roasted to barbecued and
sometimes smothered in somebody's famous
sauce. There were plenty of things I didn't
care for, and if they'd been on the table at
home, I'd have been obliged to eat them, but
here I was my own captain, and steered clear
of them. You could count on lots of vegetables
from local harvests – sweet potatoes, either
baked or candied; creamy whipped potatoes,
boiled potatoes floating in butter, beans and
peas of every variety cooked in fatback or
stirred up into a grand casserole; turnip greens
and collards with a bit of ham hidden among
the tenderly cooked leaves, corn on and off the

cob and sometimes made into pudding; tomatoes, cucumbers, homemade pickles both sweet and sour and maybe an occasional healthy salad. And, of course, there were loads of desserts – all sorts of pies – pecan, custard, lemon meringue, chocolate, apple, peach – and, Lordy! The cakes – coconut, pineapple, German chocolate, chocolate cream, strawberry, some layered high and others in baking dishes - and always yummy fruit cobblers. Sometimes, somebody churned ice cream, but that never lasted long. Everyone ate their fill and then some. And there was always plenty.

Afterwards the adults sat around talking while the kids played tag or walked through the graveyard – which was something I particularly liked to do. I visited relatives and friends who were resting there. And paid respects to those I didn't know but whose story I did – like the little boy who was run over and killed by his granddaddy - his sweet baby face immortalized on the small tombstone with lilies carved on top, and hopes that he would be an angel engraved in the stone. I knew that little boy's granddaddy – a quiet man with the saddest face I'd ever seen. His grief carried with him everywhere. And the small marker that denoted the resting place of a tiny baby who had lived only one day. I knew his parents and the sisters that had come after him. They all seemed happy, but I always felt that the mama had a little hole in her heart for her dead baby.

When some people were going back for another slice of cake or pie and the women were clearing away the dishes and packing their baskets with empty bowls and limp towels, familiar notes from the old upright piano would float out the windows of the church. The music flowed under the oaks, over the front walk, and across the cemetery, calling us home to what we called a Hymn Sing. Various musical groups from the area were always invited to participate, and the afternoon turned into a music festival. Quartets, trios, duets, and family groups of all sizes shared their talents. The chords of old familiar songs like Amazing Grace, His Eye Is on the Sparrow, Leaning on the Everlasting

Arms, How Great Thou Art, and Shall We
Gather At the River brought fresh joy and an
old comfort that felt like being covered by
your grandmother's softest quilt. The Old
Rugged Cross was my Grampa's favorite, and
no matter how many years he'd been gone
from this earth, the sweet sound of it brought
such a clutch of memory and longing to my
heart that I could not help but cry. I suppose
that's what Homecoming Sunday was all
about anyway – gathering with those you love,
filling their bellies with food, their souls with
music, and remembering those lost to us.

As a young girl growing up at the
Tabernacle, Homecoming was a hallowed day.
As a grown woman in her seventh decade, the
memory of it remains sacred still. However,
those days are long ago and far away. The
church building has been redone beautifully,
but it doesn't reflect the sanctuary that was so
familiar to me. Of course, there is central air
these days. A nice baptistry has replaced the
painting of Jesus and his sheep. The old picnic
grounds are gone – replaced with a spacious
dining hall and modern kitchen. I visit there

on occasion – usually, funerals are the reason. I see some familiar faces, but mostly those old folks who grew me up and loved me so well have gone on. Some of them reside now in the Tabernacle cemetery, which is at least twice the size it was in my youth. Some of those folks go to church elsewhere or not at all. And some have passed out of my knowing and remain only in my memory. Am I left to echo Thomas Wolfe's refrain: "You can't go home again" or John Newton's: "….and grace will lead me home"?

Country Stores

It's hard to find an old country store in operation these days. I see some old ones here and there, mostly boarded up, abandoned, and run down. I asked some folks on Facebook if they knew of any that were still open. I got all sorts of responses. Some folks suggested Cracker Barrel, and I had to laugh! Clearly, these people are much younger than me or not from around here. I mentioned worn wooden floors and hoop cheese, and some folks knew just what I meant. They gave me some good leads, and I guess I'll have to make some day trips to see some of them.

The country stores I knew were most times, wooden structures that could be of any size or shape. Some could look fairly ramshackle – as if they might fall down in a big gust of wind – but they never did. They almost always had two gas pumps out front. The interiors were dark, and the plank floors creaked somewhere or other and were often slanted or sagged at some point. Usually, the stores were heated with a wood stove that groaned and crackled in the winter and welcomed cold hands to be ritually rubbed together. Or there might be a more updated heating system, like a fancy Siegler oil heater. In the middle of summer, fans blew the stale air around to no avail. Screen doors mostly kept the flies outside. Shelves contained all sorts of offerings and varied from store to store. You could count on them having milk, bread, canned goods, hoop cheese, pickled eggs, salted peanuts, nabs, and chips. Anything else was a toss-up – unless, of course, it was a store that you frequented, and then you'd pretty much know what they'd be likely to have.

My Uncle Macon's store would have chitlins in the fall after hog-killing and fresh oysters from Atlantic Beach in the months with an 'r' in them. Sometimes, Daddy would stop by there after Prayer Meeting on Thursday nights on the way home. Mama didn't allow many snacks, and sodas were a treat. So, when I'd see Daddy coming back to the car with a carton of RC Crown colas and a brown bag with some tasty snacks, it was a real celebration!

Peck Gordon's store was a welcome sight in the summers when I barned tobacco. The summer that I helped Joe and Alice Pulley, it was a place to choose a much-deserved treat. But the summer I barned with Charles and Rose Chamblee it was a veritable banquet table at least once a week. Rather than a home-cooked meal that was the usual midday fare for tobacco workers, Rose rebelled at least one day a week – whether it was because she disliked cooking and/or because she also had 5 children and just needed a break, I didn't know or care. I was a kid, and being let loose in a country store to gather whatever I deigned nutritious was completely foreign to me. I was practically giddy with the possibilities.

Initially, I chose my most favorite things: an enormous dill pickle, potato chips, a tin of deviled ham, a Hostess twinkie, and a Nehi Grape soda. I was in heaven! Of course, I was dying of thirst not long after we started back to work and could hardly wait for the afternoon snack break when I could guzzle cups of water and devour a pack of nabs. After a few more bad decisions, I learned to hydrate myself if I was to indulge in a Salt Lick for my meal and to choose items that would give sustained energy. Rather than a dill pickle, I chose the pickled eggs. Along with whatever I chose, I started adding a slice of hoop cheese. Nobody discussed the food pyramid. I just figured it out. The adults in that crowd figured if you were old enough to get up at 4 in the morning and work and sweat 'til dark, you were old enough to make your own choices at meal time. The privilege taught me more than any lesson in school.

My Uncle Otha's store was small. There were no aisles. Food stuffs were displayed on the shelves which lined the walls. The counter was filled with crackers, chips, and an assortment of cakes and candies. Ice boxes kept the drinks chilled and delicious. His store had a nice porch on the front for the men to sit and gossip and spit. In the winter, they gathered inside around a pot-bellied stove. The store was right next door to their house, and my cousins came and went at their leisure.

I was always amazed at their easy access to such treasure. Whenever I visited, I would walk over from the house with my cousin Jean, who seemed to know exactly what she wanted and never had to linger in her decision-making. I tried to be as cool as she appeared, but frankly, I was overwhelmed with all the choices. Whatever I chose, Uncle Otha would wink, nod, and wave me away with his chubby hand. I never had to pay for my treat, and I felt honored – as if a king had just granted me a favor. Jean told me that she had a Pepsi every morning for breakfast, and I was shocked by her announcement. Really? Every morning? Even before school? Yep. When I told my mother, she shook her head and talked about good nutrition. I was unmoved. I thought Jean was one of the luckiest girls I knew.

Nowadays, country stores, as I knew them, have given way to places like Sheets, 7-Eleven, Mini-Marts, Circle K, and the like. They have plenty of groceries, toys, and what all, but absolutely none of the ambiance. Not to mention the sense of community that has

been lost. Where do folks gather nowadays?
Facebook, I suppose.

Morphus Creek Bridge

I had ridden over Morphus Creek Bridge hundreds of times before I came to know that it was haunted. I don't know when I heard the story or who told it to me. I imagine it was on a bus ride to or from school, but I can't be sure. The first story involves a family of three from the 1940s. They were traveling on the unfamiliar country road late one rainy night when their automobile crashed into the bridge railing. They were thrown from the car into the murky waters below, where the little girl drowned. Legend had it that if you went to the bridge on All Hallow's Eve at midnight, a ghostly apparition would appear - the poor little girl lost for all time and looking for her parents. Over the years, I heard other renditions. Sometimes, the whole family was killed in a tragic accident; sometimes, the father survived, but the mother and daughter died. So, on Halloween, the vision might be one of the parents looking in vain for the doomed child or the child searching for her parents. Whoever recounted the tale was always certain that this tragedy actually occurred, although they never knew exactly when it happened or who the family was. But for certain, the bridge was haunted – of that, there could be no doubt.

I was as intrigued by the ghost story as any other kid would be. So, of course, I gobbled up the tale and allowed it to take on a life of its own in my mind. It didn't seem to matter that there were several versions – I allowed for the confusion and forgetting that could happen over time. The thing I was absolutely convinced of was that something terrible happened on that bridge at some point in time, and the spirit of some poor soul was doomed to wander that place forever. Most importantly, it was possible to run into this ghoulish spectacle for real if you were willing to risk it – meaning you had to be on that bridge at midnight. Some folks allowed that the lost spirit wandered every night at the stroke of twelve – others said it could only be seen at midnight at Halloween. So, if you absolutely wanted to see this for yourself, Halloween was probably the best bet.

I longed to see something unearthly and scary as hell. And then I didn't. I traveled over that bridge regularly with my parents, and in the daylight, I kept my eyes open – just in case. But in the dark of night, I was alert and slightly worried. I could all but see a small girl in a soaking wet dress dripping muddy water from her face and limbs, her hair matted with sludge and debris, her mouth gaped open dribbling swamp water, her huge eyes hollowed and blackened from decay and ceaselessly staring into darkness and endless doom. I yearned to see her. And I didn't. On the way home from church one night, I was yammering on about this tragedy to my little brother, and Daddy stopped the car right on the bridge. I was thrilled. He turned off the car motor and the headlights. It was summer, and night sounds filled the air – crickets, frogs, wind through the leaves, occasional rustling – all of which grew louder and more eerie as the seconds ticked by. I had begun by looking intently at our surroundings but gradually I began to sink down into my seat, my hands close to my face, ready to cover my eyes to horror at any moment. The thought occurred to me that the ghoulish girl might appear at my passenger window. I moved to the center of the bench seat and leaned toward the front seat and the safety of my parents. Just when the tension became too much to bear, Mama said, "Wallace! You are scaring the children." Of course, that was exactly what my daddy intended to do. He knew the thrill of fear from his own childhood and delighted in milking ours. It was delicious fun. And he had accomplished his mission: we were properly terrified.

The Morphus Creek Bridge haunting was a frequent topic on bus rides to and from school and at Halloween parties; it was especially fun at slumber parties and sleepovers when my girlfriends wanted to terrorize one another. The legend also came up most every summer when I worked barning tobacco. There was always at least one person who knew all about it and someone completely ignorant of the whole story. So, it was up to the rest of us to nod in agreement and shudder in terror at the appropriate time to convince the novice of the story's authenticity. I remember one such summer when all the help was being moved to another barn and field. We all climbed aboard a flat wooden trailer being pulled by tractor, which meant we were zipping along country roads but at tractor speed. This particular trip had us crossing Morphus Creek Bridge, and the slowly passing scenery lent itself perfectly to the tale of horror. A teenage boy named Bobby was the orator, and a girl named Grace, who lived a few counties away, was the "Newby." I can remember sitting on the end of that trailer, bouncing on the wood slats and swinging my legs off the sides, listening to the story - once again ready to do my part with nodding and shuddering. It was daylight, of course, and we could all scan the surrounding woods carefully and peer over the sides of the bridge into the dark water below. Even in the sunshine, I could feel myself shiver at the thought of drowning in the gloomy water or encountering the incorporeal being searching in vain for lost family.

Of course, we all laughed bravely while we were on the bridge, but I felt heavy, and my eyes watched the bridge until we rounded a curve in the road that put it out of sight. I forgot all about the bridge until our day was done, and we once again climbed aboard the trailer for the ride back in the twilight. Certainly, we were tired from the day's work, but we were more somber this time as the trailer lumbered across the bridge and the site of that terrible accident of days gone by. I don't recall a single person laughing or making a joke. I think we all felt a little too exposed. It would only take one grisly hand to snatch us off that open trailer, and no one wanted to be the one to stir up harmful spirits should they be of a mind to do so. You never knew when some wicked something was looking for company or a tasty morsel.

By the time I was sixteen, I was less interested in the local legend, although I kinda sorta continued to weigh the possibility that it might be true. Even so, whenever driving in my car alone, I never once considered stopping on that bridge to see if it might be so. Driving through that misty bottom on a dark night was enough to revive the mystery in my mind and encourage me to cross quickly and be on my way.

Soon after high school graduation, I heard that some enterprising youth had planted marijuana down by the creek's edge. (Who says potheads lack ambition?) And to my knowledge, whoever it was never got busted. Perhaps the spirits that inhabited that sanctuary respected their youthful bravery or their entrepreneurial endeavors. Or maybe they were just glad for the company. That's all I know about that piece of the story.

Since my childhood days, several houses have been built on Morphus Bridge Road, just a few yards from the actual supposedly haunted bridge. I have always wanted to stop and ask the folks who live there if they've ever seen an apparition floating down their road at night. But, of course, I haven't been brave enough to do that either. I suspect that if that bridge was haunted, it was once upon a time and a long time ago. The Department of Transportation has destroyed the original wooden bridge and replaced it with a paved road and hideous concrete barriers to guard the water's edge on either side of the highway. I am not a fan of such structures. I think they lack character. Molded concrete certainly doesn't lend itself to mystery or create an air of enchantment. Any self-respecting ghost would have given up or moved on. I'm just hoping whatever wandering spirit may have been there has found peace wherever they are.

Barnin' Tobacco

Barnin' tobacco is a tough, sweaty, exhausting job but some of the most fun I've ever had. Of course, I speak from the point of view of a barn worker. Whatever tobacco farmers have to say on the subject, I humbly acknowledge and totally respect them. And I'm also talking about how tobacco was cropped in the 1960s. It's managed differently these days.

I grew up in tobacco country. My grandfather, one of my uncles, and my daddy were all tobacco farmers – although my daddy only farmed on his own for a couple of years. Most of the men at the church where I was raised were tobacco farmers. And helping "barn tobacco" was what I did in the summers to make money to buy my school clothes. The first summers I spent at the barn, I was too little to work, but I learned to help out and how to stay out of the way.

For those of you who haven't a clue, let me briefly explain the process (at least part of it) – as it was when I knew it. After setting out tobacco seedlings in the spring, tobacco plants grow to a height of about 5 feet. The leaves of the plant are harvested during July and August. "Primers," also known as "croppers" or field hands, picked the ripe leaves from the plants about 3 times (sometimes more) during a season, beginning at the bottom and moving upward as the leaves ripened. The picked leaves were placed in a "sled" or "slide truck" and hauled by mule or tractor to the curing barns. There, under an attached shelter, the leaves were tied onto sticks. At the end of the day the prepared sticks were hung inside the barn to be dried and cured. Typically, the field hands were men, and those working at the barn shelter were women.

My first summer job "barnin' tobacco" I was a "hander" – which meant I gathered leaves of tobacco by the stalk, bundled them together, and handed them to the person who was tying the leaves to a stick. The sticks were held by a wooden cradle called a "horse" as the worker (called a "stringer" or "looper") tied each bundle to first one side of the stick and then another until the stick was full of leaves. The stringer would holler "Stick!" and another worker – usually a young boy not old enough to work in the field - would take the full stick of tied leaves to racks where they hung until the end of the day. When the field hands returned to the barn at the end of the day, the sticks would be hung into the barn.

At the beginning of the season, farmers assembled workers who could be counted on to help in the fields and at the barn shelter. Once you had given your word to a farmer that you would be a primer, hander, or stringer, you were obliged to that particular farmer for the season. Wages were based on how hard and/or skilled the labor was. Primers would be in the fields from sun up to sun down. They had to know which leaves to pick and be able to keep up with the crew. Barn workers were fortunately in the shade, but stringers needed to be swift and sure. Handers had the easiest job – if you could call any of the jobs easy.

Let me tell you something about tobacco that you'd only know from an intimate meeting with those broad leaves: they are

soaking wet with dew early in the morning –
and I mean soaking!! And so are you. By
midmorning, they are completely dry. And so
are you.

Barnin' tobacco starts early – by first
light. My ride usually picked me up when it
was still dark. Primers were in the field as
soon as it was light enough to tell the green
leaves from the ripe ones. At the barn shelter,
tobacco sticks were gathered and put in easy
access for the stringers to grab as they finished
each stick. Sheets of plastic were tied with
twine around the barn workers like aprons to
keep clothes at least partially dry from the wet
morning leaves. Many stringers protected
their hands from the constant friction of the
string (which could cause blisters) by
wrapping their fingers with adhesive tape.
When that first slide truck arrived, it was on!
Within minutes, arms, hands, cold tobacco
juice, and morning dew were flying, and the
day was set in motion. And let me tell you
another thing about tobacco: if the "juice" from
the leaves gets in your eyes, it burns like fire,
and if it gets in your mouth, the taste is acrid

and awful. And let me tell you one more thing: there is no stopping for anything other than a dire emergency – which better be that you have just dropped dead. You can whine. You can complain. But you can't stop until the farmer says it's "break time".

"Break time" was like a little breath of heaven. By midmorning, the tobacco had dried, and your hands were full of tobacco gum. The morning chill was long gone, and the day was heating up enough that the wetness you now felt was your own sweat. You could order whatever soda you wanted – RC Cola, Sundrop, Grape or Orange Nehi soda, Coke, or Pepsi. You could also have a snack to go with it – round or square nabs, a moon pie, a honeybun, or the like. And there was nothing so delicious – ever!

Break usually happened after we had finished a truckload because the tobacco could not be allowed to lie in a truck bed. It had to be taken care of immediately. The break was officially over when the next truckload arrived. To be sure, the primers had taken a break also, but they were often out in a field that might be quite a ways from the barn, and we usually didn't see them until Noon when everyone took a break to have lunch – only it wasn't called lunch. The midday meal was dinner – and certainly, it was a hearty meal. Most times, farmers' wives cooked a good ole country meal: meat, potatoes, and steaming fresh vegetables, with something tasty on the side, like homemade sweet pickles or sliced tomatoes or cucumbers in vinegar. And always a delectable homemade pie, cake, or cobbler for dessert. Afterward, we relaxed while our food digested, and we'd gather a "second wind." By the afternoon, the wet tobacco was long forgotten, for the heat had set in like an unwelcome guest come to stay.

Field hands tended to be high school-age boys and young men – strong and energetic. I've seen them come in after sweating all day in the blazing hot sun, hang tobacco in a sweltering, airless barn, and rush off to play baseball that evening. Most every season, the field crew would hide at least one dead snake among the truck of tobacco for their delight and the horror of at least one unlucky hander.

What happened to the guys after that shocker usually depended on the dynamics of the group – laughter, a good-natured scolding, or someone getting chased by a barn worker with a tobacco stick (all in good fun, of course).

Barn workers could vary in age from school age to older women who might not have been all that old but seemed old to me as a teenager. Handers could be young, but they had to keep up with the stringer. Most stringers were older and more experienced. I rose to the rank of stringer the last couple of years I worked in tobacco. The first year, I didn't make as much as the older, more experienced stringers, but by the end of the season, I was more accomplished and earned a raise. I was mighty proud of myself.

Working with a crowd of young folks was always fun. There was a lot of laughing, talking, occasional gossip, joking around, and flirting. Sometime during the summer season, I usually had a crush on at least one boy – which was pretty typical from what my friends from other farms reported. And if there was a ballgame in the evenings, I usually went – tobacco gum and sweat scrubbed away and thoughts of heat and hard work long forgotten. Oh! The endless energy of youth!

Like any other section of the population, farmers vary in their perspectives. Some are cheerful, optimistic, and fun-loving. Some are crusty curmudgeons. And others are anywhere else on the possibility of personalities. There were some old coots so sour I wondered how they could get anybody to work for them – their workers had to be some desperate souls, is all I could reckon. I was lucky. I had the opportunity to spend the summer with some delightful folks and work with some fine men – all hardworking, to be sure, but easygoing in nature, respectful of others, and with a good sense of humor. And Lord knows! Sometimes, you might as well laugh as cry if you're gonna barn tobacco!

Chapter 9

Tales from the Valley

Garland

I had newly arrived at college, and having survived a broken heart (well, mostly), a fall from grace, and a life derailment, I was eager to move forward in the world. The idea of "a fresh start" fueled my days and my interactions. I imagined being the most perfect version of myself. My front was only a thin shell, and I moved carefully so as not to break my fragile persona. I wonder now how I appeared to others. What did they see?

The first person who paid attention to the new me was a tall, thin, relatively handsome guy named Garland. I think I was particularly attracted to his name. For me, the name Garland conjured images of flowers being gathered dreamily in rolling meadows and woven together by a shepherd surrounded by peaceful sheep. It also reminded me of a boy I'd known in childhood.

The boy was older than me, handsome and shy. I had some romantic notion of him but was too young for it to be anything other than something vague and faraway. He died tragically in a car accident and was forever sealed in my mind as a sort of young hero. So perhaps this new Garland was initially colored by my clouded brain seeking respite. Certainly, I was flattered by his attention.

Whenever I saw Garland on campus, I felt a flutter of excitement but was careful to conceal it. I sat down hard on my usual enthusiasm – concentrating on being a lady with class and some air of mystery. I let him do most of the talking, and so I learned that he had grown up on a farm where he worked diligently even as a child. In his teen years, he continued to do the expected chores on his family's farm, but he also worked part-time in a local grocery to earn money to buy his own car. He was proud of his work ethic and what he had accomplished – as he should have been. He admired his parents and wasn't ashamed to say so. He was especially good in mathematics and was energized by every math course he had taken. This alone impressed me – since I loathed even the simplest math. We were both enrolled in a basic psychology course, which gave us a weekly appointment together as well as fodder for engaging conversations. We took to having coffee together after class. Eventually, he asked me out, and I felt the new me was working out well.

On our first date, we went to the movies. I couldn't tell you what we saw. Mostly, I was nervous because he held my hand, and I wasn't sure if the new me should allow such intimacy. We went for ice cream afterward, and I was still worrying about the hand-holding thing. But the conversation flowed smoothly, and I decided that I should let it go. When the evening came to an end, he leaned toward me, but I demurred and said that I didn't kiss on the first date. That had been a rule for me in high school and was a big deal in the 1960s, but sometimes I'd broken the rule – depending. I decided the new Linda was sticking to the rules. I also decided that if this guy didn't like the new Linda, then this would be our last date. Garland did not disappoint. He smiled at me and said, "Of course you don't. I apologize for being too forward." Later, he told me that he would have been disappointed in me had I let him kiss me.

Over the next few weeks, I continued to be reserved and coy. It became clear that Garland liked me more than a little. He told me that he appreciated a woman like me "with class" – and the label pleased me. He made a few disparaging remarks about other girls – they were too loose, they weren't studious, they wore their skirts too short and their shirts too tight. I thought the new me might be working out, and I began second-guessing my wardrobe.

Garland talked about his future and intimated that it would include me. When I mentioned that I was considering journalism as a major, he told me that he wouldn't want his wife to work. I was slightly confused. He had not asked me to marry him. Was this his way of asking? What if he did ask me? Did I want to marry him? I hadn't even worked out the new me yet. Maybe the new me was working out a little too well.

One afternoon, Garland asked me to go with him for a drive. It was a beautiful day for it, and I thought it would be nice. During our time together, Garland talked about his ex-girlfriend. She seemed to have left a bad taste in his mouth – she talked too much, asked too many questions, wore clothes he felt were too suggestive, sometimes left trash in his car, didn't balance her check book to the penny, and placed bills haphazardly in her wallet. When he took her home to meet his parents, his mother was not impressed. Initially, Garland said that he defended his girlfriend but eventually had to agree that his mother's first impression was correct. He said he thought he could help his girlfriend improve, but she was uninterested. And he had begun to notice that she was a bit of a slob. Once, when he picked her up, he saw that she had clothes strewn about, and her pocketbook was always a mess. I made mental notes of how I might fare on this checklist. I figured that I probably didn't measure up and certainly could use some improvement of my own. When he told me he would like me to meet his parents, I cooed, "I would love that," but deep inside, I felt anxious. I suspected that his mother probably wouldn't approve of me either.

On a lark one afternoon, I went shopping with a couple of girls. We had a blast trying on clothes, modeling outfits, giggling, and being silly. I ended up buying a pair of really cute red and blue clunky shoes with tall, square heels – very trendy – as well as a royal blue miniskirt and midriff blouse. My friends insisted I looked great, and I liked what I saw in the mirror, too. We went for beer and pizza afterward and laughed ourselves silly. Their company was warm, easy, and delightful. I knew we were going to be good friends. I didn't even think about the new me. She was apparently on hiatus.

The next day, I was sitting with my new friends in the student lounge playing cards. When Garland saw me, he frowned, and I wondered what was wrong. Later, in class together, he appeared aloof and cool. When class was over, I suggested coffee, but he said he'd call me later. I was a little worried that he wouldn't, but he did, and he sounded like his usual self. He asked me out to dinner and inferred that it would be more than pizza. I was excited and donned my new outfit – elated to be able to show off my stylish clothes. Garland was courteous but stiff on arrival. My ego was a tad deflated, but I didn't say so. At the restaurant, I got lots of smiles from other patrons. One random girl even complimented my outfit, and my ego recovered. I figured Garland must still be out of sorts. After we were seated, Garland asked the waiter for water and then made a slow show of putting his napkin in his lap. Then he leaned toward me and asked, "What if I had taken you to my parents for dinner tonight?" I laughed a little nervously and said that I hoped he wouldn't have done that without prior warning. He nodded slowly and said, "I can see that you certainly would need that." Uh-oh. Garland was not happy with me. The new Linda was slipping. I decided to say nothing – that was the best way to stay out of trouble.

Garland lowered his eyes to look at the menu. So did I, and I quickly decided I would choose the cheapest thing to avoid further annoyance. But I remained quiet until he had made the announcement of his choice. I nodded and stated what I had chosen, but Garland said "no" and that I should order what he was having. I acquiesced. After we ordered, Garland asked about the two friends he had seen me with earlier in the week, and I told him their names. I went on to tell him about the good time we had enjoyed together. Garland was not amused. "So, you let them influence you?" he frowned.

"Well, no. I picked out my shoes and clothes. They just gave me the thumbs up," I explained. Garland was not impressed and then told me that he'd heard gossip about one of my new friends that wasn't flattering.

"Gossip doesn't mean it's true," I countered. Garland raised his eyebrows and then said dryly, "Gossip happens when girls put themselves in certain situations."

Yes, I knew that all too well. Guys could be in the very same situation, but they had a different scorecard. It infuriated me – the inequity of our society and Garland's acceptance of it. I also felt defensive about my new friend. Garland apparently didn't know her any better than I did. Still, he was willing to let a bit of gossip color his opinion of her. I felt my self seething – like a pot of water vibrating just prior to beginning to boil. The new Linda whispered a word of caution, and I held myself in check as Garland went on about reputations and guarding one's good character and blah, blah, blah.

Dinner came, and Garland changed the subject while I listened and tried to eat my food. My throat felt tight and dry. Every bite felt like I might choke, and I was able to eat very little. Garland didn't notice as he waxed eloquently on his view of this and that and the other – which, by the way, included card playing. It seems he didn't approve of that either. I declined dessert and excused myself to go to the Ladies' Room before leaving the restaurant. I checked myself in the mirror and decided I liked what I saw, although my face looked a little strained. I smiled at the girl looking back at me and erased the strain. A woman washing her hands looked over at me and said, "You look so cute. If I was your age, I'd wear miniskirts too." We giggled and left the restroom together. When I rejoined Garland, he let me know that several men had noticed my short skirt. Clearly, he was not pleased. However, it pleased me enormously – although I didn't say so.

On the way to the car, the new Linda was trying to get my attention – reminding me of my "fresh start." Suddenly, I realized that I really didn't know what the best version of myself was nor what she would even look like if I painted a picture of her or made a list. However, I was certain of a few things like honesty, loyalty, and kindness. Beyond that, I felt my youth and my essence still being shaped. When I slipped into the car seat, I felt my thin new shell crumble. And when Garland slid into the driver's seat, I told him a few things, and it felt like an unleashing – or perhaps an unveiling:

• I liked talking and laughing.

• I liked my new friends, and that included shopping, drinking beer, eating pizza, and playing cards.

• I liked wearing stylish clothes, and that included miniskirts.

• My room could sometimes be a mess.

• My bank statement was inaccurate – I preferred rounding up!

• And I stuffed bills in my wallet willy-nilly.

• I also liked asking questions, and I had one ready: "How about we call it a night?"

Garland didn't say a word until we pulled into the drive. He put his hand on mine and said that he was sorry if he'd upset me. I removed his hand, told him goodnight, and that I'd see myself inside. And I did just that. I don't know how long he sat there, and I went to bed feeling a little shaken but pleased with myself. After that, I saw Garland in class and around campus, but that was it. Occasionally, I could feel his eyes on me, and I wondered what he was thinking. But the good part was that I just wondered – more like an amusement. I certainly did not give a fine fat fig. I had figured out there was no old me or new me. There was just ME - rolling along and finding my way, getting knocked down and getting up again, making mistakes and making friends, learning to survive mistakes and then to forgive myself. Learning to completely like myself would take some years, – but it would come. Poor Garland had only known the me I thought I wanted to see. She turned out to be a mistake. And thank Goodness!

Ouija Wind

In 1970, my friends Vada and Debby and I spent an evening with a Ouija board. It felt exciting -- a bit on the forbidden side of life. I must admit that although I had always hoped for encounters with the supernatural or some real psychic power - the practical side of me doubted either would ever happen.

On that particular evening, in my bedroom in my parent's country home in the Shenandoah, my window was open, and so were our minds. It has been over fifty years since that night, so every nuance is difficult to recall. Here is what I remember:

Deb and I sat on my bed with the Ouija board between us as we ran the pointer. Vada sat in a chair by the bed with a pad and paper on her lap, ready to scribe any revelation. How we began is not clear, but I know we were hoping to channel a spirit. We were too naïve to know what that could mean. The pointer moved to letters that spelled out "CAROLYN." Our hopes buoyed, and we asked how she, Carolyn, came to be in the spirit world. The letters spelled "SHOTHIGHSICECREAM." Hmmmm. Vada, our scribe, translated: "Shot Highs Ice Cream." This struck me as funny – murder and intrigue in such a benign location – an ice cream shop of all places! I giggled and looked at Deb. She was giggling, too. We began to laugh. I was also thinking how ridiculous our imaginations were.............yep, "ridiculous" is what I thought. And disappointed is how I felt. Well, that is - <u>until</u> I looked at Vada. She had been sitting in a chair with her feet propped on the bed, languidly smoking a cigarette, not expecting much, her usual cynical attitude in place. But now her cigarette burned alone in the ashtray while she gripped the pad and pen and leaned forward -- her face stricken with a look I had never seen on her before. She was clearly shocked. And Vada was pretty hard to shock.

I said, "What?"

And she breathed out, "That's my cousin. She was murdered at High's Ice Cream Store."

Deb and I were stunned. Vada leaned closer and said, "Ask who did it." Deb and I, now somber and a little shaken, placed our hands on the pointer and it spelled, "NOTTOM." Vada was still looking stricken but translated this nonsensical word into two words: "Not Tom." Still confused, Deb and I pressed Vada for what she knew about this mystery, as neither of us had any knowledge of this tragedy.

Vada recounted what she knew of the crime. Three years earlier, two women working at High's Ice Cream Store near Staunton, Virginia, had been murdered: Carolyn and Connie. A man named Gus Thomas was believed to have been the killer, although there was no real motive other than a small amount of money missing from the register. Because of insufficient evidence, Mr. Thomas had been acquitted, and the murder had remained an unsolved mystery. So here we were three years later – three unassuming girls on a lark – and it seemed as if someone was reaching out from the grave. What else could we do but to ask the name of the real killer from the spirit we had summoned? We were given what seemed to be initials that I, unfortunately, cannot now recall. In further investigation with the spirit world, we were told of "letters in attic." Any other information that we may have been privy to that night is now covered in so many cobwebs I cannot tell it.

I remember feeling excited, incredulous, and a bit uneasy. I wanted to know how we were receiving this information. Who was this spirit really? God? NO. The devil? The answer came:

"WHYDOYOUQUESTIONMEWHENIH AVETOLDYOUTHETRUTH" translated as "why do you question me when I have told you the truth?" And with that revelation, we gasped, and then came a sudden gust of wind through the open window, blowing the curtains dramatically and snuffing out our candle. The lights eerily dimmed to complete darkness and then back on as if by a dimmer switch. The room became strangely cold and misty.

We were completely undone. We cast the Ouija board aside as if we'd received an electric shock and bolted out of the room. We found my parents in the den, living life as usual. We poured out our story with our words tumbling over one another but my practical parents were simply amused by our story and dismissed it as girlish hysteria – so typical of my parents.

Nevertheless, the three of us puzzled and pondered the incident into the night and for several days after that. However, we were young and interested in boys and parties and being young. Eventually, as time grew into long years, I, too, came to think of it as hysterical imagining.   Then, out of the blue -- a phrase fraught with meaning in this particular instance – yes, "out of the blue" on a Sunday morning in February 2009, I opened an e-mail from my old friend Debby, who was living in Culpepper, Virginia. It was a simple plea addressing me as "Precious Lamb" and then a short directive to go to the internet and look up "MURDER HIGHS ICE CREAM," which I did, of course, without delay.

Lo! and behold! that mysterious murder of long ago had been brought into the spotlight once again because the real killer had made a death bed confession! And, indeed, it was NOT TOM, but a woman named Diane Crawford Smith! The incredible news made headlines - including The New York Times.

Indeed, it was a bizarre tale. It seems that after the tragedy, a woman named Joyce Bradshaw stepped forward to say that a few days before the murders, she had lunch with Diane, who showed her a pistol and said she "had a bullet" for one of the girls she worked with at High's Ice Cream. Joyce had reported this to a Staunton detective by the name of Bocock after the murders but was told that Diane had passed a polygraph and the bullets didn't match her gun. The detective also told Joyce that Diane was a "crack shot," which Joyce took as a warning to shut up and did not go back to the police during the original investigation. However, many years later, with the threatening detective gone, Joyce felt free to tell what she knew. A new investigation moved forward, finding Diane in a nursing home in Harrisonburg, Virginia (about 30 miles from Staunton), dying from heart and kidney disease.

Diane admitted that in April 1967, she had shot the two women in the head in the back room of the store because she was angry with them for teasing her about her being a lesbian. Diane said, "I was just pushed so far, so I shot them, and that was it." She denied the murder was premeditated, although she could not say why she had brought the gun with her to the Ice Cream Shop. And then, in another stunning admission, Diane told investigators that she had given the murder weapon to the lead Staunton detective and that he buried it on his property. Detective Bocock had gone on to serve a long career with the Staunton Police Force, retiring in the 1980s. It was only after he died in 2006 that the real story came to light. Although Diane admitted that she and the detective were friendly and she had done some target shooting on his property, she could not adequately explain the detective's cover-up. Also, no murder weapon was found on his land. There is also no evidence to suggest that Detective Bocock and Diane had any serious relationship. The later investigation also revealed that Diane had spent some time in a mental facility soon after the double murders. Although she later married and had children, she eventually divorced and had a long romantic relationship with another woman. Another interesting twist to the story is that Detective Bocock was the one responsible for placing the blame on Mr. Thomas for the murder. Mr. Thomas was originally indicted for the murders. He went on trial for one of the murders, but because there was so little evidence, the jury quickly acquitted him. So why did Detective Bocock finger Mr. Thomas for the murders? Why did he protect Diane? Why did the detective cover-up this crime? What was his motive? And what happened to the gun? After Diane's confession, Mr. Thomas said it had been difficult having been associated with the murders for all those years. Diane died before she could be prosecuted.

The Staunton Chief of Police promised to continue to investigate but admitted, "the fact remains that there will likely be questions surrounding this case we will never be able to answer." And so, we are left with yet another mystery surrounding the High's Ice Cream Shop Murders – certainly, Deb and I are intrigued and extremely curious. Sadly, our friend Vada passed away in 2000 and is unavailable for comment -- unless we want to consult the Ouija board......

George

The first time I saw George Pappas, it was a bitterly cold winter day. He was wearing a plaid woolen scarf thrown carelessly around his neck and an elegant black wool coat with his hands casually tucked into the pockets. He did not appear to take heed of the cold but rather seemed to be on a stroll – and for all I knew, he could have been doing just that. He was tall and very handsome, with a head of thick black hair tousled by the winter wind. I was standing by the large window of a Hobby Shop that I frequented. The window ran across the entire front of the building, and when he came into view, I was unable to take my eyes off him. His physique and manner of movement simply compelled me to watch him.

The next time I saw him, I was entering the Hobby Shop as he was leaving. He courteously held the door for me and offered me a soft smile. His liquid brown eyes were large and framed by thick, velvet black lashes. His skin was alabaster. For the briefest moment, I seemed captured by an inexplicable inertia – as helpless as a victim in a web – and then his eyes moved away from me, and the moment was over. Time moved forward, and so did I. My intention to ask the owner who this mysterious stranger was fell to the wayside as the hum of liveliness that often simmered within those walls blew my question aside.

The Hobby Shop was a delightful place – open and welcoming to all ages. It was a cavernous space filled with a conglomeration of things to do and buy. The walls and shelves were filled with all sorts of needlework possibilities, from cross stitch and needlepoint to crochet and knitting – threads, yarns, hoops, and needles. There were oil, acrylic, and watercolor paints, brushes, paper, canvases, and paint by number. There was clay, wood, molds, and plaster. Scores of model planes, trains, and cars were stacked on shelves. There was an enormous worktable where several people at a time could work on their various projects or take a "how-to" class being offered. There was an even larger group of tables that held the replica of a small town and countryside with roads and railroad tracks winding all through it. There were streets and houses and buildings and cars and tiny people and lots and lots of tracks. Local boys came in to run the trains and were constantly enlarging and embellishing the landscape.

Interestingly, the boys played and planned together amenably and were relatively quiet. They showed deep respect for the owner, Mrs. Ellen Sutton, for she had earned it with such a generous gift to them. There was no charge for them to come in and play with the trains for as long as they wished. And they came after school and on weekends in every season. Some of the boys had practically grown up there. Mrs. Sutton's own son was grown, and his love for all things train had been the catalyst for opening her beloved shop. The project had grown over the years, and now it was something of a community center. Mrs. Sutton had set up tables here and there for other games as well – dominoes, checkers, backgammon, and chess. Toward the back of the store, there were two sets of stairs on either side of the mammoth room that led to a large balcony area where there were more tables set up for chess as well as comfy chairs for reading. There were stacks of comic books and hardbacks as well. Kids could trade comics or books as they chose. Underneath the balcony was a roomy storage area that opened to the back of the building. The whole idea was an amazing act of service to her community, and in some respects, the Hobby Shop was her hobby. And it served her well. She was beloved by people of all ages, shapes, and sizes. Her arms and heart were open as wide as her door to welcome whoever came in. In turn, her regular visitors would organically straighten up, sweep, take out trash, and offer her their time and assistance. She was grateful but did not take advantage of their gestures. It was an amazing experiment in grace, in my opinion. Many a friendship was fostered there, and I'm sure there were countless lessons learned. I basked in the happy atmosphere often and made a few friends of my own.

The third time I saw George, I was formally introduced to him. I had walked into the Hobby Shop on a weekday. It was early afternoon, and there were only a handful of folks in the shop. George was standing at an easel wearing a canvas apron, casually holding a paintbrush, and studying the large canvas in front of him with an air of expectation. I could not help but notice him, as he seemed the largest, most dramatic presence in the room. Mrs. Sutton called out a greeting and followed it with, "Linda, I want you to meet George Pappas. George, this is Linda Taylor." Without saying it, I heard the distinct implication that we were to be fine friends. George flashed me a charming smile and stepped toward me, but then - realizing he might be sharing paint with me -instead of a handshake, he placed his hand on his heart and offered me a slight gentlemanly bow. I was smitten. Mrs. Sutton went on gaily to say that George would likely be the new artist in residence and wouldn't it be intriguing to see what he created on canvas in the days ahead? Indeed, I thought and nodded my head.

George was certainly not a quick study. He revealed himself slowly as spun silk unwinding from a spool. And George was no ordinary spun silk, No! He was surely AuVer Sole silk – so prized in the couture industry. It was apparent that he was a voracious reader with a broad appetite that included history, the classics, science fiction, biographies, and poetry. His ability to quote verse was impressive and always elegantly suited to the topic of conversation. He enjoyed the romantics – Shelley and Keats – but also the transcendentalists – Emerson and Thoreau – as well as Gibran and Neruda. And he was fascinated by Sylvia Plath. But then, aren't we all, just a little? At least I am – that tingle of darkness and the contemplation of death have always intrigued me. I suspected it was the same for George, and it added a bit of spice to the mystery of him.

The first painting George completed was an abstract piece - oil on a large canvas, roughly 16 x 30. The piece was done in equal sections of paint in hues of green, ascending from the darkest to the lightest and fading to white at the last top section. It should have been titled "A Study in Green," but I cannot remember whether or not he even titled it. The painting sat on the canvas for some time, sans George. People who had watched his process remarked on it – some particularly praising his precision. I appreciated his work – its order, the gradually fading green hues, but not being a fan of green, I can't say I liked it very much. However, Mrs. Sutton glowed with pride whenever anyone remarked on it. It seemed that she had taken him under her wing, and she fussed over him as if he were her own son. Mrs. Sutton's best friend, Sylvia Bishop, had also taken a keen interest in George. When George did not show up at the shop for a few days, the both of them fretted and wondered if he was unwell. They were not sure where he lived, and he was not answering the phone number they had for him. They had both speculated that he had a troubled past, but exactly what that trouble was, they did not know. Although they had engaged in many conversations, George had divulged very little personal information. Still, they both felt he was a lonely soul and believed it was their duty to befriend him. I must say that I agreed with them.

At length, George showed himself, although he looked thinner than I remembered, and there were dark circles under his eyes. He dismissed the clucking about, saying that he had been sick with a bad cold and had been sequestering himself with hot tea and honey. It was apparent that he enjoyed the attention he received even as he waved us away. He donned his paint apron, put another larger canvas on the easel, and began eyeing the white space before him. I figured the artist was back in residence, and all would be right with the world soon enough. Mrs. Sutton and Sylvia were relieved by George's presence, but they were suspicious that more was afoot than George had let on. The two of them were not content to let it go without further investigation. Sylvia was an anesthetist and had more than a few connections in the medical community. Mrs. Sutton also had an army of friends who were professionals at her disposal. And so it was that after some time and a bit (or perhaps a lot) of sleuthing, the two friends uncovered some interesting facts. George was actually staying at a halfway house of sorts since his discharge from a state mental institution. How they came by this information, I am unsure, but they knew it to be solid. How long George had been in the institution was unclear, but what was known for certain was that he had been housed there due to a very tragic event. It seems that George had been born into a terrible circumstance. His mother was emotionally disturbed and had abused him in unspeakable ways. Her irrational and troublesome lifestyle had come to light by way of her neighbors, and law enforcement had removed her kicking and screaming from her filthy, rodent-infested home. Upon entry, they also found George under a bed barking like a dog, whining and shaking. The neighbors had not even known he existed. It was too horrifying to even imagine what his life must have been like. Even so, this information did not lessen George in our eyes. Rather, it served to make him appear heroic. We were all beyond impressed that he had risen from such horrific conditions. Yes, he was a tragic figure, yet he retained his mysterious allure. We more acutely appreciated his intellect and creative talent. George not only painted but also wrote poetry. In fact, at times, it was difficult to know whether he was quoting a famous author or composing his own verse on the spot. This delighted him no end, and when asked who the author of some such quote was, he would make us guess. If he happened to be the author, his eyes would sparkle, and he nearly always clapped his hands in glee.

What sealed George as a truly tragic figure were his frequent references to a young girl named Amber. He described her as an exotic beauty with luminescent, nearly transparent skin and golden hair that smelled both sweet and woodsy. He spoke of her reverently and with a certain sadness. He spoke endearingly of her frail figure, fluid movements, and gentle voice in verbal compositions that painted a tender albeit vague picture of her. It was certain that Amber was the love of his life. But who she was exactly was not clear. Was she a sibling? Or perhaps an unrequited love? We dared not ask but waited for George to reveal this to us as we feared he had lost her in some dreadful way – particularly when George once referred to Amber and added this verse from Shelley:

"We are as clouds that veil the midnight moon;
How restlessly they speed, and gleam, and quiver,
Streaking the darkness radiantly! – yet soon
Night closes round, and they are lost forever..."

George and I often went on walks together or enjoyed a cup of tea at a small café around the corner. I enjoyed his company. He was constantly inspiring me to read something that I would never have read on my own – introducing me to the likes of Robert Heinlein (Stranger in a Strange Land), Truman Capote (In Cold Blood), and Anthony Burgess (A Clockwork Orange). I am not a fan of science fiction and had, at that time, only ever read one other work of that genre. Of course, Capote was well known, but I cringed at the topic until George piqued my interest. These specific titles did not become my favorite, but the works broadened my mind, as reading tends to do. George also knew Greek mythology well. I had been a fan since childhood, so I reveled in his knowledge and perspectives. We were never at a loss for conversation. There were times when George seemed strange to me – distant and dreamy – but I had never known anyone like him. I was, quite simply, fascinated by him. It didn't hurt that his face looked like a perfectly chiseled piece of artwork that I never tired of looking at.

George's next painting was a still life of apples in a bowl sitting on a table next to an empty wine bottle. The compilation was done in hues of green with one "perfect apple" (his words) painted a luminous white at the top of the bowl. The greens were exactly the same as his previous abstract, which I found interesting, but I made no mention of this. However, the white apple particularly captivated me, and I asked George if it had any significance. He said it represented purity. I waited for him to elaborate, but he made no further comment. I was left to ponder this on my own. I suspected he was thinking of Amber.

Soon after the white apple painting, Mrs. Sutton and Sylvia uncovered another bit of news about our George. The house where George was living was owned by an older gentleman who was believed to be gay. The gentleman's sexual preferences would not have concerned either of them except for the fact that they both had some reason to believe that he might be taking advantage of George. On consideration, it might have explained George's ability to be so well dressed on a zero budget as well as his secretive MO. However, the gentleman might simply have been generous, and George's MO had nothing to do with his living situation. I was of the opinion that they were both making something out of nothing – and certainly nothing that was any of their business. Besides, both of them were very religious, and I wondered if their religious beliefs came into play here. They fluttered and buzzed about this for a time. I just listened. In the end, neither of them said a word to George, and gradually, they let the issue lie.

George's next painting was also on a large canvas. Again, he chose to do a still life. This time, the subject was eggs in a basket with yet another wine bottle sitting nearby. He began by painting the top egg on the pile a luminous white. Sylvia stood beside him, watching him paint the first egg, and asked him if the eggs were going to be perfect. He responded, *"She shines, the one white love of my youth, which all sin cannot stain."* Unfamiliar with the words, I asked if he was composing another poem. He glared at me, which was unlike him, and growled that it was a line from a poem by D.H. Lawrence. Sylvia and I exchanged puzzled glances but did not make further comment.

George's progress on the egg painting was much slower than usual. He left it alone for days at a time and then painted over things he had already painted.

As he slowly proceeded in his work, it appeared that the eggs were going to be green, with one perfect white egg at the top of the group. I resisted the urge to tease him about the green eggs (you know, from the Dr. Seuss book, "Green Eggs and Ham"). I sensed that he might be too fragile – especially after the morning he quoted from Pablo Neruda's poem, "Nothing But Death." The recitation unnerved me with these lines: "… *We die going into ourselves, as though we were drowning inside our hearts, as though we lived falling out of the skin into the soul."* It seemed that George had taken the words into his own being. It concerned me.

George seemed to be losing weight. He again had dark circles under his eyes. It was clear that he was depressed. We were all worried about him and, so one afternoon, I suggested that we go for tea. As we sat sipping our tea, George began quoting Edgar Allen Poe's poem, The Raven, which took on a darker, more personal tone as I heard George saying the words……" *Deep into that darkness peering…...tell this soul with sorrow laden."* George's dramatic effect was chilling, and as he spoke of the *"rare and radiant maiden whom the angels name Lenore,"* I knew he was referring to his own beloved Amber. My heart wondered, along with both Poe and George, if indeed there was *"a balm in Gilead"*. With the last *"nevermore,"* he grew quiet and sat there stirring his tea as I complimented his recitation. George did not look up from his brooding but began talking almost as if to himself about death and dying. It frightened me, and I felt out of my depth with him – knowing he needed help that my friendship could not give him. We took a long route back to the shop, which, at first, I thought would help loosen his dark clouds, but George was on a descent I seemed helpless to stop. He embarked on a composition of his own that turned into a bloody dirge about Amber and gleaming knives and dripping red hearts. I regretted that we were on the long route with not another soul in sight. George turned his face toward me. He was smiling strangely and seemed to sense my discomfort. When I told him that I knew that was his own composition and it was a bit too grisly for my taste, he laughed wildly. I quickened my steps – eager to be somewhere warm and friendly. I felt sick and helpless. By the time we reached the shop, I wanted to be rid of George – which only made me feel worse because I thought I was being disloyal to my friend. Still, I left as quickly as I could. At home, I reviewed the afternoon in my mind. In the warmth and solitude of my house, I began to think that I had been silly to be afraid. It was just George being theatrical and me being hormonal. George had enough trouble without me labeling him as "dangerous."

The next time I was in the shop, George declared the egg painting finished. The colors and hues were the very same colors he had used in the abstract and the previous apple painting. It was beautifully rendered but such a strange composition with the basket of green eggs, the one luminous white egg perched atop the group, and the stately green wine bottle standing alongside. George pontificated on the symbolism within his work – green the color of hope; white for purity; eggs for hope, purity, and creation; and the empty wine bottle devoid of happiness. We all hoped that this would mark the ending of his current depression, and we wondered what his next creation would be. But George did not put another canvas on the easel. Instead, he began messing around with some clay and, every now and again, helping Mrs. Sutton with her current wind chime project. He seemed adrift and was mostly gloomy and sullen. His constant topic was death and dying and Amber. An ill wind was brewing.

I came into the shop one day to find Sylvia comforting Mrs. Sutton who was apparently shaken and weepy. George was nowhere to be seen. They told me that he had been helping Mrs. Sutton with her wind chimes when suddenly he grasped an empty wine bottle by the neck, crashed it on the side of the table, and then pointing the jagged bottle at Mrs. Sutton said very calmly, "you know I could kill you with this if I wanted to." Mrs. Sutton had managed to maintain her poise and agreed that he certainly could but that she knew he wouldn't do such an awful thing. He asked her why, and she said because they were friends. He made no response but stood there staring at her and holding the broken bottle. After what felt to her like an eternity, George threw down the broken bottle and left the store. Mrs. Sutton was weak with relief and fear. Sylvia had found her holding onto the table but standing weakly where George had left her only minutes before. I had come onto the scene only a few minutes after that. Something needed doing but what? I was too young and inexperienced to have anything helpful to offer until it dawned on me that perhaps my experience with George at the tea shop and on our walk had more significance than I had allowed. Mrs. Sutton had called her husband to consult with him while I shared my tale with Sylvia. After Mr. Sutton arrived, I left the three of them discussing next steps. I knew they were wise, level headed, experienced, and had people they could call on. They didn't need me wringing my hands and helpless.

What we learned in the aftermath was that George had been diagnosed previously with schizophrenia. It was believed that his descent into his recent depression was the beginning of a psychotic episode. It was anyone's guess where that might lead. Apparently, he had been even more morose, surly, and threatening with housemates. He was believed to be hallucinating and had made threats to harm others as well as himself. Who made the decision to commit him to the mental institution, I cannot say. Nor do I know how they went about it. All I know is that George was gone from our lives just as quickly and mysteriously as he had entered. His three paintings were all that were left to remind us that he had really been there among us. Those green paintings so full of hope and purity but devoid of happiness. As a parting note, we learned that George's beloved Amber did not exist – nor had she ever existed. She was a creature of pure fantasy. Quoting from one of George's favored poets, Keats, *"she dwells with Beauty – Beauty that must die; And Joy, whose hand is ever at his lips Bidding adieu...."*

Nearly fifty years have passed, and I still remember those days with my strange friend. George will remain an unhappy conundrum – likely resigned to the tragedy of his childhood and mental illness. But I like to remember the best of him – his handsome face shining as he painted and dreamed of his "rare and radiant maiden whom the angels" and George named Amber.

Vada

Vada loved Kris Kristopherson, mountain country, scotch whiskey, and smoking pot – perhaps not in that order. She was aloof, indifferent to the opinions of other people, wild, and fragile. She was also my friend. I loved her, but she scared me a little. There was always this little piece of me that knew she could go too far and that I might go with her.

I met her during my college days in the Shenandoah Valley of Virginia. I'd seen her in the student lounge playing cards. (She was something of a card shark, actually.) I officially met her at a keg party, but she didn't pay the least bit of attention to me. On one occasion, we ended up seated next to one another in the back seat of a car, riding with a gang of folks to an event that I now can't remember. We struck up a conversation, and I found her interesting. I had no idea whether or not she liked me and sorta figured she didn't. She was one of those girls that I thought was cool but I knew I wasn't in her league and never imagined that we could be more than passing acquaintances.

I was always a little amazed that we ended up being friends. She told me once that her first impression of me was that I was a "do-gooder." I was puzzled – was that a good thing or a bad thing? I asked what she meant. She responded, "You know, a Pollyanna – a goody-two-shoes." I suspect she also meant silly and prudish, although she didn't say so. Then she shrugged in her lackadaisical way and said, "Well, you really are a do-gooder, but I guess you can't judge a book by its cover." I decided it best not to ponder that further.

Lots of guys were attracted to Vada, but rarely did she give them any encouragement. Vada was definitely not a flirt. But that didn't stop those guys from being "hangers-on" or sometimes pressing her for a more serious relationship. Even when she let them know there was no hope of anything further than her friendship, that didn't keep them from being starry-eyed and ever hopeful. I learned that she held to her heart her first lover. She called him "Roger Ann" to his face and to me privately. I knew it was her way of belittling him in an attempt to deny the power he had over her. Still, she secretly clung to a romantic ideal of him. In truth, he was not worth her time. He never appeared more than slightly interested in her – most probably because he was lazy and shallow. But, sadly, sometimes first loves live on in the hearts of young girls without just cause. And so this unrequited love seemed to me.

When handsome Vince Bascalupo showed up, I was hopeful that the unfortunate, one-sided relationship was over. I have to admit that I would never have guessed that Vada would be interested in Vince despite his good looks. He was too sweet, too nice, too polite – not that those are bad qualities at all – it just seemed to me that Vada was inevitably drawn to "bad boys," and Vince was definitely not one of those. Their improbable relationship lasted longer than I ever imagined it would, and I was hopeful for a while. But in time, Vada tired of him – which didn't surprise me in the least – but it did make me sad because I knew that she would return to her old ways. Inherently, she sought to sabotage herself – she just couldn't seem to help herself.

When my then-boyfriend proposed to me, I accepted. We planned a June wedding, and I asked Vada and another college girlfriend, Debby, to be my bridesmaids. Vada agreed and never voiced any opinion until my wedding day. Vada, Debby, and I stood together in a small room downstairs in the chapel of the church where I was to be married in a matter of minutes. Vada turned, picked up her pocketbook, took me by the hand, and looked me dead in the eyes.

"My keys are in here, and my car is right outside. Let's go. Don't do this. You don't love him." She spoke earnestly and urgently. I was stunned. Yet, in the stillness of that instant, I knew deep down in the core of my being that she was right. I certainly loved the man waiting upstairs at the altar, but not enough to marry him. But there I was in my wedding dress with my family upstairs waiting for me; guests had traveled some distance to be there, my cousin was playing Wagner on the baby grand piano, and time was running out. I should have nodded my head, grabbed her hand, and headed for her car. It flashed across my mind to do that very thing, but it seemed cowardly. The fact is it would have been the bravest thing I could ever have done – I just lacked the courage to do it. Instead, I turned my eyes away from her face, shook my head, and laughed. I have played that moment over many times in my head. It is now sealed in infamy.

The moment passed, and the day moved forward. We all marched down the aisle and toward whatever was waiting for us – me to a doomed marriage, Debby to her own distant doom, and Vada to ditch Vince and move far away from me for a time. With my friend hundreds of miles away, I was left to stumble gracelessly on my own, which I did until, at last, I landed flat on my face. I was divorced, disgraced, bereft, and lonely. When I received a letter saying she was moving back to Virginia, I felt as if I had come up for air after wallowing and choking in a rolling, turbulent sea. I could not have been more relieved to see her face. I thought at first that she would return to college, but she surprised me by landing a job. So, the two of us were employed by day and free for adventure every night and weekend. And oh, boy! Did we have some adventures? Indeed, we did.

We both loved poetry and frequently spent languid afternoons reading to one another – each of us dreaming our own dreams. We could spend hours philosophizing, considering, contemplating, and speculating on any number of subjects, from literature to music to politics to religion. We were young, energetic, and curious but without a well-laid plan or, for that matter, any plan at all. Life seemed to be an endless road before us, and we traveled it without care or urgency. Our Sunday ritual was to shake loose our Saturday night hangover, listen to Kris sing "Sunday Mornin' Comin' Down," take turns soaking in a tub, pour ourselves some scotch, and go cruising through the hill country – sometimes winding up to the Blue Ridge Parkway. It was our church. The majestic views of mountains and valleys and meadows could take your breath away. The feeling of being connected to every single thing was palpable. But always, there was a tinge of sadness and yearning. As Kris Kristofferson so aptly penned, " *'cause there's something in a Sunday that makes a body feel alone.*"

There are many stories I could tell you about this particular time together, but perhaps they should stay where Vada and I left them – scattered about in the valley and those hills and in a few bars as well – wild, luxuriant, and unrestrained. Mostly, they were wonderful – occasionally akin to divine – and sometimes they were as scary as an open grave in moonlight. Those scary times were what worried me. Eventually, those days together came to an end. After I spent some vacation time in North Carolina visiting with old friends, I decided to pursue life in my old stomping grounds. I needed the security and sanity I found there. Without a word to Vada, I proceeded to find a job and an apartment in Raleigh. I knew that I couldn't tell her without risking either her anger or her trying to talk me out of my plans. I knew I needed to have things in place before I told her. And I was right. The first thing she said was, "I thought we were going to get an apartment together," and she was right that we had briefly discussed such a venture, but it was just talk. I countered by suggesting that she move to North Carolina with me, but that was not within her realm of possibility. I knew it even as I laid out the offer. She ridiculed my decision – her tone sarcastic and bitter. Yet I knew at the heart of it she was hurt. We both knew I had betrayed her.

After I moved to North Carolina, we corresponded by occasional letters, although hers were slow in coming in the beginning. My letters to her were a way of consoling myself for having abandoned her. When I remarried, she came to North Carolina to visit me and to meet my three-year-old daughter. I knew then that she had forgiven me, and I could stop feeling guilty. She told me that she'd met a guy and I could tell that she was in love and really happy. It wasn't long afterward that I got a letter saying that they'd been married.

My husband and I went to visit them in Staunton. Sandy was good-looking, smart, gregarious, and an engaging conversationalist who didn't seem to notice that my husband was shy and quiet – and so he wasn't. We had a lovely evening. It seemed that Vada had become very domestic, and she laid out quite a feast.

I was proud of her. It pleased me to no end how happy she seemed. I thought I could stop worrying about her. She wrote me later that she and Sandy had moved into her Aunt Mary's vacant house in the country. I savored pictures of her in my mind, holding hands with Sandy on the porch swing and basking in the mountain air. It turned out to be a short-lived fantasy. Sandy was from an affluent family in Staunton who had taken great care to guard the secret of their son's alcoholism from everyone. Once he came home from college to roost and take a wife, it was out of their hands.

Vada was now the sole caretaker of a very sick man - even more fragile than she. All of this was unbeknownst to me. I embarked on what I thought would be a carefree "girls' weekend" and drove to Vada's to spend the weekend. I figured Sandy was off fishing or hunting or spending the weekend with old college mates. Nope. Soon after my arrival, Vada informed me that she and Sandy were separated and she no longer wanted him in her life. I heard all the sad and terrible stories of their marriage, saw the pain in her eyes, and heard the heartbreak in her voice. I was glad of our time together – glad that she trusted me again – glad that she could share her burden. But I knew that I would once again be responsible for worrying about her.

I returned to my life in North Carolina and became enmeshed in all of its twists and turns and intricacies. Vada and I corresponded by mail less and less. Occasionally, we managed a phone call – but those were not the days of email and cell phones. Long-distance calls were expensive, and there was no call-waiting or voicemail. Folks either answered, or they didn't. And so our connection grew faint, although she never dimmed in my heart.

In the late summer of the year 2000, I learned from our friend Debby that Vada had passed away. I heard later from my ex-husband in Staunton that Vada had been ill for quite a while before she died. I don't know any other details. Somehow, I was not surprised. I thought, how like her to choose the new century for her death – if you choose such a thing. The following year, Debby and I traveled together to visit her grave. We lit a cigarette for her, poured out a bottle of scotch, and lit a stick of incense in her memory. Then we sat on the hillside with her for a time. That spot could not be more appropriate for my friend. The view is lovely – a lush green hill cascading downward and edged by trees with blue mountains in the distance. I no longer need to worry about my friend, for I believe that Vada is at last serenely at rest – something I think she yearned for all her life. Her beloved Kris Kristopherson penned and sang the following words that could not have been more suitable than if he had written them with Vada in mind:

"Epitaph (Black and Blue)"
Her close friends have gathered
Lord, ain't it a shame
Grieving together
Sharing the blame.
But when she was dying
Lord, we let her down.
There's no use cryin'
It can't help her now.
The party's all over
Drink up and go home.
It's too late to love her
And leave her alone.
Just say she was someone
Lord, so far from home
Whose life was so lonesome
She died all alone
Who dreamed pretty dreams
That never came true
Lord, why was she born
So black and blue?
Oh, why was she born
So black and blue?
~ words by Kristopherson and Fritts

Love Stories

Rob and Kady were just about the cutest couple I'd ever seen, and, frankly, I envied their relationship – well, to be completely truthful, I envied everything about them – at least in the beginning. Their life seemed idyllic. Rob was movie-star handsome and a truly sweet guy. Kady was an enigma. She could be adorable and sassy and then elegant and sophisticated. She also had one of the best laughs ever.

Rob and my husband were long-time friends, and Rob invited us over for after-dinner drinks one evening as a way to get better acquainted. They lived in a posh section of town in a delightful basement apartment that boasted a cozy fireplace. The four of us hit it off very naturally that evening. We drank wine, played cards, and laughed a lot. It was clear that we were going to be good friends, and I looked forward to more good times together when the evening came to a close.

I learned that Kady had been a schoolteacher but was currently unemployed and just "playing house." Since Rob worked for his dad, it became clear to me that they spent a lot of time together "playing house," which I found to be oh! So romantic. My own marriage was less so, and I envied their passion. Their affection for one another was sweet but not overdone. I longed for a pet name, loving glances, and hand-holding, but that wasn't happening in my situation. And don't we always long for what we think is missing in our own life?

Being newlyweds, neither of us had much money, but we were young and creative and didn't need money to have fun. We went hiking and picnicking and visited free festivals of all kinds in the surrounding towns and counties. Kady was our event planner - mostly because she was at home with time on her hands. And we learned that dinners need not be expensive to be fun. Besides, with candles flickering on the table and a little cheap wine, who cares if we're having hamburger helper or sloppy joes? Of course, we had occasional dinners that were splendid – steaks, all kinds of seafood – oysters, shrimp, trout – pork roasts, lamb – all funded by Kady's parents who pitied their lifestyle, were aghast at their typical meals, and worried about their nutrition. So, her doting parents brought tons of food whenever they came to visit – packing their refrigerator and small freezer to overflowing. Rob and Kady found it amusing, if not a tad insulting. But not wanting to look a gift horse in the mouth, they accepted graciously. Luckily for us, Rob and Kady were generous, and we benefited from their bounty.

Kady got pregnant, and they were thrilled. I was excited, too, but jealous. In the first place, there was no way my husband would consent to having a baby. And secondly, not only would adding a baby have strained our purse, it would have also added more stress to our already rocky relationship. I decided to concentrate on being Auntie Linda as a sort of consolation prize to myself. Kady and Rob began looking for a bigger place to live – even though their current situation seemed fine to me. They found a large apartment in a trendy new complex where lots of young couples lived. It had a pool, tennis court, and a community center. It was expensive, and Rob decided to branch out to another job where he saw the possibility of advancement. He continued to work with his dad on the weekends for extra income. Kady began decorating the new apartment. She found second-hand pieces, made bookshelves out of planks and bricks (quite country chic in those days), and did needlework pillows as accents. Rob crafted their dining table, and it was beautiful. He also sanded, stained, and varnished wine barrels as side tables – very cool. He even gifted one to me, which I so appreciated. Kady's parents were eager to help out and bought them a new sofa and baby furniture. Mostly, it was a happy time, but there were occasional bumps in the road, and along the way, I learned a few things about my friends.

It came as no surprise to learn that Kady was an only child and, although she would have denied it, spoiled rotten. She had been privileged all her life. Her parents had inherited wealth, and were educated and prominent in their community. They had seen to it that Kady had the best of everything – travel, clothes, experiences, and education. She, of course, was a sorority girl. In fact, she was a direct legacy – joining the same sorority as her mom. Even so, she was very much a daddy's girl. Rob's parents were prominent in their community but for different reasons. Neither of them was educated beyond high school. Rob's dad owned a well-known service station and auto repair shop. His shop had a good reputation, and Tom was friendly and easy going, which made him popular. Rob's mom was a beauty who had married money on the first go 'round but left with her daughter after suffering several years of abuse. She left the country club crowd to marry Tom but kept friends everywhere. Although Kady's parents were polite to Rob's family, it was clear that they did not see themselves in the same league. To make matters worse, Rob had not attended college, and that put a real dent in his armor as far as Kady's parents were concerned.

But here's the thing I learned that underpinned everything else – the story of how Kady and Rob met: Kady was Rob's high school Senior English teacher. Shocker, right? It certainly was for me – but more so in retrospect than at first glance. What I mean is that I first found out from my husband, who thought their story was amusing. Although I was shocked, I withheld judgment on account of my husband. Later on in our friendship, Rob and Kady mentioned it almost in passing and with lots of giggling and teasing one another. But what I finally realized is that is why Kady was no longer teaching school. Now, I don't know that she lost her job on account of their affair, but I learned there was a bit of a scandal surrounding it. The truth of it was that Rob had never cared much for school and had horsed around a lot, been absent routinely, and failed at least one grade, maybe two. He was nineteen in his Senior year of school.

Kady was a young college graduate in her first year of teaching, so there wasn't a huge age difference, and I wouldn't classify her as a cougar. Still, it was inappropriate. Rob made it clear that he had aggressively pursued and wooed her, but she had succumbed. They did quite a bit of sneaking around during their clandestine courtship, and I don't know who found out what, but it became known. So, there was that, coupled with the fact that Kady's parents did not approve of Rob. I don't know if they knew the whole, unadulterated version of their love story, but I'm fairly sure they were clever enough to fill in any missing pieces. Of course, they would not dare blame their daughter for her part. Instead, they felt that Rob had ruined Kady's career – not to mention her life. From their perspective, she had married someone who didn't have money, status, or an education, and now their daughter was prancing around like a love-sick teenager. Rob's parents knew the whole story and thought it was cute and amusing. I also learned that whatever Kady wanted, Kady got – from her parents, from Rob, and from most folks that she knew. She just had that way about her – some people would call it charm. Others might call it manipulation.

During Kady's pregnancy, tension mounted between Kady and her parents. They were overbearing and Kady resented it, but it was hard for her to ignore their lavish gifts. Rob was usually "Switzerland," but he lived for Kady's happiness. The balance of disdain and annoyance, imperiousness and indignation, is a dance at best and a tightrope walk at worst. Someone is bound to stumble and fall sooner or later. And they did – regularly and often. Kady would have occasional tirades and periods of not speaking to her parents. Her mother would sulk for a while, but her father always caved almost immediately. Apologies and gifts inevitably followed. I don't know how they managed the stress of it. I found it supremely awful, and I never knew whether they were on or off. So, I always tread lightly until I could gauge the weather. It could be sunshine and blue skies, a raging thunderstorm, or a light drizzle. It was exhausting to keep up. Thankfully, Kady's parents were always very gracious to me, and even though I must admit they were a little much at times, I felt sorry for them. As much as Kady declared that she didn't give a fig about what they thought, she suffered frequently from debilitating headaches. I'm fairly sure they were simply a result of the constant stress.

Kady gave birth to a beautiful, healthy baby girl they named Camden Blue, and, of course, she was the most adorable and smartest kid ever to be born in the whole wide world. With no children of my own, I had to agree. The parental tension seemed to soften for a while, but by Cam's first birthday, it was back in full force. And along about then another drama entered their lives.

As it turned out, who Rob thought was his father was not really his father. It seems that Rob discovered this shocking truth in his freshman year of high school, which likely accounted for all his troubles with school. Why his mother decided to tell him, I couldn't say, but she did. The knowledge rocked Rob's world and created havoc with his heretofore-good relationship with the man he thought was his dad. So here's the story: Rob's mother, Ellen, had been married to a wealthy, abusive

319

scoundrel. When she finally got the nerve to leave him, he refused to give her a penny. Ellen went to work in a factory rather than crawl back to her abuser. As I mentioned previously, she was a beauty, and it wasn't long before she had a number of suitors. Unfortunately, the man she fell in love with was the factory manager, Walt, who happened to be married and had three children. Ellen got pregnant but refused his offer to leave his wife and marry her. Instead, she accepted an offer of marriage from her most ardent suitor, Tom, who knew she was pregnant and did not care at all. He wanted Ellen. They thought it best to let everyone think that the baby was Tom's son, and that would have been just fine, except that Walt also knew Ellen was pregnant with his child. Walt was left to keep this secret, but in truth, he carried another secret with him – the secret of his love for Ellen. When his wife died, he looked for Ellen, and even though she still loved him, she loved Tom also and was not interested in rekindling the relationship with Walt. However, she was amenable to his meeting with his son, Rob.

The introduction did not go well. Rob was angry, shaken, and refused to have anything to do with Walt. So. Walt did not pressure Rob, but he kept in touch with holiday cards and such - things that Rob would not acknowledge. Time passed. Rob met Kady, and their story happened. But Rob did not tell Kady about Walt until he received a long, hand-written letter from his biological father saying that he was not well and that his only wish was to know his son.

I suppose that having become a father himself, Rob was able to view his father's request through a different lens. He sobbed out the whole story to Kady – thinking she would be appalled. However, Kady embraced Rob and his long-lost father. The plain truth is that Kady loved drama, but, in this case, that worked out for the best. She rallied to the cry and bundled her baby and Rob up for the trip to meet the father, who had recently turned grandfather. I personally thought it was a true love story – however entangled it was. Kady's parents were disgusted and called it a circus. It was not their finest hour. Kady threatened to break ties with them altogether and refused to let them see Camden for some time. I can only imagine how this broke their hearts. Rob embraced his biological father and his newfound siblings. Both he and Kady put much time and effort into making Walt's last year the best it could be.

Now, this is the part of the story that is hazy for me because my own marriage broke apart, and I moved out of town. Kady and I kept in touch by occasional phone calls but mostly letters – and those were usually filled with Camden's progress and then her second baby – a boy whom they named after Rob. A year passed, and I went to visit Rob and Kady. If I hadn't been jealous before, well, the green-eyed monster hit me squarely between the eyes when I arrived. Kady and Rob had bought an old house in an established neighborhood. Kady had called it a "fixer-upper" in her letters. It was old, that is true, but it was also utterly charming. The street was lined with old sugar maples, red oaks, and fir trees. The house was surrounded by well-kept shrubs and sumptuous old plantings.

The front porch was wide and welcoming, with old wicker rockers and hanging ferns. Kady opened the door smiling and gracious. The smell of cookies fresh from the oven wafted out. Darling Camden ran to greet me. I met pudgy little Robbie sitting in his high chair with a happy grin on his face. Kady's knack for decorating and Rob's handyman skills were evident. I got the grand tour and found their house subtly elegant and very comfortable. It was like something from a magazine and only in my dreams. I wanted to weep for their happiness and my own loneliness. I stayed for lunch, and Kady and I gossiped and giggled after the children went down for their naps. She seemed happy, and that was cemented for me the moment I saw Rob come through the door to greet her and the children. His handsome face beamed with love for his family. It was the picture of perfection. I refused to stay for dinner – mostly because I could not bear anymore. I needed to steady myself, and that left me feeling selfish and silly.

After that, I moved away and found another life. The next thing I knew, I was reading a letter from Kady saying that Rob had moved out, and she was in the process of selling the house. I was completely stunned. I tried to call, but there was no answer. The next phone call yielded a recording saying, "This number is no longer working." All I could do was wait to hear from her. Eventually, I received a card with her new address – many miles away from her once happy home – an apartment where she was staying with the kids. She offered no clue as to what had happened. I could not imagine. I wrote to ask if I could visit. She called soon thereafter, and we arranged a time that I could visit.

I arrived to find a new complex of apartments complete with amenities. Kady's decorating was evident in their roomy abode. The children were well, but Camden was stand-offish and surly. It was clear that Kady's parents were now in good standing with her and active in her new life. Kady talked about the Montessori school that Camden was attending, Robbie's three-day-a-week play school, her old sorority sisters who were now part of her life, and trips she had taken with the children. When I asked about Rob, she was vague and mostly complained that he didn't visit the children often (never mind that she had moved over an hour away and he was still working two jobs). When I pressed, she began pointing out the fact that Rob had not gone to college, and although she had pushed him to attend the local community college, he had not done so. I couldn't believe it when she said, "Rob will always be just a blue-collar worker." So, there it was. The plain truth was that she had suddenly grown up. She was tired of playing house. She wanted the life her parents had always wanted for her, and that did not include someone who was not her social equal. If she had told me anything else, I think I might have forgiven her. Suddenly, I realized that she had left and broken Rob's heart. And that she was moving forward without a glance backward or even a slight appreciation for what she had once had. I continued to listen – hoping for a glimpse of something that would help me see this tragedy in a different light. But nothing appeared. I returned home feeling empty and sad and wondering about love – anyone's.

Several months later, I received a call from Kady. She was bubbling with enthusiasm because she had met someone. She told me he was a little older than she – handsome (of course) – an attorney in an established law firm (no surprise) – and that he was in love with her and adored the children. He had proposed, but there was one problem: he was a devout Catholic. Therefore, Kady and Rob's marriage must be annulled by the Catholic Church before Kady could become a Catholic and marry this new man. Hence, her phone call. She wanted me to serve as a "witness" regarding her previous marriage.

I hesitated, and Kady pushed on about how I probably knew them best. Then, she went on about how much she loved this new guy and how a stable family unit would be so good for the children. What could I say? I was a weak people pleaser and caught off-guard. So, I agreed. That is until the papers arrived from the Catholic Church asking me to document what I knew of Kady and Rob's relationship. What could I say? The truth? How would the truth get Kady what she wanted? And the other truth is that the whole thing thrust me back into the memories of my own other life with its heartbreak and sadness. I sank into a terrible depression. In the end, I crawled out of it. But I never answered the questionnaire, and I never heard from Kady again. Love stories don't always have happy endings.

Chapter 10

Necessary Lessons

Me Too

I was just over twenty-one, newly married, and living in Staunton, Virginia. In the original plan, I was to have returned to college after the wedding, but that didn't happen. Instead, I went to work. My first job was at Dunkin Donuts, which, for a variety of reasons, didn't last long. I'll just say that I didn't eat there for years and years after my experience.

However, I went on to find a job as an Office Assistant at the local YMCA. It was housed in a lovely old four-story red brick building downtown that had been around since 1914. The building itself was designed by a Chicago firm noted for its YMCA buildings. Cyrus McCormick, Jr., who lived in a neighboring county and was the son of the inventor of the mechanical reaper, had provided half of the building's budget. It seemed quite formal to me – a Renaissance Revival with paired Tuscan columns framing the entrance. And it was "old school" YMCA – the kind that rented out rooms to young men. By the time I was employed there, the renters were both young and old men. And the membership had opened its doors to women and girls as well. It had become family-oriented. Despite the building's formidable look, it was a delightful place. Folks came and went happily all through the day and evening. They played handball, basketball, and volleyball. They learned to swim, came just to swim laps, and belonged to swim teams. They used the exercise room, steam room, and sauna and got massages from a physical therapist. There were day camps, summer camps, tournaments, and special classes. It was a busy, friendly environment for a young person to work and I thoroughly enjoyed it. The main staff consisted of an Executive Director, a Physical Director, a Membership Director, and an Office Manager. There were folks on staff 24/7 – mostly to attend to the comings and goings of renters but also to buzz in visitors for night swims, ball games, and the like.

I worked Monday through Friday from nine to five. The location was perfectly situated for me to walk to and from work – only a few blocks. I could eat lunch downtown at various locations offering soup, sandwiches, and salads if I didn't pack my lunch. Or I could spend my lunch hour browsing in a variety of shops – clothing, newsstands, books, jewelry (window shopping only in my case), sundries, furniture, and antiques. A hobby shop was right across the street. I made friends with the owner of the shop and worked on little projects here and there – decoupage was "big" then, and I did my share of tacky stuff that didn't survive to the next decade.

My closest workmate was the Office Manager, Miss Ruth Lee, the sweetest human that ever breathed. She had worked there for fifty years – and that is no exaggeration. Miss Lee's mother had died when she was in high school. She had several younger siblings, and it fell her lot to keep house and care for her brothers and sisters. When she graduated from high school, she began working at the YMCA, keeping their books, and there she stayed. Miss Lee was a pixie of a woman – not even five feet tall. She had a pixie hair cut to match and sparkling blue eyes. She tenderly carried the spirit of that institution within her loyal heart – trudging in no matter the weather or her own health. She had never married, and soon after my arrival, she adopted me. This was supremely lucky for me as she often brought me goodies from her kitchen or something from her handiwork – knitting, crocheting, or tatting. If we weren't busy, she would shoo me off to visit my friend across the street, to loiter at the newsstand, or grab a cup of coffee with a friend. I adored her.

The Executive Director was an ambitious man who made it his business to come out of his office to personally greet any member with status or wealth in the community. He often played handball or golf with Board Members. He had a pretty wife who was a stay-at-home mom to their five children. They were both active in their church and civic affairs.

The Physical Director was a young man only about five years my senior. He was full of life, energy, and good humor. He and his gorgeous wife had a new baby not long after my arrival, and he loved to show off pictures of his young son.

The Membership Director was an older gentleman who had retired from his life's work as a well-known Insurance Agent in town. He only worked a few days a week. The rest of the time, he spent playing handball, swimming, golfing, or working in his yard with his beloved wife of many years. His son was running the Insurance Agency, and his daughter was a young wife and mother. He was very old-fashioned, and it had taken some time and careful molding to get him to embrace the YMCA's new idea of a family model that included women and young girls. I imagine he had been quite handsome in his youth, for he still retained his physique and good looks. He was a tall, imposing figure, and he had eyes that seemed to look right through you. Yet he could flash the most charming smile, and it always caught me a bit off guard.

When I first arrived, I felt his keen eyes judging me constantly, and I often wondered if I had passed muster.

I loved my job. There wasn't a single task I minded, even when it was something as mundane as filing or folding towels. I was also given various tasks that were just plain fun – sometimes, I helped with swim classes or the Women's Exercise Group. Or I might just help to stock towels in the reception area, the women's dressing room, or the upstairs residence area. I met many local people and enjoyed the congenial atmosphere. I never minded going to work, and, in fact, I looked forward to it. Even the walk to and from was an adventure – no matter the weather – rain or snow or blustery winds. On my way, I passed St. Francis of Assisi Catholic Church. Although I was not Catholic, I began to join the nuns for Mass every morning in the graceful parish. The building was an elegant Gothic revival built in the late 1800s that seemed to beckon me. It was a pleasant, meditative way to begin my day, and the priest was happy to have me – Catholic or not. The grand stained glass windows streamed light in with a tenderness that felt welcoming. I was especially fond of Saint Cecilia (the saint of music), Saint Catherine, and the Virgin Mary of the Immaculate Conception, who stood on a crescent moon. Her gown was the traditional blue, and her cloak was blue, white, and gold. Her sweet, slightly bowed head was surrounded by stars. Sometimes, on my way home, I would stop by the church and light a candle for various reasons – and sometimes, just because it felt good.

After working there for some time, I was called to the Director's office and offered the position of Membership Secretary. It was a promotion, and in addition to other duties, I would be assisting the Membership Director – yes, the older gentleman who seemed to be always deciding about me. It seems that I had indeed passed muster! Later, I learned that he would be fully retiring in a short while, and he would be mentoring me for his position. I was not only shocked but also thrilled by this news. I knew the position would be just doing more of what I already enjoyed so much –

meeting new people, mingling with old members, and promoting the "Y." It could not have been a more perfect fit for me. As I stepped into my new role as Membership Secretary, I sensed a softening in the Membership Director's attitude toward me. He remained his reserved, stoic self, but he did not appear to be constantly glaring and judging me. Instead, he treated me as if I were a colleague, which served to bolster my confidence in my ability as well as my own opinion of myself in general. Working at the Y had never been in my consciousness as a career, so it seemed to have arrived as a delightful surprise. I began to see my future unfolding there within those walls and among those people. I was happy.

Unfortunately, my home life was not going so well. It was often tumultuous and unpredictable. It didn't help that I was immature, unprepared for such situations, and lacked the skills to cope with what was happening. And to make matters worse, I had no one to share this with. My closest friends were at least a couple of hundred miles away.

Those people who were physically close were not much more than acquaintances, and I felt too awkward about my own feelings to share them. And some of the incidents that could have used some talking about were too embarrassing to share with people I didn't know well. For sure, there was no way I was spreading this unpleasantness into my happy work world. Besides, my best friend there was Miss Lee – and, bless her heart, she'd never been married, and, as far as I could tell, she'd never even had a boyfriend. No way was I telling her any of my problems. Besides, I couldn't bear the thought of her worrying about me. And so, I took my problems to the feet of the Blessed Virgin often-- knowing she alone would keep my secrets and my sorrows. I struggled alone in that way for what seemed an eternity. My heart was heavy, but I could rise above it at work and ignore the painful reality of my marriage. The reality was that my marriage had set sail, so hopefully, in the beginning, was taking on water and sinking faster than I could bail. In the end, it went down with barely a sigh.

I was alone and adrift. For several days after the initial separation, I was reluctant to speak of it at work. However, it became necessary to reveal the truth of my private life since, in my current situation, I could no longer walk to work, and driving a car meant I needed to find a parking situation. Plus, there was all the messy work of relocating belongings that could not always be handled in an evening after work or on a weekend. I cannot recall what I summoned up the courage to say – first to Miss Lee and then to the Executive Director. I didn't want to burden them with my problems, nor did I want in any way to indicate that I wasn't completely happy with my work situation. What I said or how I said it is a blank space in my mind, but I know they happened. Miss Lee and the Director were both very kind, and that was enough for me at that juncture.

I continued my work, and it seemed my promising future there would remain in place. The Membership Director did not mention my new marital status to me – although I know he was aware of it – nor did I mention it to him.

Frankly, that was a huge relief. I was aware that there was, for lack of a better analogy, a Scarlet Letter often placed on the breast plate of a "Divorced Woman" during that time. Nowadays, folks are not burdened by such judgment – in fact, it's almost blasé. But that was a different time. I had feared that my predecessor, steeped in his old-world views, would see my new status as a negative. If he did, he didn't say so to me, and eventually, he completely retired as he had planned. I was named the new Membership Director and continued on course. As sad as I was in my private life, I was balanced by the positives of my work life. Even so, I felt exposed and raw much of the time, but I was managing. Day by day, I put one foot in front of the other and moved on.

The days passed, and I began to adjust to my current situation. I had certainly never prepared myself to be a divorced person. That was something that happened to other people. Had I put those people in the "bad" category heretofore? I don't think so. It's just that I had never thought I would be in that "category."

And, Lord knows! We want to label and categorize everything, don't we? Sigh……being human is hard.

One of the things about being young is exploring all the possibilities there are in life. Exploring might mean experiencing things or just reading or talking about them. One of the things that I really liked about my job was that there were lots of people in my life – workmates, friends, and even regular visitors and members of the "Y" - who knew lots of things – different things, different ways of being. They had read, seen, and had experiences that were unfamiliar to me. Those things might be worth a satisfactory nod, or they might be completely compelling. I reveled in coming across some fascinating subject with whomever and wandering around inside their brain to glean whatever I could. Sometimes, that would send me off to see more and know more. Sometimes, the conversation was adequate, and I was done. Or it meant more delicious interchange on whatever subject.

One such subject was Neuro-Linguistic Programming or NLP. Otherwise known more commonly as hypnotism. I happened to mention my interest in a passing conversation with the Director, who told me that he had some training in this field. My curiosity was immediately piqued, and when he invited me to sit down in his office to talk about it more in-depth, I was keenly open to what he had to say. After a brief overview and some name-dropping – E.g., Satir, Erikson, Chomsky, and Castaneda – regarding methods, theories, and techniques, I was impressed and eager to hear more. He promised to give me a sample session on a day when we were not too busy, which happened one blustery, snowy day soon after that. He sat at his imposing desk in his large office while I sat across from him, ready, willing and excited to begin. It began with a meditative progressive relaxation exercise with my eyes closed. I felt peaceful and open, awaiting more. He urged me to continue to relax, deeper and deeper. I seemed to have melted into the chair. I remember being told to touch my cheek, my throat, my arm. There were more words, but I felt warm and sleepy and couldn't grasp everything he was saying. I remember being told to hug myself. And then I was to touch my breasts. Huh? Did I? Did I hear that correctly? What was he saying? There was more, but I cannot recount it.

Although I felt sluggish, a dawning horror crept through me. I kept my eyes closed, but I was no longer sleepy. I was wide awake. Horrified. Completely undone and unsure of what to do. You might think I should have known what to do. And in retrospect of fifty years, I know what I wish I had done. But I did none of those grand things that would have lifted me out of that awful moment in time. Instead, I sat there in a physical state of catatonia – unable to speak or move – although my mind was whirling at such a speed that I could not grasp a single solid thought. I would like to tell you that I told him "what for" and left his office, but that isn't what happened. The fact is, I can't really tell you what exactly happened. Somehow, the session ended, and I went back to my own desk – weak and shaken. I realize now that he had chosen a day when Miss Lee was not in the office, and truth be told, I was glad of it. I don't know what I would have done if I would have had to see her sweet, innocent face in the aftermath of that ugly experience. Somehow, the day ended, and I left. I felt bruised and beaten by the encounter. I got into my car and wept. I was more alone than I had ever been in my entire life. There was not a single soul that I felt I could tell and Lord knows! I could have used a sympathetic ear. The rest of the day is a mystery. I suppose I went home and went to bed. I certainly didn't have the energy for anything else. If I appeared downcast, folks probably assumed it was my shattered marriage plaguing my mind.

In the following days, the director seemed to be constantly arranging ways for us to be alone – taking notes in his office or helping him go through old files in a large storage room connected to his office. I felt sure these were contrived. I became adept at dodging any physical contact and changing the subject if it seemed to be sliding downhill. After a couple of weeks of these exhausting exercises, I knew I needed a comrade. Since it could not possibly be naïve Miss Lee, I decided that the young Physical Director, who was near my age, might be employed to sympathize and help me to strategize. I looked for an opportunity to talk with him without being overheard. We were upstairs in an empty residence hall when that time came. However, instead of pouring my heart out to him, it turned out that he proposed a plan for me to be rid of the ache in my heart. Yep. He thought he could "help" me since I must be very lonely – *"you know, without your husband and all."* Really? I was momentarily stunned by his suggestion, and then I laughed and acted as if I thought he was joking. I knew full well he wasn't, but it broke the seriousness of the moment, and I slipped out the door and back to the safety of my office. I cannot tell you every thought that went through my mind in the days and weeks that followed, but they were all pretty terrible. And all of them pointed to <u>ME</u> as the problem. I must have done something wrong to make these men think I was "that kind of girl." I must have misspoken in some way.

Perhaps I laughed inappropriately at some point in time. Should I rethink my wardrobe? I was filled with shame and guilt. I was also a nervous wreck. I no longer felt comfortable in that beloved building or even in my office. My visions for the future began to crumble. Just when I thought I had survived the worst that could happen, I found out there was more to endure. I was young – what did I know? I had no one I could confide in. And what would I confide? I felt dirty, foul, stained, and bad. The only thing I knew for sure was that I could not stay in that place any longer. I had to leave the job that I loved and the dreams that I had held.

Of course, by then, I was getting used to shattered dreams. What was one more? And so, I resigned. I found a job as an Assistant to the Director of Computer Services in a company in another town. Saying goodbye to Miss Lee nearly broke my heart. She was stunned that I would leave my job in light of my new position. She knew how happy I had been there. She'd heard me fairly singing about it on occasion. And what could I say to her? What could I say to anyone? Do you want to know what I said? Nothing. Not a single word. Well, not the truth, anyway. Not to a single soul. For years. And I kept this whole story to myself until the "Me Too" of recent years when it revealed scores of other women who had encountered similar treatment in the workplace – some of it way worse than what happened to me. And sometimes, those poor women didn't have a way out. They were stuck. As I listened to interview after interview that played out on countless TV shows, my heart broke open. I was, at last, able to release the guilt and shame that I had kept hidden for so long. I have joined the multitude of women – my sisters in spirit who know that awful pain, the disgrace, the humiliation. And with a chorus of "Me, too!" we have risen together. I hope my sisters have learned some of what I have also learned about acceptance and being human. It took years for me to understand the truth of being human. That truth could not be said more perfectly than by these words from Rumi-- one of my favorite poets:

The Guest House

This being human is a guest house.
Every morning a new arrival.
A joy, a depression, a meanness,
Some momentary awareness comes
As an unexpected visitor.
Welcome and entertain them all!
Even if they're a crowd of sorrows,
Who violently sweep your house
Empty of its furniture,
Still treat each guest honorably.
He may be clearing you out
For some new delight.
The dark thought, the shame, the malice,
Meet them at the door laughing,
And invite them in.
Be grateful for whoever comes
Because each has been sent
As a guide from beyond.

Home for Children

I was young, single, in a dead-end job, generally unhappy, and feeling useless. So, when somebody told me there were jobs available at a local Home for Children as a houseparent, I thought that would be a rewarding job and an opportunity to go back to college. I never made it back to college, but the rewards were priceless.

The Home for Children was located on a beautifully green and rolling campus with enormous trees and a winding driveway that curved by each of the several large houses. The homes were grand old brick structures with cavernous rooms. Each one housed from six to eight children. The house I was assigned to had eight children – two girls and six boys. They varied in age from six to twelve. Two of the boys were brothers. One of the girls and the youngest boy were siblings. There was only one orphaned child in the house – a twelve-year-old whose parents had died in a car crash. The other children all had parents but, for one reason or another, were not living with them.

I had been aware of homes for orphaned children all my life. I knew there were situations when children lived with relatives other than their parents for one reason or another. But having no family who wanted to care for you was an eye-opening perspective for me. Some of these children had been removed from their parent or parents by court order. Some children had absent parents due to drugs and/or alcohol and grandparents too aged or infirmed to care for them. Sometimes, available relatives declined to help out. Some children had simply been lost in the fray of divorced parents, with neither parent wanting to be responsible for them. It was heartbreaking. These various situations left the children hurt and confused. The children lacked the ability to identify their feelings, much less verbalize them, which led to all kinds of behaviors in their attempt to sort out and deal with what was going on in their little lives. Dealing with the children and their unpredictable behavior was challenging, frustrating, and rewarding.

I had always wanted to have a large family, and it seemed that I had landed right in the middle of a ready-made one. Only this family was far from my starry-eyed vision of the Waltons – who, as you might remember from movie or TV fame, were always kind, considerate, and loving to one another and everyone else on the planet. This real-life crew was prickly, cantankerous, sneaky, occasionally explosive, and sometimes downright mean. I never blamed them, but the bad behavior needed to be dealt with, and it wasn't long before I realized that I might be out of my depth. Some of these kids needed serious therapy.

Mornings in our home were not immune to problems, but being slow and sleepy helped me get my eight charges up and moving into their routine of dressing, teeth brushing, breakfast consumption, book bags packed, and out the door to the bus stop.

Once the last kid had boarded the bus, I enjoyed a cup of coffee and finished cleaning up the kitchen. Even though the children mostly cleaned up after themselves, there were always straggling dishes, counters, and tables to clean off and sweeping to be done. Meal planning and grocery shopping needed doing most days. Sometimes, there were school meetings to attend. Occasionally, one of the children stayed home because of illness – usually no big deal but sometimes demanding – especially if it involved more than one kid. Of course, like every other job in the world, there were always meetings with other staff – most of which were helpful. Early on, I imagined that this would be the time that I would be able to attend a class or study, but somehow that didn't happen.

Most of the houses had a married couple and a single person working in tandem. Ours was no different. We each worked five days a week, which included every other weekend. Therefore, some days overlapped, and we would all three be working together. I had two large rooms upstairs in the house with a large private bathroom between them. One room was furnished as a living room, and the other was my bedroom. Although not particularly fashionable, they were both comfortable enough. On days off, there was another house available with a kitchen, living area, and bedroom that was mercifully quiet and free of children. At first, I had the notion that I could just be "off" and stay in my own bedroom and living area, but I quickly learned that was no way to rest up for the five days to come! Even though the children mostly respected my space, there was still a good bit of noise, and the kids relied on me if I was present in the house.

The children under my care taught me unforgettable lessons about many things. Big things like love and trust and betrayal. But countless lessons on things that seem simple but turn out to be pretty big in the long run-- like how big small kindnesses really are, choosing which battles to fight, how to make the most of an afternoon in any weather, that sometimes there are things – situations and people – that can't be "fixed"; and that peanut butter and jelly is best on toast. Probably the most amazing lesson I learned is that, in a kid's view, a bad parent is better than no parent. And some of these kids had pretty bad parents.

Let's start with Mickey. Mickey's parents had divorced. When Mickey's mother died in a car accident, her parents were too feeble to care for him. Mickey's dad had remarried a woman with three children, and then they had two more children of their own. Mickey's dad figured he had five kids to feed and clothe, and that was his limit. On very rare occasions, Mickey's dad would take him for a weekend, but more often than not, he would say he was going to take Mickey for a visit, and then he wouldn't show. Poor Mickey would always wait with his suitcase packed, hope in his heart, and great determination until bedtime – by then, it was clear that his dad wasn't coming. Trying to move Mickey from his valley of disappointment into the usual bedtime routine without an explosion was a real feat. Sometimes, the poor little guy managed to hold it together until after he crawled into bed, where he would cry himself to sleep. And who could blame him? I would sit by his bed quietly and rub his back if he would allow it. There were no words that could make it better. And his crummy dad never even called to apologize for the "no-show." Nor did the derelict human even call just to check on poor Mick – ever. Yet even with this deplorable treatment, whenever Mickey got mad, his big threat was that he was going to call his dad, who would come and exact justice for Mickey. Favorite phrases that I heard often were: "I'm going to call my dad, and he'll come and beat you up!" or "I'm going to call my dad, and he'll come and get me. I don't have to stay here!" It was unbelievably sad.

Sarah and Stevie had been found in the city eating out of garbage cans. Their mom was hooked on drugs, earned money as a prostitute, and was totally incapable of attending to their welfare. Social services had located a grandmother, but she was frail and unable to take them. They were beautiful children, but they were sullen and quiet. Stevie was six years old, preferred solitude, and often balked at any demand placed on him. Sarah was ten years old, but she acted like a teenager already – experimenting with make-up and boys. A couple of times, we found her with boys in her bed after lights out. She had already seen and done much more than other girls her age.

Bryan and Johnny were handsome, dark-eyed brothers only a year apart. Johnny was eleven; Bryan was ten. They had a much younger brother, Markie, who had been sent to a foster home with a young couple because the group environment was too overwhelming and over stimulating for him. Reports showed that he was flourishing with this couple, and they very much wanted to adopt him. The boys were not orphans, but their parents were completely absent from their lives. Their father was an alcoholic and had been abusive to their mother throughout all of her pregnancies. In fact, there was suspicion that some of Johnny's slow mental development was likely related to injuries sustained while in utero. The mother suffered from severe depression and was hospitalized after becoming psychotic. At that point, the dad left the boys with their one set of living grandparents and simply vanished. Although the grandparents felt fully responsible for the boys, they were advanced in age. After the grandfather suffered a heart attack, the grandmother became overburdened. The boys visited their grandparents on some weekends and holidays. Still, even though they were basically sweet-natured, they were too exuberant to remain in the care of their grandparents full-time. The mother's mental state was never reported to be improving.

William was a blonde-haired, blue-eyed ten-year-old from an abusive home. His parents were divorced. Both had remarried and had several other children with their current spouses. Both parents did drugs and drank a lot. They also beat their children. When the new spouses got fed up with the drugs and, drinking and beatings, they took their children and left the situation. After William's dad was arrested for assaulting a neighbor and his mother had skipped town, William was left with no one capable of caring for him. Mostly, he was quiet and had a very sweet smile. Unfortunately, he was also a practiced liar and thief. You could count on one thing: he was incapable of telling the truth. I wanted to believe in him. I wanted to trust him–– just because somebody needed to––but the poor guy could NOT tell the truth if his life depended on it. He was caught shoplifting in nearby stores on numerous occasions. It was exasperating and so, so sad.

Eight-year-old Katie was one of the cutest little girls I'd ever seen – silky blonde hair, crystal blue eyes, and a smattering of freckles on her cheeks and tiny nose. Her father was not in the picture. Her mother was an alcoholic, and the court had intervened because of her neglect. Fortunately, her mother adored Katie, grieved her choices, joined AA, and faithfully collected Katie every Friday for a home visit. This sad, sweet pair lived for their time together – their faces openly reflected the fullness in their hearts when they saw each other and the sorrow when they parted. Katie's mother also called her every single evening to ask about her day.

Tony was a handsome twelve-year-old and the only true orphan on the whole campus. His parents had been killed in an automobile accident, and he simply had no other living relatives. A young man, Jim, who served as a Sunday School teacher as well as a Scout Master at the church we attended, had taken an interest in Tony that blossomed into a mutual friendship and mentor relationship. Jim took Tony to his home every weekend and holiday. Sometimes, they went camping, hiking, sailing, or to visit Jim's parents. We were all pretty sure Jim was gay, but this was back in the day when folks were mostly in the closet, and no one spoke openly about it. What we knew for sure was that Tony was happy and probably the most well-adjusted kid on the whole campus. The campus counselor concurred.

Weekends left us with fewer children than during the week. Tony and Katie were reliably out of the house from Friday afternoon to Sunday evening. Often, Johnny and Bryan were with their grandparents or Markie's foster parents. Occasionally, Mickey would be away with his inconstant dad. But I could count on William, Sarah, and Stevie being my weekend companions at the very least. Some Saturdays, we would plan outings, and some, we left open for creative play. We flew kites, played tag, planted flowers, carved pumpkins, strolled the campus, baked cookies, watched cartoons, or read. On Sunday, we walked a few blocks to church and then spent the afternoon preparing for the week ahead. Who had homework to do? Who had a project due? Who needed clean clothes? What about shoes – invariably, someone was in need of shoestrings.

If this sounds idyllic – well, there were days when it almost was. But, trust me, there was always something brewing – or exploding. Somebody was out of sorts. Somebody was mad at somebody. Somebody hit somebody. Somebody lost something. Somebody stole somebody's something. Somebody crying. Somebody screaming. Somebody bloody. It was like a three-ring circus – only more rings and more stuff happening. Even so, I loved those kids–- they completely stole my heart. So why did I leave? Well, sadly, it wasn't the kids. It was the other adults in that household. They had more drama than those eight children combined. And that is all I have to say about that. I wish I had been more mature and had possessed the tools to deal with such – but I didn't have enough strength, wisdom, or life experience. I walked away with a heart full of gratitude for my own family and the wonderful childhood I'd been privileged to enjoy – and a heart burdened heavily with love and pain for those eight children I had been honored to know. It has been many, many years ago, yet I can still recall each one of those beautiful faces. I often wonder where they are now and what happened to those precious souls. I hope with all my heart that each one of them found their way to a good life. They gave me more than I ever gave them.

*Note: Names have been changed to protect the innocent.

Insurance Company

If you were thinking an insurance company wasn't an exciting place to work, you would be exactly right. But as life would have it, you can meet some interesting folks no matter where you happen to be. And even in a place like that, there were some folks who entertained me during the self-imposed imprisonment and who also left me scratching my head.

The company was national, but the office where I worked was small. It employed a managing officer (Mr. Smith) and four other employees (Verla, Peggy, Betsy, and me). I was the last hired and "low man" on the totem pole. The boss, Mr. Smith, was an older gentleman who reminded me of somebody's grandfather. He was relatively good-looking, had white hair, wore nice suits, and smoked a pipe. Mr. Smith was nice enough, if not a bit pompous. The company didn't advertise (no joke) – rather, it depended on word-of-mouth recommendations. What that really meant was that you had to know somebody who knew somebody in order to be insured by this company. Therefore, customers were mostly elite businessmen, and Mr. Smith courted them at the golf course and other Members-only events. And, as far as I could tell, that was his big contribution to the company. We arrived to work at 8 o'clock sharp. He strolled in around 9, and someone rushed to make him a cup of coffee while he hung up his suit coat, lounged back in his leather chair, and lit his pipe. Of course, he signed and approved things but relied heavily on his long-time employee and office manager, Verla, to have already made the right decisions. She fluttered around him and treated him like royalty. Mr. Smith talked on the phone a lot – most of the conversations were lengthy and cordial, never hurried or urgent. He also took long lunches, played golf with important connections, and generally left most days about half past four. Mr. Smith seemed to be a devoted family man with a well-dressed wife, two daughters in college, and a beautiful collie – all the makings of a perfect Christmas card. Naturally, he belonged to a Country Club, had season tickets to the symphony, attended local theatre productions, and enjoyed luxurious vacations. What a life, right? I have no idea what the man's salary was, but it looked like a pretty penny to me.

In comparison, I was hired at a few dollars above minimum wage. I worked from eight to five o'clock with an hour for lunch and a couple of ten-minute breaks during the day. I was fortunate to have health insurance included with my salary, so I wasn't complaining. Let's just say, I worked hard for my money. I was constantly on the phone with clients, writing up claims and processing new applicants. There was no downtime, and the claims could be fairly intense. The good thing is that sometimes they were interesting – hearing clients explain their misfortunes could be a hoot – and it beat twiddling my thumbs at my desk or, worse, being unemployed.

I've mentioned Verla – Mr. Smith's right-hand 'man,' as it were. She was smart, capable, had been there for years, and knew everything about everything. She was fifty-something, attractive, lived at home with her father, had a daughter in college, no husband, but had a handsome regular fellow. I came to learn that Verla had survived a volatile marriage that had ended when her daughter was quite young. The two of them had retreated to her father's house. Verla's mother was deceased. Verla adored her dad and seemed overly responsible for him – treating him as if he were her child even though he was in excellent health and very active. For a long time, I assumed that her loyalty to her dad was what kept her from marrying her fella. It turns out her steady fella was also married. So there was that. I learned this from my office mate, Betsy, one day at lunch. What a shock. I mean, here was this woman who looked and acted all prim and proper, doting on her dad and daughter and singing in the church choir.

Now, going to church doesn't make you a saint, I know, but her every appearance was one of seeming to follow all the social rules. And, by my calculation, that didn't include dating someone else's husband. But, I, for one, was in no position to judge her choices, that's for sure. It just surprised me, that's all. Later on, Verla herself confided this clandestine arrangement to me, and I acted like it was news to me. I also ended up sympathizing with her. According to her, the man was married to a hateful, vindictive woman who refused to give him a divorce. Or that was his story, at least. I don't know if that was the whole truth, but it seemed to work in her world. The man certainly courted her with charm – sent her flowers, called to check in with her on a daily basis, took her to lunch often, and lavished her with thoughtful gifts. I could tell the minute he called – she folded herself inward, her face softened, her eyelashes fluttered, and oh! How that woman could flirt. She used a milder form of coquetry on Mr. Smith every day, and he clearly adored her. I never thought I knew the whole story about Verla and her beau. Maybe Verla didn't know the truth of it herself, but it was a love story for sure – as well as a bit of a mystery. I wonder if she ever thought of writing about it. I'll bet she could give Danielle Steele a run for her money.

Next in the office pecking order was Peggy. I suppose there's one in every crowd. You know the kind. Imperious, narcissistic, sarcastic, two-faced – yep, the one that rhymes with "witch." The kind of woman that always perplexes me. Mr. Smith liked her almost as much as he liked Verla – even though she was not the least bit coy – sometimes she was downright haughty, condescending, and aloof. It was as if he needed her to like him. And Verla liked her, too. Betsy was courteous, as she was to everyone, but I came to suspect that she didn't care for Peggy any more than I did.

I kept wanting to like Peggy – trying to like her – waiting for her armor to crumble and reveal a better person underneath. But she held that shield firmly in place at all times. Then again, maybe it wasn't a shield at all. Maybe it was just who she was. Peggy was one of those women who looked pretty until you got to know her. Then, all you could see was her sneering, scornful behavior that completely blotted out her previous physical appearance. I wondered how she managed to find a husband – much less keep him –

because, let me tell you right now that she wasn't any nicer to him than she was to me. No kidding. What in the world did the man see in her? I couldn't figure it out. But over the years, I've known other women just like her. It still amazes me. If somebody knows the answer, please share it with me because I remain ever curious. Peggy also claimed to be very religious – but in my observation, it was a claim without substance. Peggy had an absolutely adorable little girl that I sure hope didn't turn out like her mother. But it was the one subject that I felt on solid ground with Peggy about because, like any mother, she accepted any and all compliments about her child. It was her only redeeming behavior in my book.

Next in line was sweet Betsy – quiet, seemingly shy, and hardworking. If the office had been a social gathering, Betsy would have been the proverbial wallflower – not because she wasn't pretty – but because she was so soft and hushed that she just faded into the surroundings. Betsy appeared to take no notice of Peggy's insolent remarks. She managed to avoid being in the line of fire whenever Peggy was out of sorts (which happened on a weekly basis). Both of our workmates were prone to intrusive questions whenever Mr. Smith was out of the office – snooping and inquiring. Betsy gave neither of them enough information to use against her. As my daddy would say, she never offered them any ammunition – which served her well and was a lesson for me in future work situations. I thought of Betsy as "vanilla". Well, that is until I attended a rock concert and ran into her with her longhaired hippie boyfriend and her crowd of friends who were clearly blowing it all out. No judgment, folks. I was there with my own longhaired hippie boyfriend and my own wild crowd of people who were having an equally good time. But I must say I'm pretty sure that my mouth dropped open and I was stopped in my tracks when I first saw her. I just couldn't believe this was the same person. In the office, her dress and demeanor were neat, reserved, professional, and fairly unremarkable. Out in this boisterous scene of rock and rollers, drinking beer and partying, she fit right in. Big hoop earrings, hip-hugging faded jeans, fashionable halter top with her little belly showing, stacked wooden heels, and a wide, happy smile on her face were a stark contrast to the buttoned-up, nose-to-the-grindstone person I knew Monday through Friday. And, as surprised as I was, Betsy seemed equally as shocked when she saw me. I guess all the ladies in my life (hats off to my mama especially) had instilled a measure of social etiquette, dress, and manners that had camouflaged me more in my office setting than I had been aware of – and that realization gave me a sense of relief, security, and confidence that until that moment I had been sorely lacking. Prior to that very moment, every day in that stuffy office, I had felt like that dream where you show up naked and everybody's staring. When I saw Betsy's mouth open and gaping back at me, I realized that maybe I wasn't as exposed and vulnerable in our office setting as I felt. After our moment of astonishment, we both began to laugh. I wondered if she felt as giddy as I did. It was an instant in which we immediately realized that we were kindred spirits – no matter what game we played from nine to five Monday through Friday. What a relief! After that, Betsy and I became good friends. We shared lunch together at least once a week and sometimes went out for dinner or drinks after work. We were careful to keep our private lives entirely out of the office – never letting on that we had shared interests, private conversations, and lots of secrets. In fact, we didn't let on that we even had lunch together. Intuitively, we knew that would threaten our office mates and make our work environment more stressful.

Although I remained congenial in that office setting, I borrowed from Betsy's handbook on reticence. I curbed my natural outgoing and chatty behavior. It helped me feel less vulnerable and more secure. In the end, I felt imprisoned in that place. I felt I was living a double life. And, in truth, I was. I was unable to verbalize it at the time, but I felt artificial, disingenuous, and stifled. The day I walked out of that office for good, I could almost feel my wings beginning to sprout. It was years before I was able to soar with wings spread and free, but it was a beginning. I breathed in a huge gulp of fresh air and stepped into sunshine. I doubt any prisoner leaving bars behind has ever felt so good.

*Note: Names have been changed to protect the innocent – and even the guilty.

You Never Know....

If I close my eyes, I can still see Jane's cute pixie face with its porcelain complexion, her thick, shiny, auburn hair, and her sweet smile. We were both RNs, and we worked at a medical clinic. When I first met her, we were float nurses – meaning that we "floated" to whatever area of the clinic we were needed. We often found ourselves at lunch together, and I came to know more about her over those lunches. Jane had graduated from Wake Forest University and was not only a Registered Nurse but also held a Master's Degree in nursing. I wondered why she wasn't doing more than float nursing, but I never asked. I supposed she figured there was still plenty of time to pursue something more involved. I learned that she had two darling children, and it was clear they were her focus in life. Her husband was a handsome, successful attorney, and they had a beautiful home in a nice section of the city. They belonged to a Country Club where they golfed and played tennis. She drove a late-model

Mercedes sedan. The truth was, she didn't need to work. I figured she did it mostly because she liked people and she liked being helpful. Frankly, I was a little jealous of her picture-perfect life. But I couldn't help but like Jane. She was just as sweet as could be – a really good person and easy to be with. She was also smart and well-read. I enjoyed conversing with her, and she kept my reading list exciting.

Eventually, I accepted a full-time position in the Oncology Department. Jane continued to work as a float nurse, and because of that, I continued to see her whenever she floated to my area of the clinic. However, in this new perspective, I came to have a different opinion of Jane. Whenever nurses put in for vacation or personal leave, someone from the Float Pool would be contacted and asked to fill in for that requested time off. Those working in the department where the absence would occur were advised by weekly schedule who would be the replacement. In these cases, float nurses knew well in advance when and where they would be working. I came to dread seeing Jane's name as a substitute in our department, for she was invariably late. If the stint was as long as a week, you could almost bet that she would be absent at least one of those days – she seemed plagued with headaches and stomach upsets more than normal folks. Being short-staffed put a burden on everyone – more work, little to no break throughout the day, and generally working overtime – which led to exhaustion and frayed nerves. As much as I liked Jane as a person, I came to dislike her as a workmate. I can recall one incident in particular when she was scheduled to work alongside me. Our workday was already overbooked, and I had arrived extra early to make sure things went as smoothly as they possibly could. When the workday began, there was no sign of Jane, and I was annoyed. Fifteen minutes into the day, I received a call from Jane saying that she was not feeling well and wouldn't be in. I listened to her excuse and chewed on my lip, trying not to say anything I would regret. I breathed an audible sigh of impatience, which I am certain Jane correctly interpreted and, therefore, felt the need to embellish on the reason for her absence:

"Well, I was feeling nauseous this morning and so I took half of a Phenergan and now I'm just so tired and sleepy," she whined.

(For those of you that are not nurses, Phenergan is a prescription strength antiemetic/antihistamine often used to control nausea and vomiting. Its side effect is drowsiness.) I felt a flush of anger and silently questioned her lack of judgment. I mean, really?! Like she hadn't considered that this would be a side effect? Why hadn't she tried saltines, ginger ale, or Pepto-Bismol if she had really been planning to come in to work as she was claiming? To say I was irritated would be an understatement. I took a breath and said something like, "Well, we want you at your best when you're taking care of patients." But I confess that I probably did not say it as nicely as I could have, and we ended the call briskly. Although she appeared in the clinic the next day, and I was grateful, I still felt bothered by what I perceived as general irresponsible behavior. In a later conversation with the

Director of Nurses at the clinic, I realized that other staff shared my view of Jane. Somehow, this gave me permission to feel righteous and superior to her. I saw myself as hardworking and dedicated. I saw Jane as undependable and fickle. Even though I would never have admitted my own feeling of superiority and my self-righteous judgment of Jane, I can see it very clearly in retrospect.

Then came the morning when I arrived at the clinic, picked up the schedule, and saw Jane's name listed for my department. I inwardly groaned and prepared myself for whatever might come. Eight o'clock came, and no Jane. At half past the hour, there was still no Jane and when I was paged, I steeled myself to hear whatever excuse she was planning to offer. Instead, it was the Director of Nursing asking if Jane had arrived. When I said "no" I could almost hear her eyes rolling, and then she promised that if Jane had not arrived by nine, she would try to send someone to cover for her by at least ten o'clock. And that is what happened.

When the new float nurse arrived, I got her up to speed and we carried on with the already busy day. When I got to work the next day, the Director of Nursing called me to her office. I figured Jane wasn't coming in again and we would be discussing a plan. When I saw the Director's face, I knew it was something more serious, but I had no idea what. I cannot remember her words, but somehow, she conveyed that Jane had committed suicide the previous morning. It seems that after her children left for school she went into her garage, got into her car, started the engine, and let it run until she died from asphyxiation. Unfortunately, her children found her when they returned home from school that afternoon. Jane had been dying while the Director of Nursing and I were feeling annoyed with her. I was stunned, and I knew the Director was, too.

I don't know if there were tears in that moment, but I know they came later. I went back to work that day and went through all the motions necessary to make things happen, but my thoughts were on Jane. I wondered what on earth could have been so terrible in her life that would make her want to end it. I wondered if my attitude contributed to whatever deep sadness she had felt. I knew logically that I had played no part in her death, but it didn't feel like that. I sat in my car that evening before going home, thinking of Jane. And the tears came. I cried for her loneliness. I cried for her children. I cried for all those people who are hurting and cannot be comforted. I cried for myself – for my selfishness, for my careless judgment, for my mean spirit. And I vowed to remember Jane and the best lesson she ever taught – that you can never, ever know what people are going through. Sometimes, they are in a private hell that you know nothing about. Many years have passed since that day. Yet Jane is still there reminding me quietly to grant grace to others – no matter what things look like from the outside because you really just don't know…

Heartbreak

Trying to describe heartbreak is nearly impossible. It is invisible, and yet it is a physical pain that can be felt as palpably as a broken arm – only it's right there in the center of your chest – an ache that cannot be healed. The poet Edna St. Vincent Millay once soulfully mourned, *"Time does not bring relief; you all have lied who told me time would ease me of my pain!..."*

The first I knew of heartbreak was at the death of my Grampa when I was seven. I could not imagine the world without him in it, and there was surely a hole in my heart filled entirely by my sadness. Leon Bloy said, *"Man has places in his heart which do not exist, and into them enters suffering, in order that they may have existence."* I certainly believe that very thing happened to me on that day.

All of us have them – those places in our hearts that come about because of heartbreak. Mostly, it happens when we lose those we love. When my dog Lollipop died suddenly, leaving me without warning after she had walked me to the other side of an empty nest, that place felt windswept and barren.

Sometimes, heartbreak happens when our dreams are shattered or we lose our way. That happened to me as a young girl of seventeen. The pain of it was almost too much to bear. I would swear I could hear the sound of fine crystal breaking into a million pieces, and there wasn't enough glue in the world to mend all that brokenness. My heart was never the same. I wondered at times if my heart was no longer the traditional red machine pumping to keep me alive but instead was lying bruised and purple inside my chest, just barely doing its job, threatening to give up at any moment. I was only alive on the outside, carrying on as if it mattered.

I have often imagined that heartbreak smells like wet leaves in Autumn. And perhaps it looks like purple liriope blooming and sadly singing the end of summer. Or perhaps like broken eggs in an abandoned nest – surely Robin's egg blue.

Heartbreak is intangible, and yet it is a real thing. And that thing can feel quite substantial, certain, and perceptible. Physiologically speaking, the stress hormone cortisol can actually flood the body and cause that heavy, achy feeling in your chest. Also, there is a real diagnosis called "Broken Heart Syndrome," which the Mayo Clinic reports is temporary and treatable, and further claims that the syndrome usually reverses itself in days or weeks. But I suspect that whoever came up with that medical diagnosis et al., had never had someone break their heart. My favorite actress, Bette Davis, proclaimed, *"Pleasure of love lasts but a moment. Pain of love lasts a lifetime."*

The real danger of heartbreak is BECOMING the heartbreak itself. I think that happens to people sometimes. Remember Miss Havisham from Charles Dickens' novel, "Great Expectations" - the old spinster, once jilted at the altar, who lived for years in her yellowing wedding dress surrounded by her moldy wedding cake and cobwebs? As I languished at seventeen, I envisioned that I would become something like her. Fortunately, I survived and eventually recovered - although it drastically changed the trajectory of my life. But isn't that the way of all things? Every single thing that happens to us in life influences our decisions and the road we take. I took the pain of my heartbreak with me for many years, and I think, ultimately, that worked out best for me. I have been left to agree with the poets Teasdale and Tennyson. Sara Teasdale penned these words: *"It is strange how often a heart must be broken before the years can make it wise."* And Alfred Lord Tennyson reminded me often: *"Tis better to have loved and lost than never to have loved at all."*

Healing

During my years as a nurse, I became interested in alternative and complementary methods of healing. I explored energy work as well as massage therapy. What I found on this journey was more than I ever expected and filled with uniquely rich experiences. One of them was particularly powerful……but I will come to that in a minute.

Massage has many benefits and is much underrated, in my view. Here's a list of its perks:

- Improved circulation
- Decreased muscle stiffness
- Decreased joint inflammation
- Improved quality of sleep
- Improved flexibility
- Strengthened immune response
- Lower stress levels
- Encourages relaxation
- Improves mood
- Increases energy
- Provides a feeling of general well-being

Massage therapy is often part of a medical treatment plan to help patients return to their daily activities. It is specifically used after joint replacement surgery or injuries. Here are some specific conditions that massage can help – and, yes, I saw folks for all these reasons:

- Anxiety and/or depression
- Digestive disorders
- Fibromyalgia
- Headache
- Insomnia
- Nerve pain
- Postoperative pain
- Scar tissue
- Soft tissue strains and injuries

After graduation from a massage therapy school and while continuing to work as a nurse part-time, I began to work part-time as a massage therapist as well. At first, I worked out of a doctor's office one day a week. Eventually, I rented my own space and only accepted clients from local doctor referrals or word of mouth. And this kept me busy. Some people came once and either didn't like it, or they thought they were "fixed," and I never saw them again. Some came several times and then stopped coming when they felt better. Some folks became regular clients.

As with everything else in life, there were varying opinions, misunderstandings, misinformation, and suspicions that I encountered on a regular basis in regard to massages. Despite its clear health benefits, massage has a somewhat shady association with women of ill repute. So there's that. There's also the fact that people generally feel uncomfortable in a situation where they are lying down and naked. Many people are not comfortable in their own skin – not to mention having some stranger touch them. I did what I could to put my clients at ease, and I was always cognizant that people have beliefs and experiences that I would not be aware of, but that might affect their ability to be open to massage therapy. When clients arrived nervous and unsure, I was always glad for them when they were able to relax, enjoy the session, and participate in their own healing journey.

The story I wish to relay to you is about a woman I will call Gloria for the purpose of this story. Gloria was one of those people who would have <u>never</u> given one single thought to massage in her regular life. Gloria was a country girl born and bred. She believed in hard work and taking care of things on her own. She was not given to luxury, imaginings, or flights of fancy. Gloria had not changed her hairstyle or her job since high school graduation. She went to church every Sunday and took good care of her daddy. She was capable and strong but reserved and shy. She also knew pain was a part of life and was not likely to complain about it. But life had given her more than her share, and she came to me out of sheer desperation. I happened to meet Gloria because her sister had been referred to me post-surgery, and the sister had suggested that Gloria call me.

When Gloria called to schedule an appointment, she told me that she had sustained a shoulder injury that required surgery and many weeks of physical therapy. She also told me that her surgeon and the physical therapists were "done with" her. All these aforementioned medical professionals had told her that she had recovered as well as could be expected from her injury and that she should accept that. However, Gloria was disappointed with her recovery and unhappy with their prediction. In fact, I would say that she was angry – although Gloria would never have admitted that. I agreed to see her but was concerned that I could not give what she was looking for – especially since she had been released from her surgeon's care as well as physical therapy. In Gloria's view, "they just gave up on me".

To say that I was unprepared for what I encountered on her arrival would be an understatement. In fact, I was totally stunned. Gloria was a waif-like woman who looked for all the world like a wounded animal seeking shelter from a storm. And the storm raged within and all about her. Gloria had fallen from a set of steps about four feet in height onto a concrete pad, where she landed directly on the shoulder of her dominant arm. The bone literally had been crushed, and how it had been repaired at all was nothing short of a miracle, which had included surgical skill along with the use of rods and pins. Her range of motion was extremely limited. She certainly couldn't lift her arm over her head. In fact, she couldn't lift her arm shoulder-high. The most she could manage was a few degrees of motion. She could barely lift the weight of her injured arm and mostly moved it with the aid of her other arm. The most distressing of all was that she was in tremendous pain with any movement whatsoever. Even touching her arm would trigger involuntary muscle spasms and severe nerve pain. I'd never seen anything like it. Even so, Gloria refused pain medicine because it clouded her thinking. She attempted to be stoic, which I suspected was her usual M.O. but when the pain gripped her, she winced uncontrollably, and her facial expressions betrayed her despite her best effort.

After my initial intake and a careful examination, I agreed to do what I could, but I couldn't promise her anything. I walked out of the room to allow her to undress the best she could and get onto the massage table. As I stood outside the door, I was awash with fear and doubt. I could not think how I would even begin to touch someone so broken and in such obvious pain. I closed my eyes, gave myself up completely to the All That Is, and breathed silently, "Please, just don't let me hurt her." When I walked back into the room, she was sitting on the table because she could not lie down without triggering severe muscle spasms. I propped her up with pillows. When her spasms had calmed, and she seemed fairly comfortable – or at least what was possible for her - I moved to her head and laid my hands gently on her head, mostly because I couldn't think what else to do. I stilled myself, and from that stillness, I breathed a prayer that had no words – for there were none to be found.

Neither are there words for how I moved forward. I can remember placing my hands above her injured arm – above it, not touching, just feeling its erratic energy and the heat radiating from it. More wordless prayers poured from somewhere, and the session continued. What actually happened is – even now – a mystery to me. I had the profound knowing that this poor soul's heart had been utterly broken, and I had a sense of holding something fragile and sacred. When I came to myself, I noted that the allotted time for our session was done. My face was wet with tears that I did not know I had shed. And I saw that tears were streaming down Gloria's face as well. Somehow, I understood these tears were not from physical pain.

I told her quietly that our session was over and asked if I could assist her to a sitting position before I left the room. She nodded "yes" and I helped her sit up. I asked if she was okay and she nodded once again "yes" although she continued to weep. I stepped out of the room to allow her some privacy. When I returned, she was wiping tears that seemed to still be falling and so I just stood still and quietly. After a little while she said, "I need to tell you something." And from that place she proceeded to tell me that she had a son who had died from a brain tumor the year before.

He had been a young man, barely twenty years old, bright, handsome, and full of energy. She had raised him as a single mom and they shared a close bond. When he got sick, she cared for him tirelessly until he had died in her arms. Although this was the first I knew of this sad story, it did not surprise me and I understood the knowing that had come to me of her broken heart. But I did not say this to her. Gloria sat quietly for a minute and then spoke very slowly and carefully, as if she were trying out the words to see what they sounded like, "I know this might sound crazy but while I was on your table, I saw my son. He came toward me and wrapped me in his arms – only they were wings."

I gave her a minute to hear her own words, and then I said, "That doesn't sound crazy. It sounds like that is exactly what needed to happen." And Gloria agreed.

After that day, Gloria came regularly for over a year and, little by little, she slowly improved. First the painful muscle spasms stopped happening. Gradually, her range of motion increased – inch by inch. She shared each bit of progress with me gleefully, and we rejoiced together. Gloria was gracious in her praise of my work. Still, I knew – as sure as I had ever known anything in my life - that her rehabilitation was not my doing. I was only a conduit through which this healing was being given.

Gloria arrived one day in December, and after her session, she announced, "I have a present for you." Then she handed me a beautiful Thank You card with a gracious sentiment and her signature. I read the card through tears, and when I looked up, she said, "The present is inside the envelope." I opened the envelope wider, and there inside was a slender, rectangular piece of folded paper – the paper was the kind people use for making grocery lists. As I unfolded it, Gloria said, "I made a list of all the things I can do now that I couldn't do before I came to see you." The list read:

- Mow my grass
- Rake the yard
- Sweep the kitchen
- Mop the floors

- Put my canning pot on the stove
- Stir a pot of soup
- Reach up into my cabinets
- Reach onto the top of my refrigerator

No gift could have held more meaning. I was humbled by her gratitude and by the simple grandeur of her gift. I knew that she saw herself as healed and whole. I also knew I wouldn't be seeing her again.

I receive a Christmas card from Gloria every year, and she tells me that she is well, which makes me happy. I will never forget her. She taught me more about healing than any course in nursing school ever could.

Chapter 11

Just Because

Needles and Pins

You'd think I'd like to sew, seeing as all the women in my family liked to sew AND were good at it. To my mother's great disappointment, I did not follow in their footsteps. And let me tell you – they were some impressive footsteps. My mother's mother was a legend. The woman not only sewed – she also smocked, appliqued, monogrammed, embroidered, tatted, crocheted, knitted, and hooked rugs! There was nothing this woman couldn't do. She had five daughters, and all of them inherited her love of needlework as well as some of her other skills. These women loved to sew, talk about sewing, share sewing tips, and Lord! They loved to go to fabric stores. They could spend hours there.

My dad's mother also sewed, tatted, and quilted. Gramma loved her treadle sewing machine – she never upgraded to an electric model. Her steadfast theory was, "If it ain't broke, don't fix it." She had seven daughters – all sewed, although some did more than others.

I have all this love of sewing, all kinds of needlework, and accomplished women standing behind me. I also sleep under quilts made by my grandmothers as well as Afghans and throws made by my aunts and mother. I have drawers full of tatted doilies, crocheted covers, and tablecloths. I even have a gorgeous bedspread crocheted with tobacco twine by my great aunt. I treasure every one of these items. And I am genuinely impressed by such handiwork. Even so, I do not like to sew, nor have I ever mastered any other needlework skill. Now, that's not to say that I *can't* sew. And on several occasions, I have crocheted a long strand of something not worth mentioning. I can and have embroidered a few things – a couple of those projects are framed and hanging in my house as proof. But did I enjoy doing it? No. I did not. In fact, I hated every single stitch. Of course, when I was working furiously on each of these various projects, I would have never admitted that. I was naive and thought I was supposed to enjoy it – it was a thing that women did - so what was wrong with me that I didn't? "Shhhhh," I'd think, "just keep going." Somehow, I thought I'd learn to like it if I kept at it. That didn't happen.

I don't know when my mama started doing needlework as a young girl or when she first expressed an interest in it. Still, when I had not done either by the time I was in high school, Mama thought I should enroll in Home Economics. You may be surprised to know that I LOVED Home Ec class. I got to hang around all my girlfriends and talk and laugh and generally have a grand time. Our teacher, Miss Palmer, was as sweet as she could be – an old maid with no children of her own, and she seemed to adopt all of us. She tolerated our immaturity, effervescence, teasing, and mischief-making. We, in turn, adored her. If we were "good" all week – and, somehow, she always deemed that we were – she would allow us to cook during our Friday class, which was always delightful fun for everyone – including Miss Palmer, who tested and tasted our dishes and always proclaimed them "delicious!"

If you were paying attention, you would note that I said, "I LOVED Home Ec class." Just that. The class. The sewing part? Not so much. It's not that I couldn't do it. I simply had no patience for it. When you are making a dress, for example, you lay out the pattern pieces on the fabric and pin each one. Then, you cut out each piece and begin the task by "basting" the pieces together – which means that you use long, loose stitches to temporarily tack the garment together to see how it fits. You might see that it needs adjustment as you move along in the process. This involves endless trying things on. It also means getting stuck by a few pins along the way – and that unpleasant side effect only adds to my general irritation. And then, of course, there are countless hurdles that require particular precision – like putting on a waistband, making buttonholes, attaching sleeves, putting in a zipper, or lining the garment with a soft, silky material to make the wearing more comfortable. Miss Palmer required us to make a skirt, a pair of slacks, and a dress during our year of Home Ec. My skirt was a simple woolen straight skirt with a waistband and zipper. Well, simple for most people – not for me. I was in a lather by the time the hateful thing was finally finished, and my very kind teacher did most of the work since my waistband would have been a wadded mess if left to me. The zipper? Ay, yi, yi!!!! I put it in and took it out so many times that Miss Palmer took pity on me and just did it herself. But in my mind, I checked that requirement off and moved on to the next item on my list.

I don't know what I could have been thinking when I was in the Fabric Store with Mama looking for slack material. Still, clearly, something took hold of my good sense – or maybe my mama's excitement was infectious – or maybe I was taken over by an alien - like those characters in the movie "Invasion of the Body Snatchers." Whatever it was, I walked out of that store with a slack pattern, and not one but TWO pieces of cloth to make not one but TWO pairs of slacks – one was to be navy blue, the other a lovely Carolina sky blue. Clearly, I had completely forgotten the skirt fiasco! Or the alien inhabiting my body LIKED to sew. Who knows? And, to boot, this fabric was very special and expensive. The world had just come out with something called "bonded wool," which meant that one side of the material was woolen, but the other side was soft and had a satin-like sheen to it, which eliminated the need to line the otherwise scratchy fabric. As I laid out and pinned the pattern onto each piece of fabric, Mama cautioned me to be very careful. I shrugged off her concern and set about cutting. After the basting, I held up each pair of slacks, eyed them, and thought they looked too big for me. So, with all the confidence of a seamstress with years and years of experience (or a crazed alien body snatcher), I cut each pant leg to what I deemed the right size. When my mother came in and saw that I had cut down one pair of pants and was whacking away at the second, she asked me if I had tried them on. Nope. Nor had I even bothered with another round of pinning and basting. Mama nearly fainted dead away, then she grimly announced, "Linda, if you have ruined that material, I'm going to….." She didn't even finish the sentence. She was so enraged that she just whirled around and left the room. Would you like to venture a guess as to what happened next? Well, if you thought I had ruined those slacks – you would be wrong. By some miracle (or alien superiority), I had judged precisely right. When I had them all sewn up, they fit perfectly! My mother shook her head in amazement and declared me the luckiest girl she ever knew. And she was right.

Furthermore, whatever miracle unfolded continued as I managed the waistband and the zippers as if I were an experienced seamstress. Perhaps for one brief moment, all the skills of my ancestors were magically bestowed on me. At the time, I was full of youthful arrogance. Still, looking back, there is simply no logical explanation – unless, of course, it was the alien thing.

After that phenomenon, I began the dress project. I very cleverly chose a pattern with a Raglan sleeve and a simple A-line body – a fashion trend with no set-in sleeves. I selected a dark persimmon-colored wool for the fabric. My only hurdles would be the back zipper and the lining. I must have been living in some sort of supernatural glow because the whole thing came together like a dream. And I must say it earned me a lot of compliments and was one of my favorite dresses ever. Home Economics ended, and I earned an A+. I never again taunted fate. That was the end of my sewing career. My mother couldn't understand it. She reminded me now and again what a good (if not amazing) job I had done with my two pairs of slacks and my dress. I was unmoved. I knew they were simply an incredibly lucky break. Besides, I can honestly say that the only thing I clearly recall of the experience was how miserable I was while sitting at the sewing machine – how I hated every minute of it – and how relieved I was when the projects were over. I knew I would never sew for pure enjoyment. That was not a possibility for me. I always felt a little sorry about that and more than a little sad that it was not something I could enjoy together with my mama. I can remember the hundreds of times I had seen my mother sewing together with her mother – watching them lay out patterns, cutting them out, basting, sewing by hand and on a machine. They were bonded and of one mind. It is a sweet picture in my memory, but I am forever outside it. I have never shared even one tiny speck of their joy in needlework.

When it finally dawned on me that I was not required to enjoy sewing, nor did I need to force myself to do any sort of needlework, I felt freed to be my own woman. Only rarely do I even sew buttons on garments – even for my sweetly pleading husband. I figure he is perfectly capable. After all, he's an Eagle Scout – he should know how to do such things. Yet I am certainly not a needless woman – rather, I am a needle-less woman. And that is completely fine with me!

Camping

The first time I ever went camping, I was nineteen years old. My parents had moved to the Shenandoah Valley of Virginia. They soon thereafter joined the legions of locals who camped out regularly. They purchased a Cox camper –basically a tent on wheels - and became regulars. One of their favorite places was Camp Gerundo, which is located at the foot of the Massanutten Mountain Peak. It was close to their home and Daddy's job, so they could set up camp even during the week. That way, Daddy could easily drive to work, and Mama could run home during the week and do their laundry if necessary. They were excited about their newly found freedom. I was still living in North Carolina at the time, and they wanted me to join them as soon as I could get to the Shenandoah for a visit. As soon as I arrived, they packed up the camper and headed out, with me tagging along.

We arrived at the Campground, and after checking in, they set their camper up in what they said was their favorite spot. We were essentially in the woods, and all the "spots" looked the same to me, but what did I know? Daddy and Mama worked in tandem setting up the camper, a large folding table with a camp stove and assorted supplies, folding chairs, and laying out a large indoor/outdoor rug. I was the "gopher" - AKA "go-for" person – just doing whatever I was told. When they arranged everything to their liking, they each settled into a folding chair and invited me to join them – which I did. I surveyed the scene. A circle of rocks surrounded an empty space where I assumed they would build a campfire. A large picnic table on our campsite was within easy reach of the aluminum-folding table my parents had set up. Huge trees surrounded us. A soft breeze rustled the leaves as birds fluttered about, chirped, and sang. Occasionally, I caught a brief glimpse of a squirrel or chipmunk moving on the ground or the trees. I could hear other campers chatting or laughing at their campsites while others were just getting set up. The day was pleasant. The mountain air was fragrant with laurel blooms.

We sat quietly, enjoying the day. And we sat. And we sat. Until I ventured to ask, "Now, what do we do?"

My parents laughed and said, "We're doing it."

"You mean this is it? This is camping?" I asked.

"Yes. This is it. What did you expect?" they returned.

"Well, I don't know. I thought we'd chop firewood or something." I shrugged. They laughed, and my daddy said,

"You can go gather sticks if you want to, but we buy firewood down at the camp store."

Oh, my. I sat there wondering what I had really expected from the adventure. Somewhere in the recesses of my mind, I had pictured folks with backpacks and hiking gear. And I am sure there are many of those people around the country, but as with everything else in life, there are degrees and preferences. My parents had discovered the art of just being – which I have learned some folks never manage. Later, I discovered that I could hike at this Campground or swim in the nearby lake.

There was also singing some evenings if you wanted to participate or just listen. Sometimes, there was music – usually guitar. Sometimes, there was marshmallow roasting or making s'mores (a roasted marshmallow placed on top of a square of chocolate seated on a graham cracker and gooey and delicious). There was also ghost-story telling and general shenanigans. Mostly, it was delightful.

The bathroom situation was lackluster, in my opinion. There was a bathhouse that provided toilets and showers. They were clean and well-kept, but still, it's a public place – and even with the privacy measures......well, like I said, it's a public place. So, think about that. And there's the having to go to the potty in the middle of the night. You must take a flashlight because you need to watch where you're stepping on account of uneven ground, rocks, sticks, and the like – not to mention snakes. And then there's the rain factor when you have to go to the bathroom <u>with</u> an umbrella. And you have to go with an umbrella <u>AND</u> a flashlight, if it's the middle of the night. And for you folks who have never been camping, let me point out that at night in the woods, it is REALLY dark – meaning you can't see your hand in front of your face, literally – unless there's a full moon – in which case it's eerily beautiful. So there's that.

I guess you could say that I mostly liked camping, but it had its downside, in my opinion. So, I was still a fan when, some years later, I was married, and my husband and I thought it would be fun to go camping at the beach for a summer vacation. My parents were generous people and were happy for us to borrow their camper for the trip. Another young couple joined us, and off we went to a beach on the Carolina coast.

The campsite could not have been more perfect – well, except for a few things. We had a splendid view of the sound that provided breathtaking sunrises and sunsets. There were no campers in close proximity, so we had a great deal of privacy. Otherwise, the points to consider when camping at the beach are: (1) there is an over-abundance of sand – which seeps into every possible crevice, be it people, clothing, food, or tents (2) it is VERY hot, and shade is a minimum, and where it is available there are bugs of every variety waiting to bite and sting and annoy the hell out of you. The ocean breeze was both a relief and a villain. It brought deliverance from the heat, but it also carried thousands of grains of sand.

The vacation began well enough. Our first meal on the evening fire was a salmon stuffed with shrimp and crabmeat wrapped in foil and baked to perfection. The wine was nice, and the evening ended in a mellow glow. The morning dawned with the sounds of groaning and grunting and giggles that I slowly realized were the couple in the double bed on the other side of the camper – not ten feet from ours - engaging in sex. I nudged my husband, who was already awake and alert to the activity. He put a finger to his lips and shook his head to silence me. I mean, what in the world was I going to say? Lord, have mercy! Now, I don't want to come off sounding like a prude here. But, I mean, really! Ya know? I tried putting my pillow over my head, but it was too warm to do that for long.

I was in misery. And however long it lasted was too long. As soon as they were quiet, my husband and I exited the camper. Neither of us said a word about the ill-timed morning activity. The other couple smiled smugly at one another throughout the day, and it annoyed me no end. You'd think once would have been enough, but oh, no! They decided to "take a nap," and you can just guess what happened. But the joke was on them because inside a tent at the beach in the middle of the afternoon is <u>not</u> cool. So, we left the apparent sex addicts to entertain themselves and sweat while we found some cool shops that were cool, mostly because they had air conditioning, which we found preferable to the nearly unbearable heat. To say that our vacation was miserable would be an understatement. I can never think of camping at the beach without feeling a big fat "NO" coming unbidden up my throat and my head shaking "No-No-No" emphatically.

Lots of my relatives enjoy camping. My Aunt Dorothy and Uncle Earl were among them. They started tent camping and graduated to a travel trailer. This adventurous pair traveled all over the United States, exploring America, meeting people, and generally having a good time. They had two granddaughters, and their gift to each of them for their sixteenth birthday was a camping trip across the country in the summer after school. I always enjoyed being with my aunt and uncle, and I am sure those girls had a blast. And what a wonderful memory to have of time spent with your grandparents. I say this from the particular personal experience of my own children because when my daughter and son came along, my parents took them on many camping trips that they remember fondly.

My husband and I agreed that taking our children camping was a good experience for them. We also thought it would be an affordable vacation for our family. My husband had been an Eagle Scout, so he had outdoor skills, and I trusted his abilities. We purchased a small tent and went camping at a nearby State Park. After we had set up camp, we explored one of the hiking trails and then rowed around the lake. We built a campfire, cooked Hobo Stew, and roasted marshmallows. We enjoyed stargazing before settling down for the night. It had been a picture-perfect day. Unfortunately, the next morning was not.

As I tried to sit up, my back screamed in pain. Uh-oh. I had experienced some back troubles after the birth of my children. Hence, the pain was not out of the ordinary, but it was unexpected. Eventually, I was able to roll onto my side and get onto all fours, whereupon I crawled gracelessly out of the tent on my hands and knees. I made it to the nearby picnic table, where I was able to pull myself up onto the bench, grunting like a bear as I did so. I thought my back would get better after getting up, but alas! It did not. Our camping adventure came to an end before Noon that day, and it was many days before my back recovered. I knew that my days of sleeping on the ground were over. Since that time, I have contemplated tent camping, but I knew I'd need to make other arrangements for sleeping if I were to survive it. Procrastination set in.

Time passed. Our tent rotted away in its box. More time passed. My husband and I considered purchasing a small camper for our retirement years. Time passed. Our retirement years have arrived. And we have given up the romantic notion of camping. I have come to accept that I am not really into public showers, public bathrooms, or bugs – and most especially bears. I admire folks who camp – whether they do it in a tent or one of those fancy campers. I imagine their adventures with a sigh and in the glow of a setting that would rival the Garden of Eden. In my imagination, there are no bugs or bears or rain, and nobody has to pee in the middle of the night.

The Clothesline Incident

One summer, some years ago, my parents lived in a duplex apartment a few doors down from my family. Out-of-town relatives came to visit the both of us for the weekend. The number of visitors overflowed our guest accommodations, so my daddy set up their Cox Camper in our side yard to make room for everyone. For those of you who might not know - a Cox Camper is basically a large tent on wheels, and this particular camper held two large double beds so everyone had a comfy place to sleep. The weekend was grand, and after the crowd had gone, my husband and I relaxed in a pair of lawn chairs that evening, enjoying the quiet. Suddenly, there was shouting and indefinable loud noises from our next-door neighbor's house. It seemed the noises and shouting came first from the front door and then from the back. The sounds would quiet momentarily and then resume. After a time, a squad car appeared with flashing blue lights, and a couple of policemen went to their front door.

Our neighbors at that time were a couple about our age that I will call Donna and Denny – friendly and usually reserved. However, Denny was known to overindulge on occasion, and sometimes turbulence ensued. He moved out and then in again on a regular basis. And sometimes, the cops came to visit. We did not have easy visibility of the goings on there. We were usually on the periphery of whatever took place, with only a vague sense of whether the weather was foul or fair. On this particular night, we had a nearly ringside seat and fell prey to curiosity. We repositioned ourselves quietly into the convenient camper for cover. We lay down on the large bed with an advantageous window to secretly spy on the unfolding scene.

The police presence brought a few loud and angry words from inside their house, but soon things seemed calm, and the police drove away with no passengers, so we assumed all was well. But not for long. The back door burst open, and Denny spilled out and onto the porch, stumbled down the stairs, and was propelled into the yard, muttering to himself, clearly still angry. In the blindness of his rage, compounded by the unfamiliar darkness, he was completely oblivious to the clothesline directly in his path, and his neck met the wire at such a velocity that his body flew into a perpendicular line – his feet and head on the same latitude – and for a split second his entire body was suspended horizontally about 5 feet in midair. It was pure slapstick comedy at its best – like a cartoon come to life! Only we didn't dare laugh aloud - owing to Denny's current state of anger and inebriation. Instead, we convulsed into laughter as quietly as possible - clamping hands over our mouths. Denny's midair suspension was only momentary, and he landed with a great thud onto his back. This setback only fueled his drunken fury. He sputtered and growled and rolled around on the ground for a time but eventually managed to right himself. Weaving and cursing, he grabbed his clothesline nemesis with both his hands and commenced to try with all his might to tear it out of his way. Denny had not considered that whoever installed this clothesline had permanence in mind. The line was made of wire, and the wooden posts had been encased in cement. That clothesline wasn't going anywhere, and it held its ground as solidly as any gallant knight on horseback. It allowed Denny some leeway but, in the end, insisted on holding its firm position. It took Denny with it, hurling him to the ground a second time – much less gracefully than on his first trip down. You'd think the humiliation would have made Denny give up, but I suppose he determined that he wasn't going to be beaten by something so mundane and ordinary as a clothesline. With an animal yowl, he rose again to do battle with the dastardly clothesline. This time, he widened his stance, grasped the clothesline with bear-like paws, and proceeded to yank forward and backward with strong hurling motions, cursing all the while. His movements only succeeded in setting the wire into an equally strong gyroscopic motion that sent Denny into a spinning free-fall backward, where he came to another tremendous thud onto his back and was left looking up haplessly into the night sky. Being utterly and supremely defeated by a clothesline was more than Denny could bear. He howled and cursed some more and then dragged himself up to standing. He swayed and lurched toward the clothesline but thought better of launching another attack this time and made his way warily around the post to an unsuspecting outbuilding where he kept tools and whatnot. My husband and I stuffed pillows into our mouths to stifle our laughter. We listened to Denny hurl tools and swear words around the toolshed until, at long last, his tirade subsided. Eventually, he shuffled out of the shed, mumbling with much less energy. Considerably subdued, he moved on down the street into the night. The clothesline had won. The end. The show was over. We closed the camper and went to bed. The next morning, that clothesline stood quietly and unassuming as usual. But there were a few people a bit wiser about the power of that clothesline than they'd been the day before.

Over the years, when something or other has triggered our memory of the clothesline incident, my husband and I can see the whole scene replay itself in our minds. And this time, we laugh right out loud.

Ode to Tortellini

August 2nd, 2013, was one of the worst days of my life. I ran over my old cat, Tortellini. It was awful, and I felt as if I owed her some tribute for her years on the planet. This is what I wrote the very next day after I was able to somewhat collect myself:

Tortellini has lived at our house for 18 years. For at least 17 of those years, she has hung out in our carport at her pleasure. She ate, napped, and lounged as she pleased. Whenever we arrived home, she leisurely moved out of the way of our car -- so leisurely, in fact, that we would have to pull in very, very slowly – to encourage her to move along. Sometimes, this was a source of amusement to us. Sometimes, if we were in a hurry, it was an annoyance. She didn't seem to know the difference – nor did she care. She just moved at her own pace………but she always moved. For some reason, yesterday – even though I was in no particular hurry -- she did not move along. I saw her lying there, pulled up to the edge of the carport, and waited patiently, following our prescribed pattern – our human/cat dance. Finally, slowly pulling up onto the pad and thinking she was rising, stretching, doing her cat-thing. When I realized that she had not risen, I came completely undone.

I am left now to wonder what happened. Why didn't she get up as she's done 1,000 times before? Had she been hurt and was unable to get up? Had she been hit by a car? Had she been in the process of dying from old age? Are these only questions that I ask myself in order to rationalize the awfulness of what I've done? I will never know. All I know is that she is gone from this world, gone from our lives and that she will be missed.

Tortellini came to live at our house on Judd Street in the Fall of 1995, about a week after I stood in our yard, hands on hips, and proclaimed to the Universe: "We need a cat!" -- because we were being overrun with squirrels. I really meant it. I was irritated by the bodacious attitude of the haughty creatures who practically knocked on our door to demand that we fill up the bird feeders for them. Those words left my lips and evidently went directly to God's ear. No more than a week passed when a mangy, thin, tortoise-shell-colored cat showed up on the edge of our yard. She was cautious but hungry and clearly looking for food. We set out a bowl of milk for her as she peered from behind a bush and waited for us to leave. She lapped it eagerly after we were out of sight. We left a bowl for her every day for a week. She would wait until we were out of sight and then slink over to the bowl and eat like a poor beggar. We peeked at her through our kitchen window and wondered where she'd come from. She figured we were a food source, and we figured she had run out of luck. By the end of that first week, we bought cat food. Six weeks later, her fur was looking better, and she stopped running to hide when we walked outside. A week after that, she brought five kittens to show us.

The kittens were more than we had bargained for, but we didn't have the heart to do anything more than admire her babies. She was clearly proud of them, and who doesn't enjoy watching kittens play? Besides, her brood was unique among cat litters. All five of them were very different – not a single one alike. One kitten was a boy with short, solid black fur. Another male had long black fur with a small speck of white at his throat. The third boy was a perfectly marked seal point Siamese that could have been sold as a pure bred. The remaining two kittens were girls – one a beautifully marked calico and the other a tortoise-shell, like her mother, but with long, fluffy hair. They were a fascinating sight!

No wonder she was so proud. Even so, we were realistic and knew that six cats could easily turn into sixty. So, we trapped them one by one and had them spayed and neutered. Tortellini was the first to visit the clinic. The vet said, "If that poor cat could talk, she would thank you. Her poor old body is worn out from giving birth. There is no telling how many litters of kittens she's had." We figured she was old and that she would live out the few years she had left with us. Who knew that would stretch out for 18 years? The vet didn't offer us an estimate of her age that day. Now,

I wish she had so that I could register a good guess about how old she actually was. Was she 20 years old? (which would have meant she was 2 years old when she arrived on Judd Street) Or was she older than that?

During the 18 years that she lived on Judd Street, Tortellini claimed our yard – all of it – as her domain. She lounged on the carport, the front porch, in my herb garden, on our patio, on the patio furniture, on the stone bench by our pond, or under the grapevine. She dared any dog we owned to chase her or even to disturb her chosen space in any way. Our old cairn terrier, a cat hater extraordinaire, would snarl and growl at her, but he kept a respectful distance. She flaunted our rules in his face – as we forbade him to bark or snap at her, she would wind herself around him – looking demurely at us and glancing back at him with (what I'm sure was) a smirk on her face. He would try to look taller as he indignantly ignored her. It was hilarious. Our sweet Sheltie she clearly adored and would allow herself to be gently herded about the back yard. Tortellini opened her eyes after a nap on the stone bench by our pond and stared down our hound mutt. Then, she stretched out her paw and leisurely extended her claws – just a lazy threat before closing her eyes and going back to her nap. The hound decided she wasn't going to be any fun to chase, and that was the end of that.

Tortellini remained the Eternal Feline Matriarch. She ate out of her own bowl at feeding time – occasionally allowing one of her children to share her bowl. At other times, she would smack their intruding whiskers, reminding them that she was still THE Cat Queen. Her children, even as adults, sought her attention. She continued to bathe, caress, and reprimand them as she chose.

Tortellini wore an old face all the years I knew her. Her eyes always seemed tired but wise to the ways of the world. I sensed she had seen things and been places that were not nice, not pleasant, not good. I liked to think she was happy living on our corner. Sometimes, I felt that she could look right into my soul. It was as comforting as it was unnerving. I believe she came to 119 West

Judd Street because I invited her. After all, I needed a cat. And she kept her end of the bargain. The squirrels stopped knocking on our windows and demanding we fill the bird feeders. In fact, they kept their distance – staying respectfully in their trees and out of our windows. Her hunting skills diminished the voles that damaged our lawn and kept the number of mice to Zero. She left us occasional presents – a squirrel's tail, blue jay feathers, a vole. We were careful to never let her see us throw these gifts in the trash. We knew that they were trophies and signs of respect. We also knew that they were especially precious coming from an old hunter who had known hunger and want.

I will miss seeing her around in her old haunts – especially those where she languidly soaked up sunlight to warm her orange-brown fur and peer at me from her regal yellow eyes. I hope she has reincarnated to another of her nine lives -- a life in which she doesn't owe a human being a single thing. She deserves a good life, a fine life -- because she has paid her debt and then some.

Chapter 12

A Matter of Perspective

Xs & Os

I recently learned that my ex-husband passed away. The news struck me like a stone. My feelings were a strange mix, my sadness multi-layered, and all of it took me down a road I had not traveled for a very long time.

My ex-husband, Brent, found me at a time in my life when my heart had been completely broken and my self-confidence shattered. I was deeply depressed, taking too many risks and making unhealthy choices. Brent came along and became a steadying influence. He was smart, confident, and a popular guy on campus. He was as charming as he was aloof, drove a hot car, was a total card shark, pool hustler, skilled chess player, and impressively well-read. I'd never known anyone like him, and I found him intriguing. When he asked me out, I was surprised and flattered.

He swept me into his circle of friends, who were the most varied group of folks belonging to any young man I knew. His crowd included childhood friends, fraternity brothers, locals from an out-of-the-way beer joint and pool hall, a wounded Vietnam veteran, a sweet family who owned a small grocery, a curmudgeonly newsstand owner, a nice lady who owned a hobby shop, an elderly watchmaker, and an old lady who needs her own fairy tale simply because her name was Polly Peterfish. Brent was a constant surprise and an amazing fellow. I wish we had just stayed friends because he was someone fun to know, and he cherished his friends. But it's hard to remain friends when your marriage has fallen apart.

I refuse to paint him as a bad guy, although I confess that I did at first – mostly because it kept me from looking at myself. The truth is that we both hurt each other, and we lacked clarity and maturity. It is true that Brent had quite a temper, but I pushed all of his buttons - that is for sure! Besides, I was an unacknowledged emotional wreck, and he wound up with damaged merchandise that he had no idea how to fix.

There were many things about our marriage that were good, and it warms my heart to think of them. We could talk for hours about any number of things – most especially literature. We liked the same kind of music, ranging from classical to Rock'n Roll. Brent was a huge history buff who also loved the town he grew up in and knew its history well – often regaling me with a story about its ancestors, architecture, or geography. We enjoyed spending Sundays exploring the Shenandoah Valley or the Blue Ridge Parkway. And we both loved a picnic, which we combined with those explorations. Our Friday night ritual was cooking something special – like oysters or steak – or trying a new recipe that we'd found earlier in the week. Brent had a wicked sense of humor and could make me laugh even when I didn't want to. So what happened? Honestly, there was not one simple thing that I could point to. What I am wise enough to know now is that another person cannot make you happy when you are not happy way down deep. And way deep down, I was miserable, and only I could fix that – only I didn't know that then, nor did I know how to go about it.

My actions and feelings during our marriage plagued me for years after our relationship ended. It is no wonder that one night, I had a particularly disturbing dream about Brent. The dream was charged with symbolism – including a long, winding road, mountains, a fence, signs I couldn't read, and finding my wedding ring lying on a stone wall. On waking, it was so clear and so distressing that I could not but wonder and worry that something had happened to him. I pushed down my fear and any reticence and bravely called him on the phone. I was both relieved and terrified when he answered. I took a deep breath and launched into my reason for calling him – basically, I'd had a dream that had me worrying something was wrong. As soon as the words were out of my mouth, I imagined him thinking, "yep, she's still crazy." But he surprised me by addressing me in a very gentle tone. He thanked me for calling to check on him and for thinking of him. He said that he was perfectly fine and was sorry that I'd had a bad dream but was glad that it had pushed me to call him because he had been thinking of me and wanted to know that I was doing well. He went on to say that he had long wanted to apologize for anything that he had ever done to hurt me – that he'd never meant to – that, in fact, he had loved me very much and was sorry for how things had ended. How could I not apologize for my own contribution to the downfall of our marriage? Tears flowed down my face, but it felt more like a dam breaking. We talked about where we were currently in the world, and it seemed that both of us had managed to find a life apart that was happy and good. I was never so glad to have had a bad dream and equally glad to have acted from a purely gut feeling. Our conversation had a good outcome that I believe pleased the both of us.

That phone conversation could have been the last time we ever connected. But it wasn't. Some years later, my now husband

and I took my mother to visit her sister in the Shenandoah. My husband wanted me to give him a tour of my old haunts, and that is how we ended up in Staunton, Virginia. I drove by a couple of places I had worked, beautiful Gypsy Hill Park, my old apartment, my old house, and, of course, we drove by the famous birthplace of President Woodrow Wilson – which happens to be located near Mary Baldwin College. As we drove along the beautiful tree-lined streets, I pointed it out. I mentioned that my ex-husband worked there as the Director of Computer Services. My husband said that I should go in to speak to him, and he parked the car. I thought it was funny at first, but then I realized that he wasn't joking. Then I thought to myself, "why not?" And that's how I found myself walking to the administrative buildings and asking for directions to Computer Services – which turned out to be very easy to find.

I walked into the Computer Services Department to find a sunny secretary at the reception desk asking how she could help me. I asked if the Director was in and if I could see him. She quickly buzzed his office and announced that he had a visitor. He said, "Sure," and she pointed to the door of his office. I admit that I had a moment when I thought I should run, not walk, right back to the car and skedaddle right out of town. But I bravely stepped through the door to find Brent behind a large desk, but with his back turned toward me. I checked that I was wearing a smile and tried to calm my hammering heart. Brent swiveled his chair to face me, and the minute he saw me, he leaned back, putting his hands behind his head, smiled, and said as casually as if he had just seen me the day before, "Well, hello, Darlin' – what brings you here?"

The guy was his ultimate cool self, and I remembered why I'd been attracted to him all those years ago. It steadied me, and we fell into a comfortable conversation. When he realized my current husband was outside in the car, he leaped up and said, "Well, I'd like to meet him." And that was how those two guys ended up driving around town together as if they'd been friends forever. Brent was full of historical information, of course, which delighted my husband. It was surreal. When we dropped Brent back at the college, he hugged me good-bye and whispered in my ear, "I like him." It made me laugh because, in many ways, they were so similar – it just made sense.

Brent and I connected on Facebook - which, even though his posts were rare, it allowed me to peek into his life. He lived a good life with a wife and two daughters. His daughters seemed to share his sense of humor, and I could tell they were close. I have no idea if he peeked into mine. Our connections were mostly birthday and holiday good wishes. At one point, I noticed that he and his wife had just completed a cross-country trip to the Grand Canyon some months prior to my husband and I planning our own trip out West. I emailed Brent asking for tips and his itinerary. I wasn't surprised to see that my current husband had planned almost the exact same itinerary, allowing for similar drive times and rest stops. On our return home, I reconnected with Brent by email, thanking him for his travel tips. After that, our connection resumed its regular cadence. I could always count on hearing from him on my birthday. Well, that is until last year. I noticed the absence of his greeting, but that was it. When December rolled around, I went to his page to wish him a happy birthday, and that's when I saw it. His daughters had turned his page into a Memoriam for their dad. I was shocked and sad and had a myriad of other feelings as well. I was compelled to reach out to his daughter through Facebook Messenger to express my condolences. She was sweet and gracious and clearly heartbroken. I wished I could have hugged her. There were a thousand things I wanted to say to her about her dad, but I felt I'd said what was socially acceptable. Anything more could have gone wrong.

What I can say now, without reservation, is that my first husband was a good man, and I am glad to have known him. He added to my life a rich experience that, however painful, helped me grow into the person I am now. And these days, I like myself, which certainly wasn't true all those years ago. Grieving for an ex-husband is weird, so I haven't said much until now – but I acknowledge my sadness as well as my love for him. The world is not the same without him in it. I liked thinking of him holding down his corner of it as only he could.

War Memorials

I had been seeing on the news that various people and organizations were facilitating trips to War Memorials for veterans of WWII. Every time I saw one of those news stories, I thought about my dad. He was a veteran of this war who served in the Pacific Theatre – Iwo Jima, to be exact. I wondered if he had been alive would he be interested in attending. I don't know, but I imagine not.

When my brother and I were children, we were not allowed to watch war movies on television – ever. One Sunday afternoon, my parents were not at home, and my brother and I decided to watch "The Longest Day," which was being shown on television. It was a recounting of D-Day, which starred John Wayne and other big-name celebrities. We were absorbed in the movie and surprised when my parents arrived home sooner than we had expected. Daddy walked into the room, sat in his big armchair, and began to watch the movie with us. My mother called to me from another room. I walked into the kitchen, and she whispered sharply, "I've told you not to watch war movies. Change that channel." I was uncomfortable defying my mother's wishes but said, "Mama, Daddy is watching it. I can't just go in and change the channel." My mother glared at me. I slunk back into the living room. The movie rolled on. I began to think that my mother was just being bossy because _she_ didn't like war movies. It never occurred to me that my dad did not change the channel because my brother and I were already engrossed in the movie. Unfortunately, I was more than a little ignorant. I thought the movie was wonderful. John Wayne was commanding and confident. And, of course, we would win the war. So, there would be a good ending, right? To this day, I can't answer that question in the affirmative. What happened at the end of the movie was that my dad rose from his chair, went into his bedroom, and closed the door. Even with the door closed, I could hear the awful racking sobs coming from his big chest. I was shocked and sickened by the sound. I looked at my brother's face – it registered the emotions I was feeling. I knew he felt as badly as I did, but neither of us knew what to do about it. He left the room to go where? I don't know. I went to my room and closed the door. It didn't help. I could still hear those earth-shaking sobs - they seemed to go on for an eternity. Our dinner that evening was somber and quiet. There was no congenial conversation. I could barely look at my parents. Daddy looked pale, and Mama looked worried. I was glad to be excused from the table and slither back to my room. This time there was quiet. It was twilight. I lay on my bed feeling sad and altered in a way I could not understand. It is only now that I know I had been given the understanding that my father was not immortal and, as much as I believed he was my protector, there were some things he could not protect us from. Neither my brother nor I ever had to be warned against watching war movies after that incident.

There were some things I knew about the war and my daddy. What I knew of the war came from books and History classes. As it involved my daddy, I knew from a picture that was proudly displayed at my grandparents' house. It was a glass frame with a picture of the American flag waving painted on it, and it housed a photograph of my dad standing on the beach wearing a bathing suit. His hair was thick and wet from the ocean. He was tall and broad-shouldered with a spear in one hand and a tiny fish in the other. He was clearly laughing and happy. The back story I was told by someone (not my dad): he was wounded on Iwo Jima when an enemy soldier threw a hand grenade into his company of American soldiers. Without thinking, Daddy picked up the explosive and threw it away from his companions but, in doing so, was wounded in the explosion that soon followed. Shrapnel sprayed into his face and blinded him. His family had feared the worst, but he recovered from his wounds. He was, however, left legally blind in his left eye. The picture of him with his prize fish portrayed a greater triumph than one could know without the back story. It told his parents that their son would return from the war healthy and whole, at least from outward appearance.

Daddy often regaled us with stories of his army days. But they were mostly about his days at Fort Macon, where he had risen to the rank of Master Sargent and was an instructor. Usually, the stories were funny or recounted hard work or unusual circumstances. He made friends from all over the United States – this country boy who had traveled little outside of his farming community before the war. "Join the army and see the world" was certainly true for him. He traveled North to New York, New Jersey, Pennsylvania and Maryland. He traveled West to Oklahoma, Texas, and California. He met the families of his friends and sampled cuisine very different from his mama's Southern cooking. He was proud of those adventures, and it broadened his appreciation for other ways of life. When he recuperated from his wounds in Hawaii, he declared that it was the most beautiful place he'd ever seen. But he rarely spoke of the war, and when he did, it was in a somber, quiet voice that made me be still and listen. I rarely asked questions – mostly because my mother had warned against it.

It was a rule in our house that if either my brother or I awakened during the night and wanted to enter the open door of our parents' bedroom, we must call out to them. One night, I awakened from a bad dream with my heart pounding. I leaped out of bed and ran into their bedroom. I was thinking I would go around the bed to my mother's side and crawl in with her. We all respected that Daddy rose early, worked long, hard hours, and needed rest. As I padded by the bed, I heard something whiz through the dark air, felt sharp wind close to my face, and was suddenly in the strong grip of Daddy's large hand. His voice boomed through the night, "Don't you ever come in here like that!" It scared me nearly to death. I began to cry. Daddy was at once tender and his baritone soft and repentant, "Honey, I didn't mean to scare you." He pulled me into his arms and hugged me. Then he put me beside Mama, and she held me and stroked my hair,

"Shh. It's alright." I knew it was, but I was unnerved all the same. The next day, Mama explained that when Daddy was in the war, he had learned to stay alert for noises even when he was sleeping, and that was why I should always call out to them before entering their room in the dark. In my youthful innocence, I could not truly appreciate this in the way I do now. But I had understood the momentary terror that was in the room that night, and it belonged to me as well as my dad. I never forgot it.

Over the years, I have heard men speak of the war in the presence of my father. I have heard them make remarks to my dad, trying to draw him in. But I never heard him enter such conversation. Usually, he removed himself – sometimes physically. It always made me uncomfortable for him. He was usually so congenial. He managed to avoid such conversations without embarrassing the other person or them even realizing that he was dodging the issue.

During the long years of the war in Vietnam, my dad sympathized with the soldiers who were fighting and losing their lives, as well as those who were returning home to crowds of protestors. Yet he was torn. I knew he understood those who protested the war machine and the draft. I was among them. My father was a born debater and loved a good argument. Normally, he would have taken me on. But we did not argue about these issues. And on the controversial issue of Lieutenant Calley, who was found guilty of the My Lai Massacre, he was mostly silent.

The years moved on. I forgot about war. My mind was on my children and other issues when the war began in Saudi Arabia. I had been having lunch with my parents. The television was on, and Mama and I were listening to the news about the war. I had forgotten about not watching war movies, not startling my dad in the dark of night, not talking about the war. I think my mother had, too. Mama and I were listening intently to the news. Daddy was in the next room. Suddenly, my dad was there in the room, standing nearer the television than we were. I became keenly aware of his presence and less aware of the General who was speaking on television. When the speech was over, my dad turned to us, his face sadder than I can tell, then his head bowed, and he said in a weak, trembling voice – very unlike himself, "War really is hell." He buried his face in his big hands and sobbed quietly. It had been 45 years since World War II, and still, it weighed on him so heavily that it was almost visible at this moment. I wanted to comfort him but knew that I had no power to do so. I gave him the respect of remaining quiet and still. Eventually, he went into his bedroom. Mama said he stayed there most of the rest of that day.

Not long after that, my son Alex and my nephew John (just children then) were playing a board game called WAR. Of course, they were talking about war strategies and equipment. It was an endless fascination for these cousins. They were in the living room at my parents' apartment, and I was cleaning up from lunch and could hear them talking. My dad walked into the room, and they assaulted him with questions about war equipment - tanks, rifles, and such. And then they asked him if he'd ever seen a flame thrower. He was silent for a moment. Then he spoke in that quiet voice that made them as still and intent as it had always made me, "Yes. I've seen a flame thrower. We used them on Iwo Jima to root out the Japanese soldiers who were entrenched there. I saw what happens to a man when he is hit by one. The smell of burning flesh stays in your nostrils for a long time. I hope you boys never have to see such things." Their excitement about the weapons of war was quelled. I was stunned. It was the most I'd ever heard him say about the war.

The last year that my dad lived, he was very ill in the hospital. At one point, he became unresponsive – nearly comatose. Our family stayed countless hours at the hospital. One day, I was at home getting ready to go to the hospital when the phone rang. It was one of the nurses from his unit who told me that I needed to come quickly because my father was awake but extremely agitated. I raced to the hospital. When I arrived at his unit, I learned that he was indeed awake but possibly psychotic from endless days in an intensive care unit with lights burning both night and day. He had bodily thrown a therapist from his bedside to the door of his room. Even at 80 years of age, he was as strong as a bull. He had grabbed a male nurse by the collar and lifted him off the floor. The nurse recounted the event to me and was astounded by my father's strength. When I walked into the room, he was gripping the hand of a nurse so tightly that I feared he might break her fingers. He turned to look at me, eyes flashing, and then he ordered me, "Go to the house and bring my guns. They are trying to kill me. Get your brother and Bradley. I need help." I managed to distract him, but only briefly. In the days that followed, he imagined all sorts of things, but all of them involved struggles with some unknown enemy. His doctor said he was suffering from PTSD. I wondered at this. My dad had never seemed anxious or worried. He did not drink or otherwise self-medicate. He never talked about the fighting, the battles, nothing about the war itself. Even so, I knew this diagnosis was accurate. I was humbled by the realization of what war can do to a person – even a strong, disciplined man like my father. It had scarred him deeply, but one cannot see the scars of the soul.

Once, my husband and I went to see the movie "Saving Private Ryan." It won rave reviews for its realism. It was almost too much for me. I could hardly stay in my seat. For certain, there were long periods when I closed my eyes and covered my face, but the sounds of killing, of death, of dying were not drowned out. I could not imagine being any closer. I knew for certain that had I been in any branch of the service, I would not have survived emotionally even if I had escaped the bullets and bombs. I was given a window into the world that my dad must have lived in during those terrible years of war. I gained a new appreciation for his strength of will.

When Daddy died, he was given a military burial because he had earned a Purple Heart and a Silver Star. At his request, his simple wooden casket was draped with the

American flag. After the memorial service at the church, we gathered around his casket at the cemetery. Soldiers fired a salute. Then, the air was filled with the haunting refrain of a bugle playing "Taps." The soldiers marched in unison, removed the flag from his casket, and began folding it. They were very young men, and it was soon evident that they had not had enough practice as they struggled to do it correctly. They stopped and started the folding process several times before they finally got it right. I am sure they were embarrassed. I found it amusing and had to stifle laughter. I looked at my brother, who sat beside me. He was trying not to laugh, too. We smiled at each other. We are both sure that our dad was somewhere close by, enjoying this as well. He would have had sympathy for those young men who had joined the Army to defend their country and were now struggling to maintain their dignity in this somber moment. He would have told them not to take things too seriously and not to worry because everyone makes mistakes. And he would have hoped that they would be strong and return safely home to their families. But given the choice to visit a War Memorial, I'm pretty sure he would have declined. I'm sure he had more than enough war memories. He would rather go fishing.

Floors

I began thinking about floors a few days ago. Lord! Don't ask me why such stuff comes into my head. It just does. And this is what came of that thinking.

I'll just start with the word: floor. A benign word, as words go. Usually, it is a noun, and we most immediately think of it in reference to the base of a room or the lower inside surface of a hollow structure such as a cave or a body part (like the floor of your mouth). When we talk about the ocean floor, we mean a ground surface, but when we talk about the stories of a building, we are referring to the structures that divide the building – the first floor, second floor, third floor, and so on. Yet bridges also have floors, and they aren't on the ground.

Floor is also used as a verb, for example, when a room is floored. Or when a vehicle is accelerated rapidly, as in "he floored the sports car." My favorite verb usage is the literal meaning of floor, as in "to knock or bring down," and even better when someone is floored – as in flabbergasted or dumbfounded.

And how about all the ways we use this simple word: floor lamp, floor length, floor manager, floor plan, and floor show – just for starters? And we also talk about "getting in on the ground floor" , "being on the cutting room floor"; "keeping our feet on the floor"; "having the floor", "holding the floor,"; "being floored by a punch or a statement." I have personally "cut a rug" on a few "dance floors." I also connect with the floor each morning when I do yoga – or some might just call it "floor exercise."

And speaking of floor exercise, I recently read that a floor is THE best exercise tool, and each one of us has it conveniently at our disposal. Getting down to the floor and getting up from the floor is a very good exercise in itself. If you don't think so, just try getting down to the floor and getting back up about ten times right now. See what I mean? Jon Kabat-Zin, a famous professor of medicine, author, and meditation teacher says: "Just getting down on the floor for a while…..can change your whole orientation toward the moment and the day and what is transpiring." I happen to think he's right.

I know a story I could tell you about the time I saw someone floored – literally, as in knocked down to the floor. It was a terrible sight to behold. That someone went flying up and then backward into the air, where they hit a wall and then slid unceremoniously to the floor like a wet dish rag thrown into a sink. But that is a long, sad story best left untold here. Let me just say that when I hear "he was floored," that is the picture that flashes through my mind.

Fortunately, other happier things regarding floors also came to mind during my pondering - in particular, a favorite story often told in our family. Sometime in the late 1940s, not long after WWII had ended, my parents, along with my aunt and uncle, went out for an evening of fun. None of them were married at that point in time. They were young and had survived the Great Depression and a terrible war. Celebration was in the air. On that happy night, my daddy and my Aunt Nellie (my mama's sister) stepped onto the dance floor of a nightclub and began doing a popular dance of that era -the jitterbug. Apparently, they were pretty good, or perhaps they were just performing with gusto because a crowd gathered around them and threw money as they danced. Only pennies, of course, but a penny was certainly worth more back in those days, so Daddy and Aunt Nellie stopped to pick up every coin before they left the dance floor laughing.

My parents built a house of their own sometime in the mid-1950s. My mama was delighted with the new kitchen and all its new-fangled appliances. But she was most proud of her oak hardwood floors, which were laid in every room of our house except for the kitchen. Mama took good care of them – dusting, cleaning, waxing, and polishing them often. In the early years, all that waxing and polishing was done by hand – my hands were likely as not the ones helping. The polishing was the fun part because Mama turned it into a game that included my brother and me. We each donned at least two pairs of the thick woolen socks my daddy used when he went hunting. Then, we started polishing those floors with our sock feet. It was slow going at first, but eventually, the wax smoothed out, and we could get a good slide out of our efforts. The game was over when we could slide swiftly and easily for several feet all over the floor. At least one of us would fall down during the game, but it didn't matter. We just got up and kept going. Sometimes, we just fell down laughing. It was the one chore that my brother and I never minded one bit. After some years, on a special occasion – birthday or Christmas, I forget which – my daddy bought my mama a floor buffer. Such a gift doesn't sound the least bit romantic, but it delighted my mama entirely. My brother and I didn't share her excitement because, well, it was a floor buffer, for one thing. And for another thing, we figured it sort of ended our sock-sliding fun. But then we discovered that when I was running the buffer, my little brother could hop on for quite a ride. If Mama caught me giving my brother a ride, she'd make me stop – claiming we might break her beloved floor buffer. But let me tell you right now, there was no way in the world we could have broken that monstrosity. It was all I could do to control such a powerful machine. It was a veritable tank. That thing could spin brushes and pads over those floors and leave them gleaming in no time.

Now, my mama's floors were certainly beautiful and well-maintained, but they couldn't hold a candle to my Aunt Mary's floors. Aunt Mary lived in an older house that had wide floor boards that I think were pine. They were stained dark and varnished to a gleam. Aunt Mary kept them glowing and spotless. When I tell you that you could practically see yourself in them, I'm not kidding. They were amazing. And they were the only floors that outshone my mama's.

When I was in middle school, I was fortunate to take ballroom classes. As much fun as the classes were, the highlight was the Ballroom Parties that our instructor hosted on a regular basis. The parties took place in the Lions Club building in my hometown. That dance floor was one of THE best dance floors ever – whether it was a waltz, fox trot, cha-cha, bop, or a rousing polka. You could spin and glide as easily as a skater on ice. And Shagging on that floor was heaven. The only thing better is Shagging at the beach. For those of you who might not know – especially my British friends – the Shag is a DANCE (sorry if you had something else in mind); some refer to it as the "Carolina Shag." This dance originated in the South along the Atlantic Ocean during the 1940's. Some believe its birthplace was Cherry Grove Beach, South Carolina. Others believe the term was coined in Carolina Beach, North Carolina. For sure, it is a Carolina "thing". And this Carolina girl loves to Shag. There is nothing quite like doing the Shag at a beach pavilion with sand on the floor and salt in the air.

At the North Carolina Museum of Art in Raleigh, there is a beautifully preserved Roman mosaic floor panel from the 2nd Century AD. It is composed of various types of marble and glass. The design includes geometric and floral motifs and an endless knot design, all enclosed in a braided border. I have admired it on countless visits, and the child in me wants to step on it – just because. But, of course, it is just for looking at – not for standing on. On one visit, the mosaic floor panel was not on display in its usual place. I asked a guard about it – thinking perhaps I had misremembered its placement. The guard told me that it was being cleaned because there had been a private event at the museum, and one of the guests had spilled a glass of red wine on it. Lordamercy! I'm glad I wasn't anywhere near that gala event. I can just imagine living that legend down – *did you know that Linda Griffin was at some froo-froo thing at the museum, and she spilled her wine on that ancient mosaic floor?* "No!" *"Yes, she did, and the curator has had it removed for special cleaning – well, that is if they can even GET it clean. You know how red wine stains!!!"* Whew. Fortunately, the floor panel is back in place and looking none the worse for the wine spill.

But now I want to tell you a story about a <u>kind of floor</u> AND someone who <u>got floored</u>. My Aunt Dorothy nicely combined both of these categories. One sunny summer morning in the Shenandoah Valley of Virginia, my Aunt Dorothy was late into her eighth decade of life when she most unfortunately slipped on her kitchen floor, fell, and broke her hip. My uncle was not at home when it happened, and unable to get up, she lay on the floor for several hours before he returned. This predicament could have been a bad ending for a woman of her age, but she proved to be her usual resilient self. After the doctors put her back together again, she spent a few weeks in a rehabilitation facility and returned home as good as new. Once she was home, I traveled to Virginia to visit her and found her as chipper as ever. I marveled aloud about her drastic accident and the dire circumstances that followed. I said, "Aunt Dorothy, I know you must have been scared lying there all that long time!"

She replied, quite nonchalantly, "Not really. It was a nice morning, and there was a good breeze blowing. I was glad that I had opened the windows in the breakfast room and kitchen earlier. The floor was nice and cool. We had a new tile floor put down a few months ago, and I hadn't seen the pattern up close since I picked it out. I had forgotten how pretty it was. I was glad I chose the one with those little blue flowers." I could only smile at her serene perspective and nod in agreement. Although she had landed ON the floor, I'm pretty sure she wasn't floored – literally or figuratively. I suppose this proves Jon Kabat-Zin's point, doesn't it? "Just getting down on the floor for a while…..can change your whole orientation toward the moment and the day and what is transpiring."

Lollipop

My son was moving out. Leaving home. And he was taking his two dogs with him. The thought struck me like a lightning bolt. My house would not have a dog in it. My husband and I had been married for over thirty-five years, and we had never been without a dog in our lives for any significant length of time.

When we were first married, we adopted a poor, starving dog that strayed onto our property and into our hearts. We named him Hap and thought we could save him, but he couldn't accept the kindness of strangers, and eventually, he wandered away and never returned.

After Hap's departure, we found an English Shepherd that we named Maggie Mae. She did not much like being inside and preferred to roam the neighborhood. We lived in a rental property and had no way to fence her in. But I doubt she would have tolerated such an existence. We lived in a small community where everyone knew everyone. And everyone knew Maggie. She made friends with all the neighbors and had a daily route, which led to every friendly, dog-loving soul within a mile's radius. Whether at the grocery store, gas station, or church, we were frequently apprised of her visits and how they saved treats for her – biscuits or bones or leftover stew. At length, she disappeared as well. I have always suspected that someone stole her because she was such a beautiful girl. In vain, we called and continued to look for her for many months.

When we bought our first house, we had a cat that we enjoyed. But cats can be solitary, mysterious creatures, and as much as you might love them, you always have the feeling that you are serving them – which is not the same connection you have with a dog that is always happy with your company. When we moved to our second house (which turned out to be our forever home), a friend offered our four-year-old daughter a spunky little terrier that she named Sparky. He was lively and just right for a young girl. But he was also adventurous and would often slip out of the gate and be off like a shot. On one of his forays into the neighborhood, he got into some poison, became ill, and died. It was a sad and terrible experience.

Our daughter, Whitney, mourned Sparky and wrote notes to him about how much she loved and missed him. And so, when I heard that some friends had collie puppies, I thought we should see if a puppy would cheer her. Whitney chose what appeared to be a ball of fluff and named him Scottie. His actual name (he had a real pedigree – the first ever in my life) was proclaimed to be "Whitney's Lad from Scotland." Collie puppies are full of energy, and Scottie was no different. Scottie's father, Jonathan Livingston, was the largest collie I'd ever seen – and Scottie certainly inherited that gene. Although Whitney was only five, she was a good pet owner, and she took Scottie for a walk every day to burn off some of his puppy energy (although he still chewed on everything you didn't want him to and got into trouble on a regular basis). One of our neighbors would report to me frequently, "I saw Scottie taking Whitney for a walk yesterday." And that was about the size of it. Eventually, Scottie mellowed, and he adopted all the humans in our household – guarding each of us through the night by moving from room to room and settling by each bed for a turn. When our son, Alex, was born, Scottie lay often by the crib and was intensely interested in the new human in our house. Alex learned to read with his arm around Scottie's neck as the dog sat patiently, listening to every word. When my son took to sleeping on his closet floor, Scottie allowed his huge fur coat to serve as a comforting body pillow. And once, Scottie fended off a swarming nest of angry yellow jackets as he circled my small son to take their painful stings himself. He continued barking and snapping at them until I was able to rescue little Alex from the attack. Scottie loved my children without measure. He died the summer before Whitney left for college. We had a funeral service under the grapevine in our backyard, lit incense, read Frost's "Nothing Gold Can Stay," and sang "Amazing Grace." All four grandparents, a friend of

Alex's and a friend of Whitney's, joined us in mourning him.

Whitney did not want to leave her brother alone without a dog friend, so they began to research what kind of dog might suit our family. I asked them to consider a more manageable size and less hair. They settled on a Cairn Terrier. Alex thought since the breed hailed from Scotland that it would be a nod to his beloved Scottie. Cairns are small and do not shed. We found a Cairn pup – the last in the litter – who seemed to be waiting for us to come pick him up. And we did. He was a little butterball of black fuzz. The kids named him Bilbo Baggins after their favorite character from J.R.R. Tolkien's fantasy adventure "The Hobbit." This dog turned out to be a whole other story for another time. Suffice it to say, Bilbo was an Alpha male who constantly vied for leadership of our family pack. This made bonding with Alex impossible, and after multiple failed attempts at Dog Training - yes! He even failed the Good Citizenship test – we eventually accepted the fact that Bilbo only grudgingly acknowledged leadership from

ME. That left Alex still without a dog, and after some time, I gave in to Alex's pleas to get a Sheltie. I had only known a couple of Shelties in my time, and they were all exuberant dogs – a little crazy, to be honest – and I worried that Alex wouldn't be able to manage such a creature.

Serendipity found us at the home of a couple whose sheltie had given birth to a litter of five puppies. One of them waddled over to Alex and settled her fluffy fanny directly onto Alex's foot, claiming him to be her person from that moment forward. And so he was. Alex named her Cristina, and I never saw her crown, but I'm very sure she owned one. Cristina was a beauty, quite regal, perfectly calm, and steadfast in the knowledge that Alex belonged to her. Bilbo fell completely in love with her and, totally under her spell, allowed her to reign supreme. Bilbo lived to be thirteen and died of liver cancer. By then, Cristina was five years old, and Alex thought it would be good to have a companion dog – although I suspect he had realized that dogs don't live as long as humans, and another dog would be insurance of a sort. Alex loved Cristina's herding instinct and wanted to bring another herder into our pack. And that's how we ended up with a corgi named Einstein who did not herd anything except treats and toys. By the time Einstein was five and Cristina was ten, Alex had landed full-time work hours and wanted to live on his own. We began apartment hunting for dog-friendly places. And that is when the realization hit me that Alex and his pups would be leaving. Having got used to having two dogs, I could not imagine having zero dogs.

My husband and I discussed dog possibilities and, not relishing the idea of puppy training, thought we might look at adult rescue dogs. We investigated a local sheltie rescue since we had enjoyed Cristina's company so much. The organization came out to do a home inspection, and we passed with flying colors. However, each available dog was rife with problems – not housebroken, known for excessive barking, serious health problems, etcetera. We were disheartened and looked at another local shelter that housed all sorts of dogs, mainly mutts. I scanned their website daily – too big, too small, not housebroken, too energetic. I wasn't discouraged, as there seemed to be an abundance of dogs looking for a home. Then, one day, I clicked on the sight, and there was a dog looking back at me with the most soulful eyes I'd ever seen. The shelter had dubbed her "Lorelei" and described her as a "hound mix" that had lived as a stray. She was what I considered a medium-sized dog and weighed in at thirty pounds. I showed her picture to my husband, and he said, "Sure. Let's go visit her."

I made an appointment with the rescue facility to meet "Lorelei" along with our adult daughter. I thought an extra set of eyes and a dose of common sense couldn't hurt when making such a commitment. Once there, the workers brought "Lorelei" out to meet us. She was friendly, and we started off with her on a leash to see how she responded to that. "Lorelei" was uncertain but docile. We had a ball with us, and when we removed her leash and threw the ball, she surprised us all by "fetching" it as naturally as if we had been playing this game with her since she was a pup. She seemed to be a happy dog, fetched untiringly, and stayed easily with us as we roamed the large property. "Lorelei" was a black and tan, short-haired hound that seemed to be part beagle and part some other kind of hound. Her ears were floppy but too short to be a real beagle. They were more like those of an English Foxhound. She looked like a dog wearing a coat that belonged to a bluetick hound with large black spots – as if she'd gone to a dog party and taken the wrong coat from check out. She was simply a puzzle. It was her eyes that won us over. They were lined with black like Cleopatra's kohl black accent and colored a deep, rich brown like melted chocolate and sadder than any dog I'd ever seen – as if she knew a loneliness that I could only imagine. My daughter voted "yes," and so did my husband, and the next thing I knew, she was in the back seat of our car riding home with us. I had elected to sit in the back with her – uncertain of how she might handle the car ride. The minute I crawled in beside her and gazed up at her, I knew her name could never be "Lorelei," and I said to my husband, "We should call her Lollipop." I had never known a dog by that name and had never entertained such a thought. It was as if she "told" me that was her name. My husband agreed, and when he said, "Do you want to be Lollipop?" she looked quite agreeable.

On the ride home, a sense of dread washed over me. It felt like "buyer's remorse," and I told my husband that we had made a mistake. We didn't need a dog, and we didn't need her. We should take her back to the shelter. And the more I said these words, the more sure I was that we needed to return her – that we shouldn't keep her. My usually amenable husband was silent as I raved on. Finally, he told me very firmly that we were not taking her back, that we were going home, and that we were definitely keeping her. I railed at him that if that is how he felt she was going to be HIS dog – not mine. I didn't want her! What had I been thinking???

My husband calmly pulled the car to the side of the road and moved from the driver's seat to the back seat with Lollipop. Then he told me that since she was going to be his dog, he would sit with her and that I should drive them home. "Fine by me," I pouted, and I got under the wheel and drove the three of us home. Once there, my husband did all the things that needed to be done for her. He took her to investigate her new home and backyard, and he fed her. He talked to her and petted her. I staunchly ignored her. At bedtime, she came into our bedroom and curled up into a small ball on the floor right next to my side of the bed. I agreed to let her be since it was her first night but vowed that wasn't going to be her "place." The next morning, my husband let her out to potty and fed her. When we went to the grocery store later on, he decreed that she should learn to hang out with us. Okay. I shrugged. It was raining, and when my husband went into the store, I agreed to walk Lollipop in the parking lot with an umbrella. Then we waited by the store's entrance for him to finish shopping. Lollipop sat patiently by me and looked up at me now and again for reassurance. I tried not to look into her eyes and continued to hold to the notion that she was my husband's dog alone – not mine! I continued in this vein of thinking until the next day when my husband left for work, and, not being confident that she would stay within our fenced backyard, I agreed that I would take her for a walk. I had Lollipop on a slip leash because I thought I could manage her better. Unfortunately, I had not counted on a large, loud trash truck startling her and her ducking out of the leash and racing down the street without me. For the briefest of moments, it occurred to me that if she ran away, we would be rid of her, but my naturally tender heart also melted as I thought of how she would be alone and scared and hungry – a stray once again – living life the best she could manage on her own. I took off after her as she fled with her tail tucked down the street nearly a half block ahead of me. As I ran, I realized I was no match for her speed and felt a flood of guilt at my previous wish that she would just run away. I figured calling her would be useless, as she surely did not know my voice or her name. Still, I called out,

"Lollipop!" And to my surprise, she turned toward me and came running back, seeming glad to see me. I couldn't believe it! When she drew near, she lifted her head to accept the leash, and I knew she wasn't going anywhere.

Later, at home, I called my friend Maureen and laid out the whole mixed-up story of adopting this mutt and my crazy feelings. I was nearly in tears when I finished and breathed out, "What in the world is the matter with me? Do you think I'm going crazy?"

Maureen responded with her usual keen insight, "Linda, this isn't about a dog."

"What do you mean?" I queried. And she landed this nugget of wisdom right into my heart,

"This is about Alex leaving home."

And in that very instant, I knew she was exactly right. Later, after our telephone conversation ended, I apologized to Lollipop. As I put my arms around her soft head, I realized that she also knew the truth as well and would never hold my insane reaction to her against me. And from that moment on, she began walking me to the other side of an empty nest. She knew that was her job in life all along, and I could never have done it without that sweet dog, my Lollipop.

If I had known……

If I had known those summers of my childhood weren't forever, I would have listened longer to the busy grasshoppers whirring across the country fields and the chirping of ink-black crickets as night fell. I'd have lain just a little longer on the quilt with my cousin, watching clouds making picture shows against the crystal blue sky. I would have run my toes through the hot sand of our driveway just one more time before skipping up the back steps to have a tomato sandwich for lunch and just one more time in the delicious cool sand under a twilight sky when Mama called me in for supper. I would have sat just a little longer in the doorway of my grandaddy's tobacco barn to smell the rich gold leaves drying there. I would have stayed with Daddy all the while he turned the ice cream churn and heaped on a little more ice and salt as he worked to make frozen deliciousness for us on a sweltering hot Sunday afternoon. And I would have asked for just one more scoop of its cold, creamy

473

sweetness. I would have stayed longer in the kitchen listening to jar lids popping and sealing the cans of green beans and tomatoes that Mama and I labored all morning to finish, knowing how good they would taste on the cold winter nights to come.

Had I known the autumns of my childhood would end all too soon, I would have risen just a little earlier to feel the first chilly morning of autumn, to see the last of the morning glories blooming and caressing the spent garden, and watch the mist lingering on the river. I would have paid more attention to the smell of newly sharpened pencils, the feel of excitement coming from my classmates on the edge of beginning a new school year, the sound of the high school band on the eve of the first football game of the year, and I'd have ridden just one more time around on the Ferris wheel at the State Fair. I would have watched my daddy's bird dogs running in the field just once more before turning away, walked a little farther into the woods with my daddy, and asked him about one more tree I spied whose leaves were falling around us in the autumn wind. I would have watched more closely as my mama made her giblet gravy for the turkey roasting in the oven, lingered longer after the Thanksgiving meal, soaking up the stories my relatives loved to tell.

My childhood winters abide warm and sweet in my memory, but oh! How I long for the sparkle of sunshine through frosted panes in the early morning kitchen with my mama setting a steaming bowl of oatmeal on the table. I would like to wait until the last of the rich yellow butter had melted completely and swirled out into the sweet cream before taking one single bite. How I would savor the thrill buzzing through my every fiber, anticipating Christmas morning's fullness coming down. And oh, my! The true joy of a winter snow – no school, tramping through fields blanketed in milky whiteness, crystals glistening on every tree branch, playing outside all day and never minding the cold. I would dawdle when Mama called just long enough to witness the icy horizon swallow the sun in one crisp gulp.

And those eternally soft yellow-green springs have gone the way of my other childhood seasons – budding and flowering in a pallet of colors – rich, spectacular, singular. Finding a new litter of kittens hidden in a box in our garage, watching my daddy till up soil for a new garden, smelling its earthy smell, seeing my mama kneel to lovingly sow her zinnia seeds, searching eagerly for colored eggs hidden among verdant grass and burgeoning foliage. How could I have known that such moments are not endless?

Seasons continue to come and go, but there are pieces of them that have faded as the years have progressed and moved me into adulthood almost without notice. And now, as I enter my seventh decade, I recall those little things that seemed so ordinary at the time – so very precious now.

Summer is still summer, winter is still winter – and yet not. Now, I see them through a very different lens…